Jayne Ann Krentz is the critically-acclaimed creator of the Arcane Society world, Dark Legacy, Ladies of Lantern Street and Rainshadow Island series. She also writes as **Amanda Quick** and **Jayne Castle**. Jayne has written more than fifty *New York Times* bestsellers under various pseudonyms and more than thirty-five million copies of her books are currently in print. She lives in the Pacific Northwest.

Visit Jayne Ann Krentz online:

www.jayneannkrentz.com
www.facebook.com/JayneAnnKrentz
www.twitter.com/JayneAnnKrentz

By Jayne Ann Krentz

***Ladies of Lantern Street Novels*:**

By Jayne Anne Krentz
writing as Amanda Quick

Crystal Gardens

***Arcane Society Novels*:**

By Jayne Ann Krentz
writing as Amanda Quick

Second Sight
The Third Circle
The Perfect Poison
Burning Lamp
Quicksilver

By Jayne Ann Krentz

White Lies
Sizzle and Burn
Running Hot
Fired Up
In Too Deep

By Jayne Ann Krentz
writing as Jayne Castle

Dark Light
Obsidian Prey
Midnight Crystal
Canyons of Night

***Dark Legacy Novels*:**

By Jayne Ann Krentz

Copper Beach
Dream Eyes

***Rainshadow Island Novels*:**

By Jayne Ann Krentz
writing as Jayne Castle

The Lost Night
Deception Cove
The Hot Zone

Other titles by
Jayne Ann Krentz
***writing as Amanda Quick*:**

With This Ring
I Thee Wed
Wicked Widow
Lie By Moonlight
The Paid Companion
Wait Until Midnight
The River Knows
Affair
Mischief
Slightly Shady

Other titles by
***Jayne Ann Krentz*:**

Light in Shadow
Truth or Dare
Falling Awake
All Night Long
River Road

THE HOT ZONE

A RAINSHADOW NOVEL

JAYNE ANN KRENTZ WRITING AS
JAYNE CASTLE

PIATKUS

First published in the United States in 2014 by Jove Books,
The Berkeley Publishing Group,
A member of Penguin Group (USA) Inc., New York
First published in Great Britain in 2014 by Piatkus

A CIP catalogue record for this book
is available from the British Library.

ISBN: 978-0-349-40174-4

Printed and bound in Great Britain by Clays Ltd, St Ives plc

Papers used by Piatkus are from well-managed forests
and other responsible sources.

MIX
Paper from
responsible sources
FSC® C104740

Piatkus
An imprint of
Little, Brown Book Group
100 Victoria Embankment
London EC4Y 0DY

An Hachette UK Company
www.hachette.co.uk

www.piatkus.co.uk

THE HOT ZONE

For Lyle and friends: Party on!

A Note from Jayne

Welcome back to Rainshadow Island on my other world—Harmony.

Everyone on Rainshadow has a past; everyone has secrets. But none of those secrets is as dangerous as the ancient mysteries concealed inside the paranormal fence that guards the forbidden territory of the island known as the Preserve.

The secrets of the Preserve have been locked away for centuries, but now some of them are coming to light—and they are dangerous, indeed.

I hope you enjoy the Rainshadow novels.

Chapter 1

THE DUST BUNNY WAS BACK.

Sedona heard the soft, muffled chortle and rushed to the barred door of the small, windowless chamber. The lab was deserted for the night but there was ample illumination. The Aliens had vanished a few thousand years ago but they had built their maze of underworld catacombs to last. And they had left the lights on. The quartz walls of the small cell and the chamber that housed Dr. Blankenship's research equipment glowed with an acid-green radiance.

Because of the constant light it was impossible to tell whether it was day or night up on the surface, but she was pretty sure it was night because Blankenship's two seriously bulked-up assistants had left a while ago, talking about dinner. The pair had names but she had privately decided to call the one with the short, razor-cut hair Buzzkill. The other man had completely shaved his head. She had nicknamed him Hulk.

They wore a lot of khaki and leather, but even without the clothing cues she would have known that they were ghost hunters. She had worked with Guild men often enough to recognize them when she saw them. One big clue was that they were obsessive about their amber. They wore amber in every conceivable way—in their belt buckles, in their earring studs, in the hilts of their knives. She knew they probably carried more amber as backup in their boots. No self-respecting Guild man ever went down into the catacombs without plenty of amber, and all of it was tuned. Good amber set to the correct frequencies was the only way to navigate in the heavy currents of senses-distorting psi that flooded the Alien tunnels. Lose your amber and you were lost forever.

She heard another muffled chortle. This time it came from beneath one of the lab workbenches. There was a flash of motion near the floor. The dust bunny scurried out from under the bench and fluttered across the room to the door of the cell. He looked like a large ball of fuzzy dryer lint studded with a pair of baby blue eyes. There were six paws and a couple of ears but they were nearly invisible in the fluff of his fur.

At some point she had decided to call him Lyle. She wasn't sure why. The name just seemed to fit, and giving the dust bunny a name served to make him seem more real. She needed all the solid, tangible links to reality that she could get. Last night when Lyle had first appeared she had still been fighting her way up through the thick layers of the drugs that Blankenship used to keep her heavily sedated in a waking dreamstate. She had no idea how long she had been held prisoner. Her days and nights were filled with nightmares and disturbing visions.

At first she had assumed that the dust bunny was just one more hallucination, albeit a comforting one. She had wondered if it was a sign that Blankenship's experiments had finally pushed her over the precarious border between sanity and chaos.

Lyle had appeared thrilled with the energy bar that she had given him from the stash in the cell. He had squeezed easily through the bars in the door and hopped up onto the cot. He had chattered at her with increasing urgency until she finally realized that he was trying to get her to leave.

"I can't go anywhere," she had explained. "The door's locked."

She had sat beside him for a long time, taking comfort from him. He had departed shortly before Buzzkill and Hulk returned. There had followed another horrible day of Blankenship's experiments. It had taken every ounce of willpower she had to fake the waking dreamstate. What she really wanted to do was scream her rage and claw Blankenship's eyes out of his head.

That night she had despaired of ever seeing Lyle again. But he was here. Her spirits soared.

"Hi," she whispered. She crouched and reached through the bars to pat Lyle. "Good to see you again, buddy."

Lyle rumbled. He had a small, shiny metallic object about an inch and a half long clutched in one paw. He fluttered through the bars, bounced up onto the cot, and waved the bright thing at her.

"A gift in exchange for the energy bar?" she said. "Thank you."

When she took the present she saw that it was a small emergency firestarter. They were known as flickers and they were standard-issue emergency equipment for Guild men. Fire was one of the few useful sources of energy that worked in heavy psi environments because it could be made to burn across the spectrum from the normal into the paranormal. Sophisticated, high-tech gear like guns or computers either failed to function at all or else exploded in your hands.

She considered the little flicker. A plan quickly formed in her head. It wasn't much of a plan but when you were desperate, any sort of plan held a certain appeal. At most the flicker would generate only a spark of a flame. Still, that might be enough for her purposes.

"Hmm."

Lyle muttered impatiently and bounced some more.

"Yes, I know," she said. "Time to get out of here. I don't think I can get through another day pretending to be in a dreamstate."

When she had finally begun to drag herself out of the oppressive nightmare landscape she had intuitively known that she had to conceal her recovery. If Dr. Blankenship realized that she had awakened, he would very likely double the dose of whatever hallucinogen he was using on her.

She considered her options. She had comprehended

two facts yesterday during the course of the experiments. First, for whatever reason, Blankenship and his men were extremely wary around her. They evidently considered her dangerous. That was a good thing, she told herself, probably the only thing that had kept Buzzkill and Hulk from molesting her while she was in the dreamstate. But she dared not give them any reason to use physical restraints as well as medication to keep her under control.

The second discovery she had made was that the experiments Blankenship was conducting had something to do with her talent. She had no idea what had been done to her but she was sure she still had her ability to open and close the paranormal gates of the Underworld. Unfortunately her ability to work the energy gates was of no obvious use when it came to escaping the lab.

Lyle growled, impatient with her failure to get with the program.

"I would like to come with you," she whispered. "But I can't fit through the bars of this cell."

She had been contemplating that problem since she had awakened. The first obstacle was the lock on the cell door. It was an old-fashioned padlock. A key was required to open it.

Buzzkill and Hulk had keys.

Even if she succeeded in escaping the cell and getting past the two bulked-up assistants, she would still face the challenge of getting out of the tunnels. Without tuned amber she would never find her way back to the surface.

There was plenty of amber embedded in the lab apparatus but it was all tuned to operate the simple instruments that were designed to function in the heavy psi atmosphere—not for navigation.

Lyle rumbled softly again. She could feel his small frame vibrating with a sense of urgency.

"We need a distraction," she said. "I've got a sort of plan but it's one of those ideas that had better work the first time because I'll only get one shot at it."

If she failed, Blankenship would overwhelm her with his ghastly dreamstate drugs.

"Here goes nothing, Lyle."

He blinked and sleeked out, his tatty fur plastering against his little body. He opened his second set of eyes, the ones he used for hunting. They burned molten amber. He vaulted up onto her shoulder.

"Right," she said. "Let's do this."

She took a deep breath, rezzed the little flicker, and touched the small spark to the edge of the pillow.

That was when she found out what Blankenship had done to her para-senses.

With a terrifying whoosh of energy, the tiny flicker spark literally exploded into a firestorm, engulfing the cot in seconds.

"Crap," she whispered. She stared at the raging fire, too stunned to comprehend for a few seconds.

Smoke was not a problem in the heavy psi environment. It dissipated quickly in the atmosphere, but the fire she had inadvertently started was something else again.

In her panic she intuitively rezzed her senses to the max.

And discovered to her amazement that she could control the flames.

"Impossible," she gasped.

But she was doing it. Frantically she reached out with her talent, struggling to control the currents of the fire. It took a moment or two but in the end she realized it was not all that different from working gate energy. She beat the wall of flames down until only the bed was burning.

Fascinated, she concentrated harder and generated more energy. The tide of flames surged and ebbed at her command.

Satisfied she had the fire under control, she opened her mouth and screamed.

There was no need to fake genuine fear. She was committed now.

Lyle growled. The claws of his small paws sank through the fabric of her shirt. He could have escaped the cell but he made it clear he wasn't leaving without her.

Two figures appeared in the doorway of the lab. Sedona screamed louder, flattening herself against one wall of the cell as if trying to avoid the flames.

"Shit," Hulk said. "The crazy bitch is awake. She set a fire. How in green hell did she do that?"

Buzzkill started forward, dragging a key out of one pocket. "We'll figure that part out later. Right now we've got to get her out of there. Blankenship will be pissed if he loses his precious research subject."

"Yeah, well, he's not the only one who will have a reason to be pissed. In case you haven't been paying attention, we need that little witch."

"Don't you think I know that?" Buzzkill said. "I told you the woman was going to be trouble. She gives me the creeps the way she looks at us with those weird eyes."

"What the hell is that thing on her shoulder?" Hulk said. "Don't tell me she's got a rat."

"I think it's a dust bunny," Buzz said.

Sedona screamed again.

"Shut up, already," Buzzkill growled.

He stabbed the key into the lock and swung the door wide.

"Come on," he snapped. "Get out of there." He glanced back at Hulk. "Be ready to grab her. Give her a shot of the sedative to keep her quiet while we put out this fire."

"It'll be a pleasure," Hulk said. He reached into the pocket of his leather vest for a small syringe case.

Lyle growled. Sedona clutched the flicker very tightly in one hand and fled from the cell.

Buzzkill did not try to stop her. He left that job to Hulk, who was already moving to intercept her. One big fist reached out to close around her arm.

The instant he made physical contact with her she rezzed her new talent, clicked the flicker again, and set fire to his shirt.

Hulk yelled. The expression on his face was a mix of astonishment and panic. He released her and staggered back, batting wildly at the flames that were leaping from his shirtsleeve.

"What in green hell?" Buzzkill paused in the act of trying to beat out the flames and turned to stare at Hulk.

"The bitch set my shirt on fire." Hulk clawed at his

vest and T-shirt, ripping the clothes off his massive chest and shoulders. "It's the heavy doses of the formula that Blankenship has been giving her. If she wasn't crazy before he started his experiments, she sure is now."

"Stop her." Buzzkill charged out of the cell. "Pull a ghost. Hurry, man. She's getting away."

Sedona ran for the door. Lyle clung to her shoulder and urged her on with small hissing noises.

She was only a few steps from the arched doorway of the lab when a ball of hot green psi-fire coalesced in front of her, blocking her path. She slammed to a halt, nearly dislodging Lyle. He recovered his balance and snarled at the violent energy ghost that Hulk had generated.

The technical name for the dangerous ball of psi was UDEM—Unstable Dissonance Energy Manifestation. There was nothing of a supernatural nature about ghosts. They were composed of specific frequencies of Alien psi that those with a special talent could work.

Pulling unstable dissonance energy out of the invisible currents of psi that flowed throughout the Underworld was, in Sedona's opinion, the only thing Guild men were really good at. There was no doubt but that Hulk was a very powerful hunter. The seething ghost in front of her was the largest she had ever seen. The currents pouring off of it lifted her hair and raised goose bumps on her arms. A cold sensation shivered through her. A ghost this large could be deadly.

"Got her," Hulk said. He started toward Sedona, rage burning in his eyes. "You're going to pay for that little fire trick."

"Be careful," Buzzkill warned. "She already set fire to you once. She's a gatekeeper. Everyone knows they're weird to begin with. No telling what she is now that Blankenship's been using the drugs and radiation on her. Knock her out with the ghost."

Hulk halted, clearly torn. But in the end self-preservation won out over damaged pride and anger.

"Yeah," he said. "The ghost will work just fine."

The ball of green energy started to drift toward Sedona. In another moment it would come close enough to burn her senses. She had some natural immunity because of her gatekeeping talent, but no one could withstand the full onslaught of a powerful ghost. The best she could hope for was that the unstable energy manifestation would merely render her unconscious. The worst-case scenario was that it would kill her.

No, she thought, death wasn't the worst possibility. She had already sustained one bad psi-burn in the Underworld. Another severe burn might send her into a permanent dreamstate. She would spend the rest of her life here in Blankenship's lab or some low-rent parapsych ward. No question about it—death would be a better outcome.

"This could go real bad," Sedona said to Lyle. "Better run while you still can. Go on. Shoo. Get out of here."

She tried to pluck him off her shoulder and send him toward the door. But Lyle just growled and dug in his claws.

"Okay," she said. Her pulse pounded in her veins. "Looks like we're a team. Neither of us leaves the other one behind, right?"

Lyle rumbled.

"Unlike some Guild bosses I could mention," she added.

The green ghost was drifting closer now, forcing Sedona to edge backward until she came up hard against an unyielding block of green quartz.

Buzzkill and Hulk stood still, breathing hard, and waited for the green ghost to come into contact with Sedona's aura.

"Better not let it kill her," Buzzkill said. "Remember, we need her."

"Yeah, yeah," Hulk said.

But Sedona could see the feverish excitement in his eyes and hear it in his voice. He was at the edge of his control. That was never a good thing but it was always really bad when it happened with a ghost hunter. A Guild man who couldn't control his talent was liable to do a lot of damage, especially down in the Underworld where there was so much energy.

She took a deep breath, rezzed the flicker, and simultaneously pulled hard on her senses.

Flames exploded in the atmosphere between her and the ghost. She fought to control the stormy currents of fire. This time it was easier. She had more control. Power swept through her. The flames obeyed her every command.

A heady sensation threatened to overwhelm her. She was strong—stronger than she had ever been in her entire life.

She marveled at her own creation. She'd possessed plenty of talent before that last job in the Underworld, but she'd never been able to do anything like this.

"Wow, Lyle. Very high-rez, huh?"

Lyle chortled and bounced a little on her shoulder.

"What's she doing?" Buzzkill whispered hoarsely.

"Shit." Hulk was clearly stunned. "She's some kind of fire talent now. Everyone knows they're psycho. I told you, she's a total whackjob."

"A whackjob with nothing left to lose," Sedona warned. A terrible excitement was flaring inside her. "Watch and learn, gentlemen. Watch and learn."

The firestorm she had created was in the direct path of the oncoming energy ghost. At any second the two would collide.

"Oh, man, this is not good," Buzzkill said. "I can feel the energy levels rising in here. There's going to be an explosion. Stop her, damn it."

"I can't stop her," Hulk said. There was a panicky tightness in his voice. "That's the biggest ghost I can pull. If you think you can do something, be my guest."

"We've got to get out of here." Buzzkill sprinted toward the door. "This place is going to blow."

"What about the woman? You said yourself, we can't lose her."

"There's nothing more we can do," Buzzkill yelled. He did not pause on his charge toward the door. "Blankenship can find himself another research subject. Stay here if you want. I'm leaving."

Sedona concluded that *nothing left to lose* had become her personal motto. She pulled more power. The firestorm surged.

"You stupid, crazy bitch," Hulk shouted. "You're going to die if you don't shut down that storm."

Sedona laughed.

"Those damn experiments turned you into a real freak," Hulk gasped.

He gave up trying to control the ball of hot energy that he had generated. As soon as he stopped channeling his talent, the ghost fizzled and winked out of existence.

Sedona sent the leaping flames of her firestorm toward Hulk. But he was already on the run, pounding toward the doorway. He followed Buzzkill out into the glowing green hall and was gone.

Sedona waited a moment or two, savoring the exhilaration that had ignited her blood. She could have stood there for a long time, admiring the storm she had created. But Lyle chortled and reality slammed back.

Reluctantly, she lowered her senses. The firestorm dissipated. An eerie silence descended on the lab.

"Okay, that was a real rush," she said softly.

Lyle chortled. He was once again fully fluffed but all four eyes were still open.

She opened her hand and stared at the shiny flicker. A shiver of dread replaced the fading euphoria.

"What did Blankenship do to me?" she whispered.

Lyle muttered, displaying some impatience.

"Right." Sedona steadied herself. "I can worry about the details later. Time to vacate the premises."

She crossed the room to the storage chest that held the few things she'd had on her when she was kidnapped.

She found her pack. There wasn't much inside it, just the usual emergency essentials that she always carried when she went down below into the tunnels on a job. There was also a cell phone but she knew it would not work until she got aboveground.

Two items were missing.

"They took my locator and my backup tuned amber," she said to Lyle. "Bastards."

She looked at Lyle.

"I'll bet you know the way to the surface, don't you?"

Lyle gave no indication that he understood the question but it was obvious that he was eager to leave. He bounced some more on her shoulder and made encouraging noises.

"Okay, buddy, I'm depending on you. Anything is better than hanging around here waiting for Dr. Blankenship and his pals to come back."

She slipped the strap of the pack over one shoulder and started toward the doorway.

The sight of the glass-and-steel strongbox sitting on a workbench stopped her. She shuddered, nightmarish memories slithering and coiling through her mind.

"Hang on," she said. "Something I want to do before we leave."

She went down an aisle formed by two long, steel lab benches to the strongbox. For a moment she studied the container, wondering if there was any way to destroy it and the contents. The thick glass glinted malevolently in the paranormal light. The steel was heavy gauge. The whole thing probably weighed nearly a hundred pounds.

There was a lock on the strongbox, but, like the lock on the cell door, it was a simple, old-fashioned padlock. She could not open it without a key. Not that she wanted to even touch the contents, let alone steal them. But she did not want Blankenship using the serum on some other hapless research subject. The crystal seemed to be important to the drug-making process.

There was no way to destroy the box or the strange gem inside. She did not have the time or the upper-body strength required to carry the container away from the lab and conceal it somewhere in the catacombs. The only option she had was to lock the strongbox so tightly that no one else could ever unlock it.

Setting a small gate lock on the box was easy enough. Setting one that no other gatekeeper could unlock took some concentration but the job was done in a matter of minutes. When she was finished there was a fine, eerie radiance around the strongbox. Anyone who touched it would get a scorching psi-burn. Anyone foolish enough to try to open her lock would trigger an explosion that would likely prove fatal to whoever was in the vicinity. With luck such an explosion would be strong enough to destroy the jewel.

"Done," she announced to Lyle. "Now we can leave. I'll lock the door on the way out."

She was halfway back down the aisle of lab benches when a gleaming steel test tube holder caught her eye. There were six glass tubes filled with the serum set in the holder.

Another wave of anger washed through her. She

reached out and swept the metal holder to the floor. The glass test tubes shattered, spilling the contents across the green quartz.

She was about to move on when she noticed a small plate bolted to the test tube rack. She paused and took a closer look at the lettering. PROPERTY OF AMBER CREST HOSPITAL.

She glanced at the other instruments on the bench. The little amber burner and the microscope bore the same label.

There was no time to dwell on the implications. She kept moving.

Outside in the gently illuminated hallway she paused again to rez her senses. In an instant, hot energy blazed in the vaulted doorway. She created a gate and then wove an intricate lock into the oscillating currents.

When she was satisfied that no other gatekeeper could unlock the gate, she stepped back and studied her surroundings.

She was in a vast green quartz rotunda that must have been at least three stories high. A dozen arched doorways opened off the circular chamber, all of them glowing with psi.

"Okay, Lyle, it's up to you now. Take me back to the surface, pal. If you don't, I'm going to die trying to find my way out."

Lyle chortled, unconcerned, and peeled the wrapper off the energy bar he had acquired along the way.

Tentatively she started toward one of the tunnels. Lyle didn't stop munching but he made a rumbling sound that she took for disapproval. She changed direction and went toward another arched doorway. Lyle took another bite and rumbled again.

Then, evidently concluding she was no good at navigation, he finished the energy bar and bounded down to the floor. He trotted off toward a third hallway.

Sedona followed him into the maze. Nothing left to lose.

Ten steps later she glanced back over her shoulder. She could no longer see the rotunda. She was well and truly lost.

She followed Lyle through the sense-dazzling catacombs, questions circling endlessly in her mind.

If she did survive she would have to confront the reality of her new talent. Individuals with more than one kind of talent were extremely rare. Everyone knew they were inherently unstable. The experts had determined that the human mind simply could not handle the heightened level of stimulation that occurred when a second or third talent developed. Multi-talents almost always went mad. If they did not die young, they ended up in locked para-psych wards and were kept under heavy sedation.

Her life had taken a very weird turn.

Chapter 2

SHE HAD NO IDEA HOW MUCH TIME PASSED BEFORE LYLE led her up an ancient green-quartz staircase and out into the ruins of an Alien outpost. It was nighttime. The strange, ethereal towers of the dead town glowed with luminous energy. The windowless structures had been abandoned centuries earlier but they showed no evidence of weathering.

When she went through the gate of the high quartz wall that surrounded the ruins she discovered that they were in a stand of trees. She could hear the sounds of traffic in the distance.

"Thanks, Lyle," she said. "You are hereby designated my best friend in the whole world."

Lyle chortled and bounded up onto her shoulder.

She took her phone out of her pack and was not surprised to see that there was no charge left on the amber battery.

"Probably couldn't get a signal out here, anyway," she said to Lyle. "So much for calling Brock to let him know I'm okay. He must be worried sick. Probably has a privately financed search-and-rescue team combing the Underworld, looking for me."

The thought that her new husband was searching for her night and day warmed her as nothing else could have done. She had to let him know as soon as possible that she was alive and well. Okay, maybe not entirely well, but definitely alive.

She followed the sound of traffic to a road. A short time later a trucker stopped for her. She climbed up into the cab and sat down with Lyle in her lap.

"I really appreciate this," she said.

"Sure." The trucker eyed Lyle. "Is that a dust bunny?"

"Yes." She patted Lyle. "He's sort of adopted me."

"Heard they were dangerous. They say that by the time you see the teeth, it's too late."

"Lyle won't hurt you, I promise."

Lyle chortled and blinked his baby blues a couple of times.

The trucker smiled and pulled back onto the road. "He's real cute. Where you two headed?"

"The nearest town."

"First stop is Crystal City."

Crystal City was the home of her father's family. There would be no help for her there.

"Where do you go after Crystal?" she asked.

"Should be in Resonance City sometime before dawn."

She brightened. "That works. That's where I live. I've got some cash on me. I'll buy you breakfast."

"Fair enough." The trucker gave her another searching glance and then concentrated on his driving.

"What day is this?" she asked after a moment.

"Wednesday," the trucker said.

"No, I mean what is the date? I've lost track of time."

The trucker glanced at her, brows elevated. "It's the second of October."

"Oh." She swallowed hard.

"How long have you been gone?"

She nearly stopped breathing.

"Just a couple of days," she lied.

She had left on the last contract assignment more than three weeks earlier. Brock would be beyond worried.

A short time later the lights of an isolated set of buildings glittered amid the trees at the end of a long, private drive. There was a gate and a guardhouse at the entrance. She caught a fleeting glimpse of a discreet sign at the junction of the road and the drive. AMBER CREST PARA-PSYCHIATRIC HOSPITAL.

"What is that place?" she whispered.

"Para-psych hospital," the trucker said. "Run by the Gold Creek Guild. Supposedly it's where they treat the really bad psi-burn cases. But rumor has it, that's where the big Guilds house the worst of the worst—the monsters and freaks. It's a high-security facility. Had to make a delivery there once. You wouldn't believe how hard it was to go in and out. We're talking armed guards, hot fences, and cameras everywhere."

Sedona shuddered. Lyle cuddled closer, as if trying to reassure her. She patted his tatty fur and watched the darkened road come up in the truck's headlights.

Amber Crest treated the monsters and freaks. *What had she become?*

They pulled off at a truck stop diner for breakfast at three in the morning. Sedona paid the tab. An hour before dawn the truck rolled into Resonance City.

"You can drop me anywhere," Sedona said. "I've got enough money left for cab fare."

"You sure you're going to be okay?" the trucker asked.

"Oh, yeah. I've been looking after myself for quite a while now."

"Not doing a real good job of that, if you ask me. Getting lost out there in the woods and all."

"I'll be okay," she promised. "My husband will be waiting for me."

The trucker got a troubled expression. "You're married?"

"Yes," she said.

There was no reason to add that her freshly minted marriage to Brock Prescott was only a Marriage of Convenience, not a true Covenant Marriage. MCs had some legal standing but the reality was that they could be cancelled by either party with no legal or financial hassles. A lot of people took an old-fashioned attitude toward MCs, deeming the institution a polite fiction designed to paper over an affair. That was true, Sedona thought. Nevertheless, it was a commitment of sorts.

She decided not to mention that Brock was probably the only one who would have been searching for her the past three weeks. She was the offspring of an illegitimate union. Her parents were dead and her blood relations on both sides had officially disowned her as soon as they were legally allowed to do so. She had gotten the papers informing her that she had no claim on either of her birth families the day she turned eighteen.

She climbed out of the truck at another all-night diner, intending to call Brock. It was four o'clock in the morning but he wouldn't care about the time once he heard her voice.

The waitress allowed her to use the house phone but when she dialed Brock's number she got tossed into voicemail. She called a cab instead.

A short time later she emerged from the cab in front of Brock's elegant town house. She had moved in with him the week before her last assignment.

Rain was falling heavily. She hurried up the walk, but by the time she got to the front door she and Lyle were both drenched.

Clutching Lyle in the crook of her arm, she leaned on the doorbell.

"Home, at last," she said to Lyle.

Lyle chortled.

After a moment lights came on somewhere inside the town house. An almost overpowering sense of relief swept through Sedona. Soon she would be throwing herself into Brock's arms.

"He's going to be so surprised," she said to Lyle.

The door opened. It wasn't Brock who stood in the hall.

"Sedona?" Diana Easton, Brock's administrative assistant, stared at Sedona in shock. "Good grief, you're a mess. What in the world are you doing here?"

"I could ask you the same question." Sedona took in Diana's dainty robe and filmy nightgown. "But I think I already know the answer."

Lyle growled at Diana.

"Is that a rat?" Diana asked.

Sedona ignored her.

Footsteps sounded on the stairs.

"Diana?" Brock called. "Who is it?"

His rich, well-modulated voice reflected his social status. Brock Singleton Prescott was wealthy, well-educated, and very well-connected. His family moved in the highest social circles of Crystal City. Two years ago he had become the CEO of the family empire, Prescott Industries.

"You'll never guess," Diana said a little too sweetly.

Lyle growled again.

Brock emerged into view, still tying the sash of his robe. He was tall, with chiseled features, a toned body, and an innate sense of style that enabled him to look just as good in a bathrobe as he did in one of his hand-tailored business suits. He stared at Sedona, stunned.

"The Gold Creek Guild authorities told us that you

were lost and presumed missing," Brock said, sputtering a little in shock.

"My life has gotten complicated," Sedona said.

"Yeah, well, I, uh, filed the divorce papers two and a half weeks ago."

So much for throwing herself into his arms, Sedona thought.

Lyle rumbled darkly.

"It's okay," she whispered to Lyle. "We'll be fine."

Brock frowned. "What the hell happened to you, Sedona?"

"Long story," she said tightly. "What about my stuff?"

"It's in storage," Brock said, evidently trying to be helpful. "Isn't that right, Diana?"

Diana smiled again. "Old Quarter Storage Facility. I'll get the key."

She vanished into the depths of the town house. Sedona was left looking at Brock.

"Just one question," she said.

"What?" he asked uneasily.

"Did you ever look for me?"

"I told you, I was informed that you had gone missing on your last job and that you were in all probability dead."

Sedona nodded. "So you didn't even bother to search for me."

"The Guild boss who hired you for that last mission assured me that a team had been sent out but that it found no trace."

"Right. Here's a tip going forward. Next time a Guild boss tells you something, don't assume he's giving you the truth. A Guild boss has no trouble lying through his teeth if it suits him."

Diana reappeared with a key and a business card. "Here's the address of the storage facility."

Sedona took the key and the card. Without a word she turned and went down the front steps.

"Sedona?" Brock said behind her. "Do you need some money for a cab or a hotel?"

She stopped and turned around. Somehow she managed an ice-bright smile.

"Go to hell, Brock."

She turned back, tucked Lyle more securely under her arm, and walked into the rainy night.

"Looks like it's just you and me, Lyle," she said.

Lyle chortled.

"Nothing left to lose."

Chapter 3

"YES, I DO SEE YOUR RESERVATION HERE IN THE COMPUTER, Mr. Jones, but the only cottage that we have left is quite small." Sedona put on her brightest innkeeper's smile. "Number Thirteen, Graveyard Cottage. No view of the bay, I'm afraid. It looks out over the local cemetery."

"Sounds like the place has a lot of atmosphere," Cyrus Jones said.

She had overheard the hunters refer to him as Dead Zone Jones. She had no idea why they called him that, but she was very certain of one thing—there was nothing dead about him.

His voice—low, dark, and freighted with power that was both very masculine and very controlled—sent shivers through Sedona's senses. She could have sworn that she heard wind chimes clashing softly in another dimension.

She knew the eerie music was her intuition pinging her. It was a recently discovered and decidedly unsettling aspect of her new weirdness. She was still getting accustomed to the strange vibe. She didn't always know how to interpret the chimes. But in this case she was pretty sure they signaled danger of a kind she had never before experienced.

Jones was the boss of the newly established Rainshadow Ghost-Hunters Guild. He had arrived, along with a gleaming black SUV and very little luggage, on a private charter ferry.

The October night had long since descended when the ferry docked in the Shadow Bay Marina, but Sedona had watched Jones's arrival from the lobby window of Knox's Resort & Tavern. She had not been alone. Most of the town had turned out to get a look at the island's first Guild boss.

He'd received an unusually colorful welcome. Shadow Bay had never seen fit to invest in extensive streetlighting. But this was Halloween Week—a weeklong festival instituted by the new mayor as a way to promote tourism on Rainshadow. As a result, the town's single shopping street was festooned with hundreds of orange and psi-green lanterns. The garish illumination extended from the Haunted Alien Catacombs attraction that had been set up in an old warehouse at the marina all the way to the town square. Most of the shops and eateries along the route were open and filled with visitors.

Jones had driven the SUV off the ferry and parked it in the marina lot. The shopkeepers and island residents who happened to be in town had watched him take a large black leather duffel bag out of the back of the vehicle. He had walked up the street, moving through the macabre glow of the Halloween lanterns with the ease of a man who owned the night.

In the course of his hike to the entrance of Knox's Resort & Tavern he had stopped several times to speak with the people lined up on the sidewalks. He had shaken a great many hands before he came through the lobby door.

Now he was standing in front of Sedona and she didn't need the chimes to warn her. Common sense was all it took to know that if she wasn't very careful, Jones was going to screw up her carefully structured new life on Rainshadow Island.

Cyrus contemplated her across the width of the inn's front desk. His gem-green eyes burned with a little heat. She was not an aura reader but a woman didn't have to have that particular talent to register the heat in a man's aura, not when the energy field was so strong.

"I don't care about the view," Cyrus said. "I won't have a lot of time to admire it." He glanced rather casually at her name tag. A faint smile edged his hard mouth. "I'm here to get a job done, Miss Snow."

Chimes clashed softly, rattling her senses. She had no idea why he found her name amusing but the knowledge added to her unease. She did not doubt for a moment that the powerful members of the Guild Chamber—more formally known as the Joint Council of Dissonance Energy Para-Resonator Guilds—were well aware of what they were doing when they tasked Jones with establishing a new Guild territory on Rainshadow. If he set out to do a job, the job would get done.

It was just her luck that she was the new manager of Knox's Resort & Tavern. Less than a month ago she had come to Rainshadow seeking a refuge; a place where misfits felt at home. The good people of Shadow Bay, long accustomed to dealing with the weird, had welcomed her, and Lyle, too, with open arms.

She had known, deep down, that it was probably all a little too good to be true. She was right. A week ago the town had been overrun with ghost hunters. Okay, maybe *overrun* was an exaggeration—the Rainshadow Guild was still a small operation, as Guilds went. But when you had a resort full of them, it certainly seemed as if they were on the island in vast numbers.

Housing a bunch of rowdy hunters was not her worst nightmare. She experienced more hellacious dreams on a nightly basis, thanks to Blankenship and his two assistants. And it was undeniably true that the Chamber was paying the outrageous prices she had demanded for the room-and-board arrangements for the men. Her boss, Knox—he only used his surname—was thrilled at the way the money was rolling in. *The Guilds always pay their bills,* he'd explained on several occasions.

At the moment Knox was behind the bar in the adjoining tavern, doing his best to lighten the wallets of half the hunters in town. Hot Rocks beer and Green Ruin whiskey were flowing freely.

It was bad enough having to house a lot of hunters for an indefinite period of time, Sedona thought. She really did not want to have to deal with the new boss of the Rainshadow Guild.

It was no secret that this was Jones's first job as the CEO of a Guild. It was not entirely clear what his previous position had been, but she would have bet good amber that he had been promoted out of the ranks of the Chamber's mysterious security division. They had fancy titles for the hunters who conducted Guild-sanctioned investigations—security specialists or something along those lines. But an enforcer was an enforcer, regardless of whether he worked for a mob boss or the Chamber.

Chamber enforcer to Guild boss was not a common path of advancement through the Guild hierarchy, but she had heard of other such instances. Adam Winters, the new Guild boss of Frequency City, was rumored to be a former enforcer. The Chamber probably assumed that if a man was tough enough to hunt the human monsters who possessed lethal amounts of paranormal talent, he was tough enough to control his own territory. She hadn't met a lot of enforcers in the course of her work with the Guilds—they were a rare breed and they tended to keep low profiles. But those she had known all had an ice-cold edge.

Cyrus Jones had that edge and a lot more going on. Dark secrets whispered in the atmosphere around him. It wasn't just raw power that she sensed. She was pretty sure she was picking up the vibes of the kind of mag-steel will that was required to handle a high-rez talent.

The edge was there, too, in the ruthless planes and angles of his hard face and his lean, rangy, broad-shouldered build. He was wearing the classic ghost-hunter uniform—khaki trousers and shirt, leather boots, leather jacket, and heavy leather belt. All of it looked well-worn. All of it sent the message that he had seen a lot of action in the Underworld.

Like every self-respecting hunter he wore amber. There were chunks of it set in his buckle, his watch, and the hilt of the knife he wore on his belt. And that was just the visible amber, she thought.

Sedona knew that it had come as a shock to the hunters who had recently arrived on the island to discover that here on Rainshadow, even well-tuned amber wasn't strong enough to steer a person safely into and out of the forbidden territory known as the Preserve. Only those with unique talents could handle the paranormal forces inside the psi-fence.

But the Guild wasn't on the island to deal with the problems inside the Preserve. That was the job of the Rainshadow Foundation. The Foundation had brought in the Guild to do the one thing ghost hunters did best—neutralize the chaotic forces and assorted hazards that were always waiting down below in the catacombs.

The maze of ancient tunnels on the island had only recently been discovered in the aftermath of some very powerful storms. Researchers and explorers from the corporate and academic worlds were eager to go into the Rainshadow Underworld to start collecting data. But that kind of expensive and dangerous—and potentially quite lucrative—fieldwork required security. For as long as anyone could remember, the Guilds had had a monopoly when it came to providing escort and protection services for those going underground.

"I'm sure you'll want space to set up a temporary office, Mr. Jones," she said. "This morning when I saw your name in our files I called Anna Fuentes down at the Bay View Inn. She said she's got a lovely two-room suite with a connecting door. It will be perfect for a field office. Very conveniently located to the center of Shadow Bay, I might add."

"I don't need the extra room," Cyrus said. "The Guild will be renting space from the owners of the Kane Gallery."

"I see."

She gave him her patented, no-room-at-this-inn smile and drummed her fingers on the counter. Fletcher Kane and Jasper Gilbert, both retired ghost hunters, owned the gallery. They would be only too happy to accommodate the new boss. Once a Guild man, always a Guild man.

"Would you mind giving me my key?" Cyrus asked. "I'd like to unpack and get settled."

The amusement in his arresting green eyes told her that he was well aware he had won the battle of wills.

She was saved from having to surrender the key by the roar of masculine shouts that erupted from the adjoining tavern.

"I've got a hundred says you can't toss him more than ten feet."

"You're on. Make room, people, make room. We need some space here."

Chairs and tables scraped on the old wooden floor. There was some excited chortling.

Alarm arced through Sedona. She stared across the lobby at the door that connected the tavern to the inn.

"Good grief, they've got Lyle," she said. "Damn it, I knew your hunters were going to be nothing but trouble."

She dashed out from behind the counter and raced across the lobby to the tavern entrance. She was aware of Cyrus following behind her but she ignored him.

The shadowy tavern was crammed with hunters. Knox was behind the bar, polishing glassware with a white cloth. He was grizzled and rotund with the weathered face of a retired commercial fisherman. He peered over the rims of his reading glasses, clearly pleased with his customers' revelry. Sedona knew exactly what he was thinking—the more the hunters drank, the more money they spent.

The Guild men had pushed the tables and chairs aside to make room for two hunters who stood opposite each other. There was a distance of about ten feet separating the pair. One of the hunters was holding Lyle in both hands. Lyle was fully fluffed and chortling with excitement.

As Sedona watched in horror, the hunter tossed Lyle toward the second man.

"Stop that!" Sedona shouted.

No one paid any attention. The second hunter deftly caught Lyle in both hands. Lyle chortled wildly, buzzed on dust bunny adrenaline.

"One pace back," the first hunter said.

Both hunters stepped back, lengthening the distance between them.

Sedona heard side bets going down around the room.

"Five says Duke can't catch the dust bunny."

"I've got twenty says Tanaka won't be able to control the trajectory, not with the dust bunny wriggling like that."

"You're on."

Tanaka, a lean, dark-haired hunter who wore his hair tied back with a strip of leather, prepared to launch Lyle into the air.

"No, don't you dare throw him," Sedona shouted. She lunged toward Tanaka. "Give him to me."

But she was too late. Tanaka had already completed the toss. Lyle was airborne. He chittered exultantly as he sailed across the room.

Moving with an unnerving quickness and, as far as Sedona could tell, almost no sound whatsoever, Cyrus was suddenly there in the flight path. Deftly he snagged Lyle out of midair and plopped him down on one shoulder.

Lyle whooped with delight. The crowd of hunters, however, fell abruptly silent. Those who weren't already on their feet slid off their bar stools and stood respectfully. No one actually saluted. The Guilds were technically not military organizations. But they operated in a quasi-military fashion in the Underworld, and they were subject to a strict chain of command. The new boss was in the room and everyone knew it.

"Sorry to interrupt the game, gentlemen," Cyrus said. "But the lady would rather you didn't toss the dust bunny around like a beanbag."

"Understood, sir," Duke said. "No dust bunny tossing.

Welcome to Rainshadow, Mr. Jones. I'm Sergeant Duke Donovan, Special Underground Operations, sir."

"Thank you, Sergeant," Cyrus said. "As I'm sure you are all well aware, I'm here to establish the Rainshadow Guild, and you are going to help me do that. Each of you has been handpicked to participate in this project because of your high levels of talent and your experience. I look forward to working with you."

There was a chorus of *"Yes, sir."*

"Tomorrow morning I will be meeting with the local authorities to get a full briefing on what I understand are some unusual conditions here on the island," Cyrus continued.

"Yes, sir," Duke said again. Excitement lit his eyes. "They've got monsters here on Rainshadow, boss. Real ones. Attridge, the local police chief, found the remains of a second carcass just inside the Preserve this morning. Word is, it looked like a giant snake covered in weird scales. No one has seen anything like it on the island, and they say that there's nothing big enough inside the psi-fence that could take down a huge snake. But something took it down."

"The theory is that freaks of nature are coming out of the catacombs at night," Tanaka added.

"I read the initial reports," Cyrus said. "We will deal with the problem. Now, if you will excuse me, I'm going to finish checking in to my room. After my meeting with the authorities in the morning, I want to see the entire team in my office, which, I understand, is next door to the Kane Gallery."

"Right, boss," Duke said. "I'll make sure the team is notified."

"Thank you," Cyrus said. "Now I would advise you gentlemen to get some sleep. We have a lot to do here on Rainshadow and we will start doing that work tomorrow."

There was another round of respectful *"Yes, sir."*

Cyrus turned his back on the crowd and walked across the room to where Sedona waited. He handed Lyle to her. Lyle chuffed contently a few times and settled down on her shoulder.

"May I please have the key to my cottage now?" Cyrus said.

Knox came out from behind the bar and made his way to where Sedona and Cyrus stood. "Give the man his room key, Sedona," he said. He beamed at Cyrus and offered his hand. "Welcome to Rainshadow, Mr. Jones. Name's Knox. I'm the owner of this here establishment. Proud to have you and your men amongst our clientele."

"Thanks," Cyrus said, shaking his hand. "Call me Cyrus."

"You bet. We don't stand on formality here on the island." Knox peered at Sedona over the rims of his glasses. "Tell you what, why don't you show Cyrus to Graveyard Cottage while I close down the bar? I can handle things here. Time you went home, anyway."

"I'm sure Mr. Jones can find the cottage by himself," Sedona said. "He's a Guild boss, after all. I'll just aim him in the right direction."

Cyrus raised his brows but he did not say anything.

"Nah, it's a little hard to find," Knox said. He smiled broadly at Cyrus. "On account of it's sort of hidden in the trees. We don't use it much, but we got it cleaned up when we realized that there would be a lot of hunters descending on Rainshadow. Didn't know Sedona had held it until it was the last available room, though. Tell you what, why don't I have her shift a couple of the hunters around so that we can get you into one of the nicer cottages?"

Cyrus looked at Sedona. "That won't be necessary. Graveyard Cottage sounds like it will guarantee me some privacy."

"Oh, yeah, no problem with privacy out there at the cemetery," Knox said. He looked at Sedona. "Get the man his key, honey. It's a long, hard trip here to Rainshadow. Expect Mr. Jones wants to get some sleep tonight."

"Right," Sedona said.

Grimly aware that she was flushing an unbecoming shade of pink, she crossed the lobby. Rounding the counter, she snagged the last key off the hook on the board, and bent down to retrieve two flashlights from under the computer. She straightened and tossed one of the flashlights in Cyrus's general direction. He caught it as easily as he had snagged Lyle out of midair a short time earlier.

Cyrus examined the flashlight with interest. "I'm going to need one of these to find my way home at night?"

She did not like the casual manner in which he used the word *home*. It made it sound like he would be hanging around for a while. Which was certainly true, she reminded herself. Like it or not, there was now an official Guild presence on the island and it wasn't going to go away. But with luck, Cyrus would soon find himself permanent housing.

"There aren't any streetlights out by the cemetery," Knox explained. "Actually, we've only got a couple on the island. One is over at the police station and the other is down at the marina."

"I won't need your flashlight," Cyrus said. He put the one Sedona had given him on the counter and unclipped the one on his belt. "I've got my own."

Knox chuckled. "That's a Guild man for you. Always prepared."

Cyrus gave Sedona a thoughtful look. "So, no streetlights and a view of the graveyard. Sounds perfect for me."

"Oh, yeah." She managed another sparkling smile. "I'm sure you'll find Graveyard Cottage a delightful, luxurious retreat from the stress of your daily routine."

Chapter 4

CYRUS AIMED THE FLASHLIGHT AT THE WEATHERED SIGN over the stone gates that guarded the graveyard. SHADOW BAY CEMETERY. An old-fashioned wrought-iron fence surrounded an assortment of weed-studded, overgrown grave markers.

One of the gravesites was fenced off with what looked like a mag-steel cage. It was deep inside the cemetery grounds, but he could have sworn he felt a whisper of Alien psi leaking out of it.

"Is that Graveyard Cottage?" Cyrus asked. "Am I going to be sleeping in an open grave?"

"I did try to warn you that the accommodations were a little rough," Sedona said.

Amused by her excruciatingly polite tone, he jacked up his senses a little. For a couple of heartbeats he allowed himself to indulge in the dangerous, reckless, intensely sexual thrill he got just from being so close to her.

He had been damned curious to meet her but he had not anticipated the hot vibe of sensual awareness that had ripped through him the moment he entered the lobby of Knox's Resort & Tavern. The rush was much more powerful now that she was standing within arm's reach.

Probably just the raw heat of attraction, he warned himself, jacked up by the fact that she was a strong talent of some kind. Add the factors of night, a nearly full moon, and the edgy vibes that emanated from the very heart of the island, and you got a mix that was highly combustible—at least on his end of the connection. All he had detected from Sedona thus far was a cool, wary watchfulness, however.

It was her possible para-psych profile that he had been warned about, but now that he was close to her he could not summon up any serious degree of caution. Just the opposite, he thought. He wanted to take risks with Sedona Snow.

There was a photo of her in the file that he had read before leaving for Rainshadow. The picture had failed utterly to capture the mysterious aura and the possibly dangerous allure of the woman, Cyrus thought. She wore her shoulder-length near-black hair in a severely elegant knot at the nape of her neck. Her eyes were the color of molten amber, hinting at the talent beneath the surface. Her delicate features were etched by intelligence, a fierce independence, and bone-deep determination—not cookie-cutter, fashion-runway beauty. This was a woman who came to a man on her own terms—if she came to him at all.

The dust bunny on her shoulder somehow went with the total package, he thought. He was walking through the night with a very interesting little witch and her familiar. A man was entitled to a few fantasies. It was Halloween Week after all.

"Relax, Mr. Jones, no need to sleep in a grave," Sedona said. "You'll have a real bed. Your cottage is over there in the woods."

He glanced back through the cemetery gates. "I assume that steel cage is protecting the entrance to the Underworld?"

"Yep, that's the gravesite of an early resident of the island, William Bainbridge. At least, everyone assumed it was his grave until a couple of months ago when it turned out that it was actually a hole-in-the-wall entrance to the catacombs. The Rainshadow Foundation installed a new, high-tech psi-and-steel fence to keep people from trying to go below."

"Has it worked?" Cyrus asked.

"About as well as any fence works. You know how it is. There are always thrill-seekers, treasure-hunters, and kids who can't resist a *Keep Out* sign. The theory that there may be genuine monsters wandering around down in the catacombs has proven to be a more effective deterrent than the cage."

"I saw the photos of the two half-eaten carcasses."

"The research team from the Foundation has concluded that something new has been added to the ecological mix inside the Preserve," she said. "But they haven't been able to figure out what's going on. The only viable explanation so far is that the recent violent storms here on Rainshadow opened up another entrance into the Underworld somewhere deep inside the fence. The creatures certainly haven't been using Bainbridge's grave. Someone would have noticed, trust me."

"But there have been no reliable sightings of live monsters according to the file."

"No," Sedona said. "The researchers have a theory about that, too. They think that the creatures can emerge only at night when the psi levels are highest inside the Preserve. The experts don't think that the monsters can handle daylight, not even inside the psi-fence. They were obviously evolved to live in a heavy-psi environment. Everyone seems fairly certain that the creatures can't come out of the Preserve, either."

"It's always dangerous to make assumptions when it comes to things that go bump in the night in the Underworld."

"Tell me about it," Sedona said.

Each word was etched in ice, Cyrus noted. Interesting.

"As I understand it, all the researchers have to go on so far are two half-gnawed carcasses," he said.

"Right. The Foundation people managed to retrieve them. They'd both been pretty well mangled, first by whatever killed them and then by the critters that live inside the Preserve."

"And everyone is sure that there were never any

sightings before the recent storm activity here on Rainshadow?"

"Well, that is a matter of opinion," Sedona said. "The thing is, people have been seeing things inside the Preserve ever since the first explorers landed on the island. For years people who manage to crash through the fence have stumbled back out—if they got back out at all—in a dazed, disoriented condition. Some of them have sworn they saw monsters, but most people think the survivors were hallucinating wildly."

She led the way around the far side of the cemetery fence and stopped in front of a weathered, single-story cabin. Moonlight glinted on the obsidian-dark windows.

"Quaint," Cyrus said.

"We like to think so," Sedona said. She went up the front steps and crossed the small porch to the door. "Welcome to Graveyard Cottage, your new home away from home."

He followed her up the steps. "I'm guessing there's no room service."

"No, but breakfast is included." She used the key to rez the lock and then pushed open the door. "It's served in the tavern from five thirty until seven thirty in the mornings. Judging by the amount of food your hunters have been consuming, I would suggest that you show up early if you want to eat."

"Thanks for the warning."

"Anytime."

She stepped through the doorway and rezzed a wall switch. Lyle chortled. He bounced down off her shoulder and scuttled around the place, exploring. Cyrus dropped his duffel on the scarred hardwood floor and examined his surroundings.

A couple of lamps glowed, revealing a spare, rustic space furnished with an ancient sofa, a rather battered table, and a couple of rickety-looking chairs. There was a well-worn area rug in front of the fireplace and faded curtains on the windows. All of the pieces looked as if they had been picked up at a low-rent yard sale. There was also a small kitchenette. Through a darkened doorway he could make out a tiny bedroom.

Sedona watched him. "Like I said, they've got a very nice two-room suite at the Bay View Inn. Great view of the marina."

He had to give her credit. She didn't give up easily.

"This will do nicely," he said. "Lots of rustic charm."

"Yeah, right. Well, if you change your mind, let me know. There's a supply of firewood in a shed out back. Here's your key."

Her fingers brushed against his when she handed him the key. He had already braced himself for what he anticipated would be a few sparks of pure energy. He was not disappointed. Small flashes of lightning crackled across his senses. Everything inside him tightened.

He could tell from the way Sedona flinched and took a sharp little breath that she had been caught off guard by the zing of awareness. Her eyes widened but in the next heartbeat she got herself back under control.

She stepped quickly back out of range, doing her best to make the retreat look like a normal action. But he knew better. She was not as oblivious to the currents that resonated between them as she wanted him to believe. Knowing that was enough to satisfy him—for now.

"Come on, Lyle, time to go," Sedona said. She scooped Lyle up off the floor and plopped him on her shoulder. She summoned up another cool smile. "See you in the morning, Mr. Jones."

"Call me Cyrus," he said.

"Whatever." She headed for the door.

"Hold on, I'll walk you to your place," he said.

"Thanks, but that's not necessary. I've got my flashlight."

"It's night, the fog is rolling in, and I'm told that here there be monsters."

Her jaw tightened. "I thought I made it clear, they haven't escaped the Preserve."

"Yet. I'll walk you to your place." He kept it polite but nonnegotiable.

She watched him with a speculative expression, lips pursing a bit. "And just what, exactly, will you do if we are attacked by a monster?"

"I have no idea," he said. "But I will try to come up with something helpful."

"Is that your usual approach to problems?" For the first time she sounded genuinely amused.

"It's kept me alive in the Underworld until now," he said.

"Can't argue with that." She turned and went out onto the porch. "Okay, suit yourself, but as it happens, my place isn't far from here."

"Someone waiting for you?" he asked.

"Nope. I live alone, except for Lyle, of course."

She reached up to touch the dust bunny. Cyrus allowed himself to breathe again.

He followed her outside, dimming the lights as he went through the door. Sedona had already rezzed her flashlight. He got his own going and then kicked up his senses again, not focusing on Sedona this time, but on the night around them.

Rainshadow was an intriguing place, he decided. There was an ambient energy in the atmosphere. The fog coming in off the bay was getting heavier but it was normal fog, not the strange paranormal-infused mist that he had read about in the Foundation reports. The near-disaster that had come close to destroying Rainshadow a couple of months back had been averted. Everyone had breathed a sigh of relief—until the monsters started emerging from the catacombs.

"Where, exactly, is your place?" he asked.

"Not far," Sedona said. "Number Twelve, Cemetery View Cottage. It's the second hardest-to-rent room at the resort, which is the reason I got it."

"My cottage being the hardest to rent, I assume."

"Uh-huh."

He considered the heavy darkness around them. "Please don't tell me that you walk home alone every night."

"I don't usually work nights. Knox handles that shift most of the time. He lives in the cottage nearest to the lobby and the tavern. But I've been helping him out in the evenings this week because we're so busy."

"I'm surprised the Foundation hasn't evacuated the island."

"That's not a realistic option," Sedona said. "The residents of Rainshadow tend to be a tad stubborn. Unless those critters start coming out of the Preserve and strolling down Main Street, I doubt that any of the locals could be convinced to leave. By the way, for future reference, I'm pretty sure there's a rifle or a mag-rez pistol in just about every house on the island."

"Just about?"

"I don't have one. But I've got Lyle, here."

Lyle chortled contentedly on her shoulder.

"And you have your talent," Cyrus said quietly. "Think either will work against the monsters?"

There was a short, highly charged beat of silence.

Sedona halted and turned to face him, the beam of her light aimed at his feet. He pointed his flashlight downward as well. The light was reflected around them in the swirling fog.

"You know who I am, don't you?" Sedona said. "I thought you probably did."

"I do my homework," he said. "I know you're a gatekeeper and that you used to do regular contract work for the Guilds. I also know that you disappeared for nearly a month awhile back. When you reappeared you did not apply for any more work with the Guilds. You moved here, instead. According to the file, you were probably badly burned on your last job."

"And now you're worried that I might be a problem,

aren't you? Who knows? Maybe you're right. You want to know what really happened to me awhile back? Let me give you the short version. Kirk Morgan, the boss of the Gold Creek Guild, made it look as if I had been lost on that last job. The truth is, I was kidnapped and sent to a secret Underworld clinic that is probably run by Morgan's Guild. I was held against my will and kept in a waking dreamstate while a mad scientist shot me full of drugs. I escaped with Lyle's help. When I got home, I discovered that my MC husband had divorced me and that absolutely no one had bothered to search for me. I figured I had nothing left to lose, so I decided to start over again here on Rainshadow." She paused. "And there you have it—absolute proof that I am a psi-burned, delusional gatekeeper who is living in a paranoid fantasy world."

He contemplated that briefly. "Sounds like your life has been interesting lately."

"Don't pretend that the Guild file you read didn't indicate that I'm in all probability a whacko."

"Yeah, that's what it says in the official file," he agreed. "But I also read another file, one that was given to me by a private investigation agency, Jones and Jones. Ever heard of it?"

The question stopped her cold. Then she grew thoughtful. "No. Are you telling me that you had me investigated by a non-Guild security agency?"

"I like to be thorough."

"Is that a way of saying that you didn't trust the official file?"

"I never trust the official file," he said.

"Very wise of you. We're talking about the Guilds and the Chamber, after all."

"I'm getting the message that you don't have any fond memories of your time with the Guilds."

"You know that old saying, that a Guild boss never leaves anyone behind?"

"What about it?"

"I am living proof that is a flat-out lie." She took a breath. "Kirk Morgan follows another motto: When things go south, cut your losses."

"He left you behind?"

"We were guiding a corporate exploration team through the Rainforest. It was a big contract. The corporation wanted the boss, himself, to take the lead that day. That was Morgan. He screwed up and led us straight into an energy river. You could say it wasn't entirely his fault. The river shouldn't have been where it was. The sector had been mapped. But you know how it is down below."

"Unpredictable."

"Exactly," Sedona said. "For a time it looked like we might lose some people and a lot of expensive equipment. But river energy is a lot like gate energy. I was able to redirect the flow of the currents long enough to get Morgan and everyone else to safety—everyone except me, that is."

"What happened?"

"I'm not sure, to be honest. I was supposed to be the last one to make the crossing. One minute I was dealing with the currents. In the next minute I felt someone come up behind me. At first I thought that I had lost count and that not every member of the team had made it to safety. I started to turn around to see who was there. I felt a small, stinging pain in my upper shoulder. I thought I'd been bitten by an insect. But someone clamped a thick cloth over my mouth and nose. I started to struggle and immediately lost control of the energy river. When I woke up I was in the underground lab, locked in a drug-induced waking dreamstate."

"You're saying you were kidnapped." He kept his voice neutral.

Sedona exhaled slowly. "I'll never be able to prove it, of course. There's nothing like a Guild cover-up. So I am officially a burned-out gatekeeper. What made you run a private background check on me?"

"Nothing personal. I ran a check on a lot of folks here on the island before I took this job. And I looked extra hard at those who were believed to have some talent."

"People like me," Sedona said.

"People like you."

"Well, just in case you're tempted to send me away to a para-psych hospital, you should know that I've created a file of my own."

"Is that right?"

"Yes," she said. "It contains my version of what happened to me during the three weeks I vanished. It's stored in a digital file that will automatically be made public all over the rez-net within twenty-four hours if anything happens to me."

"I see."

"I know that the Chamber will deny the existence of

the lab and claim that I'm just another badly burned gatekeeper. But we both know that the online conspiracy freaks feed on stuff like my story. The media and the bloggers would go wild. I'm sure the Guilds would survive, but they don't like that kind of bad press." Sedona paused for emphasis. "They might tend to blame the boss who allowed the problem of Sedona Snow and her delusions to blow up in their faces."

"The boss here being me."

"You," she agreed.

He whistled softly. "Blackmailing a Guild boss. I'm impressed. That takes guts."

"Just thought you should know."

"Your threat is duly noted. Now I've got a question for you. Can I count on you if we need a gatekeeper down below, here on the island?"

"What?" She stared at him, clearly stunned.

"You heard me. It's a simple question. Are you open to a Guild contract in the event I need you when we start clearing the tunnels?"

"Are you serious?"

"I'm a Guild boss. Of course I'm serious."

She hesitated. "Do you think you're likely to need a gatekeeper?"

"Here's what I know. This island is a very strong geothermal nexus. Energy gates and energy rivers are always a possibility underground at nexus points. In addition, just to add to the potential problems of the natural forces in the area, the reports indicate that the Aliens evidently used this island as a bioresearch lab. If that's true, they probably conducted a lot of very dangerous, very desperate experiments with the local flora and fauna."

"That's what the experts from the Rainshadow Foundation have concluded, yes."

"If that theory is correct," Cyrus continued, "there is every reason to expect that the Aliens conducted some of their experiments underground as well as on the surface. No telling what we'll run into down there."

Sedona exhaled slowly. "True."

"I'd like to know there's a gatekeeper available if we need one."

She was quiet for a moment.

"Why didn't you bring a gatekeeper with you?" she asked finally.

She was wary but he could tell that she was also intrigued. Confronting her had been a risk but he had done his research on Sedona Snow. He knew a lot about her and he knew something else as well. Whether she admitted it or not he was very certain that she wanted to go back into the catacombs.

Once you had worked in the ancient, glowing tunnels, you always wanted to go back down. Everyone—even those with scant measureable talent—got a buzz from the strong paranormal currents that flowed through the maze. But for those who were extremely sensitive to Alien psi and were capable of controlling some of the powerful forces down below, the rush was like no other.

"I didn't bring another gatekeeper because I knew you were here," he said quietly. "You're a Class Five, one of the best."

"I *was* a Class Five." She tightened her grip on the flashlight. "According to your damned file, I'm probably a certified whacko now."

"All I care about is talent. Are you still one of the best?"

She was silent for a moment.

"Do you really think your men would want to work with me if they knew that I had been psi-burned?" she asked.

"I'll handle my crew. All I want to know is if you're willing to go back down into the catacombs to work gate energy."

She got quiet again. He did not try to push her into an answer. The fog thickened around them. Something rustled in the bushes. Lyle's second set of eyes popped open, gleaming amber-hot in the night. He made a soft rumbling noise, bounded down to the ground, and disappeared into the foliage.

"He goes out a lot at night," Sedona explained. "There are other dust bunnies here on Rainshadow. I think they like to hunt together."

"He seems to have bonded with you. Where did you find him?"

"He found me in that underground lab I told you about. If it hadn't been for Lyle, I would still be there."

He could hear the shudder in her voice. Whatever the truth of the situation, he did not doubt that she believed her version of events.

"This lab where you were held," he said carefully. "Any idea of what happened to you while you were there?"

"I told you, I was drugged most of the time."

"Any idea who ran the experiments on you?"

She hesitated, very wary now.

"He called himself Dr. Blankenship," she said finally. "He had a couple of hulks for assistants. Big guys. Looked like they'd been using a lot of steroids."

He pondered that for a moment. "I don't suppose you have any idea where the lab was located?"

"No. They took all my amber. Lyle is the one who got me back to the surface. All I can tell you is that when I emerged from the Underworld I flagged down a truck on a highway near the Amber Crest Para-Psychiatric Hospital. Some of the lab equipment Dr. Blankenship used came from Amber Crest. I saw the tags on a few of the instruments."

"Huh. Think Blankenship worked at Amber Crest?"

"I have no idea. It's all I've got and we both know that's not very much." She watched him with great caution. "What are you thinking?"

"I'm thinking it might be a good idea to track down Dr. Blankenship. Someone should have a chat with Kirk Morgan, too."

"Trust me, they'll both deny everything, and there will be no way to prove them wrong," she said. "They've got the power of the Guilds behind them. They're well-protected."

"You don't have a lot of faith in the ability of the Chamber to police the Guilds, do you?"

"Nope. I won't trust anyone connected with the Guilds ever again."

"You're out here, alone in the dark, with me," he pointed out.

“That’s different. I’m safe here on Rainshadow. The Foundation runs things on this island, not the Guilds.”

She wasn’t wrong on that score, he thought. The Rainshadow Foundation was controlled by the powerful Sebastian family. The Sebastians were a force to be reckoned with. They had invited the Guild in to clean up the Underworld but if they changed their minds, they could just as easily send the Guild away. In addition, the island’s police chief, Slade Attridge, was a former Federal Bureau of Psi Investigation agent with connections throughout law enforcement. All indications were that Chief Attridge took his responsibilities to the residents of Shadow Bay very seriously.

Cyrus smiled.

“Something amusing?” Sedona asked suspiciously.

“I was just thinking that you made a very good decision when you moved to Rainshadow,” he said.

“Works for me,” she said. “This is a town full of people who don’t fit in very well in mainstream society.”

“You consider yourself to be one of those misfits?”

“Since the day I was born.”

Sedona stopped in front of another cottage that was cheerfully decorated for Halloween. Orange and green lanterns were suspended from the porch ceiling. A hollowed-out pumpkin carved with ghoulish features sat near the front door. A skeleton draped in a flowing psi-green cape reclined on a rocker.

“I’ll bet you get a lot of trick-or-treaters here on Halloween night,” Cyrus said.

“I’m hoping for a crowd,” she said. “It’s my first

Halloween on Rainshadow, though. I'm afraid the kids might skip my cottage, what with the graveyard nearby and all."

"How could they resist a house near a cemetery on Halloween?"

"I've got my fingers crossed," she admitted. She went up the steps to her front door. "Good luck hunting those Underworld monsters, Mr. Jones."

He watched her from the bottom of the steps. "You never answered my question. Can I count on you if I need a gatekeeper down below?"

She turned back to face him. "My standard fees are high," she warned. "And I'll have to charge extra because of the unknowns here on Rainshadow."

"Thanks," he said. "That's all I wanted to know."

She pushed open the door and stepped into the small, dark space. She rezzed a lamp and paused to look at him once again.

"Aren't you just a little bit concerned that I might not only be psi-burned but crazy?" she asked.

He smiled. "No."

"Why not? I've got all the hallmarks. Three weeks I can't account for in the Underworld. Tales of secret research labs and strange experiments. That kind of stuff is right up there with stories of Alien abductions and lost worlds underground."

"I've met a few real crazies in my time," Cyrus said. "I have what you might call a feel for them."

"I don't feel like one to you?"

"No," he said.

"Why do you say that? Everyone knows the human monsters can hide in plain sight."

"Trust me, Sedona Snow, you're not crazy. An off-the-charts talent, probably, but not crazy."

He turned and started to walk away into the night.

"Mr. Jones," she called softly.

He stopped again and looked at her over his shoulder. "Cyrus."

"Cyrus." She sounded as if she was test-driving the name, waiting to see if it felt right to her. "What makes you think I'm an off-the-charts talent?"

"Got a feel for those, too. Lots of them in the Jones family. Our history makes us a little more open-minded when it comes to dealing with unconventional talents, conspiracy theories, and secret labs where strange experiments are conducted. Good night, Sedona Snow."

Chapter 5

HE WALKED BACK TO HIS COTTAGE THROUGH THE FOG, unclipping his phone as he went through the front door. Marlowe answered on the second ring.

"Jones and Jones," Marlowe said. "And for the record, cousin, it's getting late here in Frequency City."

"I found her," Cyrus said. He shut the door, rezzed the light, and lowered himself onto the sagging sofa. "You were right, Sedona Snow is here on Rainshadow. Whatever happened to her during those three weeks, it was bad. She described a real nightmare experience to me."

"Assuming her memories are accurate and not the by-product of a bad psi-burn."

"Assuming that, yeah."

There was a short, tight silence on the other end of the line.

"She's still alive?"

"Alive and looking quite fit."

"It's been nearly a month now since she surfaced. Maybe she somehow managed to get hold of a fresh supply of the drug."

Cyrus thought about his impressions of Sedona. "It's possible. We don't know much about the latest version of the formula. It might not show any outward indications at this stage."

"But she's still alive," Marlowe repeated.

"And looking damn stable, as far as I can tell."

"Any sign that she might be more powerful than she was before she was kidnapped? Any indication that she has acquired additional talents?"

"No, but give me a break here. I just met her this evening. Somehow asking her if she has become an unstable multi-talent didn't seem like a good way to introduce myself. She did give me a brief rundown of what happened to her last month when she disappeared for a few weeks."

"What's her story?" Marlowe asked.

"She claims that she was kidnapped in the Rainforest while on a job for the Gold Creek Guild. She says she was held in a waking dreamstate somewhere in the catacombs where a Dr. Blankenship ran experiments on her."

"What kind of experiments?"

"She didn't describe them," Cyrus said. "We haven't had what you would call an extensive discussion of the subject. She's a tad anti-Guild at the moment. Thinks Kirk Morgan, the boss of the Gold Creek operation, may have conspired with the kidnappers."

"That's not beyond the realm of possibility," Marlowe said. "How did she escape?"

"I don't have the details on that angle, either. But she did say that Lyle helped her get out of the Underworld."

"Lyle?"

"Lyle is a dust bunny."

"Really?" Marlowe's voice brightened. "She's got a dust bunny companion?"

"Yep, just like you."

"That could be significant."

"Why?"

"Well," Marlowe said, "I can't see a dust bunny bonding with one of the monsters."

"That's because you've got your own dust bunny sidekick. Marlowe, dust bunnies are cute and smart and some of them seem to enjoy human companionship, but that doesn't mean they only bond with the good guys. Lots of bad guys have pet dogs."

"Dust bunnies are more particular than dogs."

There was no point arguing the subject with Marlowe, Cyrus told himself. His cousin adored her own dust bunny pal, Gibson. Time to get the discussion back on track.

"About this Dr. Blankenship," he said.

"I'm already working on it. I'll see what I can find."

Cyrus heard the clicking of computer keys in the background. He pictured his cousin at home with her new husband, Adam Winters, the powerful CEO of the Frequency City Guild.

Cyrus got up and went to the window to look out at

the view of the graveyard. He was aware of a wistful sensation. Marlowe and Adam were clearly very much in love. The bond between them was so strong, even those around them were aware of it. He knew his own odds of achieving that kind of long-term relationship were very slim, indeed. They called him Dead Zone Jones for a reason.

"I've got one other small piece of information for you," he said. "Sedona remembers that some of the lab equipment she saw while she was being held was tagged as the property of Amber Crest Para-Psychiatric Hospital."

"Amber Crest?"

There was more rapid clicking followed by a couple of pings.

"Hmm." Marlowe sounded thoughtful now. "It's a psi-burn hospital run by the Gold Creek Guild."

"Kirk Morgan's operation."

"Right. Hang on. Nope, no Dr. Blankenship on the staff."

"Keep looking," Cyrus said.

"Don't worry, I will. This is the first real break we've had since we heard those rumors awhile back. Every other lead has been a dead end."

Cyrus was amused by the enthusiasm in Marlowe's voice. "You're really into this investigation, aren't you?"

"Are you kidding? The possibility that someone has come up with another version of that old Arcane formula is huge. Jones and Jones hasn't had a case involving the drug in the two hundred years that we've been on Harmony. That formula is a legend in the Arcane archives."

"Don't get too excited. The thing about legends is that there are always a lot of lies mixed in with the truth."

"That's what makes them legends. Speaking of which, how's the monster-hunting going there on Rainshadow?"

"I haven't even started. I arrived on the island two hours ago. I haven't unpacked."

"And already you have confirmed that one of Arizona Snow's many-times great-nieces is there and that she was involved with some folks who sound like they have reformulated the drug. Nice work, cousin."

"Gosh, thanks. Now, if you don't mind, I'm going to get some sleep."

"Lucky you. I'm going to be working all night on these new leads."

There was a *click* as someone else came on the line.

"No, she is not going to work all night," Adam Winters said. "We just found out she's four weeks pregnant. She is going to get the sleep she needs."

"Pregnant?" Cyrus said. "Hey, that's great. Congratulations."

"Thanks," Marlowe said. "We're excited. Don't tell anyone else in the family, though, okay? We haven't made the announcement."

"I'm stuck here on Rainshadow," Cyrus said. "Who am I going to tell? Good night, and let me know as soon as you find anything, Marlowe."

"Will do," Marlowe said. She paused. When she spoke again, her voice gentled. "Don't worry, Cyrus. You're going to find the right woman someday."

"Tell that to Arcanematch, will you? Congratulations, again, and good night."

He ended the connection before Marlowe could offer him any more crumbs of comfort and reassurance. Unlike legends, there were some things in life that were impossible to change. The nature of his talent was one of those things.

Arcanematch, the society's exclusive matchmaking agency, didn't give up on very many clients, but they had given up on him.

Chapter 6

SEDONA WATCHED THROUGH THE WINDOW UNTIL CYRUS disappeared into the fog and the trees. It didn't take long. She caught glimpses of the beam of his flashlight for another moment or two and then he was gone.

She turned away from the window and went to the small kitchenette. Opening a cupboard, she took down the bottle of brandy that she kept there. For medicinal purposes only. Tonight she definitely needed a little medication.

She splashed some of the brandy into a glass and de-rezzed the living room lamp. The little night-light that she had installed the day she moved into the cottage automatically came on, casting a pale glow that illuminated the entrance to the hallway. She sank down into the big, over-stuffed reading chair and propped her feet on the hassock.

Nights were very dark on Rainshadow. The heavy presence of the densely forested Preserve, which occupied most of the island, cast a long shadow. That shadow was most intense after dark. It was a fact of paranormal physics that psi-energy of all types was strongest in the absence of sunlight. It wasn't a supernatural thing, simply one of the immutable laws of nature. Sunlight and other forms of normal light interfered with the energy from the paranormal end of the spectrum.

She sat in the deep shadows of the living room for a while, thinking about Cyrus Jones. Mostly she wondered if he was telling her the truth when he said he didn't think that she was a whacko. There was no reason to trust a Guild boss—every reason not to trust one—but she had the sense that he believed that she was stable.

Then again, it would be really dumb to try to second-guess a Guild boss's strategy. They were by nature inclined to be extremely secretive. In her experience, the powerful men who ran the Guilds were also dangerous. Traditionally, they controlled their various territories with a degree of ruthlessness that would have done credit to the leaders of organized crime syndicates.

Some of the Guild CEOs were more notorious than others. It was true that the Chamber was under new management. It claimed to be determined to clean up the reputations of the organizations it oversaw. But old habits die hard. Most of the high-ranking Guild men she had met protected their privileges, perks, and powers with all the money and manpower at their command. There were a few women in the Guilds but they tended to be in the rank and file. They were rarely promoted into the higher echelons.

The vast majority of ghost hunters at every level of the organizations were male. The reason was simple. One of the greatest hazards down in the tunnels were the so-called ghosts—unpredictable manifestations of highly unstable dissonance energy. The talent required to control that kind of energy was linked to testosterone. Ergo, most ghost hunters were male.

But other sorts of talents were needed on the tunnel teams, as well—her kind of talent, for example. Maybe Cyrus Jones really did want to get on her good side because of the possibility that he might require her services in the Rainshadow catacombs. Still, there were other high-rez gatekeepers. He could have brought one of them along with him to the island. But he hadn't brought one because he had known that she was here and presumably available.

Coincidence? I think not.

Never trust a Guild boss, she reminded herself. Nevertheless, the thought of working underground again stirred her senses. It also raised some unsettling questions. Why would Jones be so willing to risk the safety of a team by employing a gatekeeper who might be unstable?

Even as she asked herself the question, the answer whispered through her thoughts. Jones knew something about the Disaster—maybe something that she did not know. Maybe she was the real reason he was on the island.

Watch it, she thought. *You're becoming as paranoid as the other residents of Rainshadow.* Then again, paranoia had some definite survival value. She had taken a risk telling Jones about the file that she had set to release to the media in the event anything happened to her. But it was all she had in the way of a threat.

She drank some more of the brandy and forced herself to confront the very real possibility that Jones was on the island because he wanted to use her in ways she could not yet fathom.

If that was the case, it probably made sense to play along, at least for a while. Maybe Jones had answers to some of the questions that had haunted her since the Disaster. But what would be the price she would have to pay to get them? Guild bosses were not known for their compassionate and understanding natures. One thing you could depend on when it came to a Guild exec—he had his own agenda.

She had to hand it to him; he had certainly known what he was doing when he had offered her the prospect of going back down into the tunnels. Everyone who worked the Underworld knew how addictive the catacombs could be. The stronger the talent, regardless of the nature of that talent, the stronger the rush. There was nothing else like it—except going into the Preserve. But the forbidden area of the island inside the high-tech security fence was off-limits unless you were lucky enough to accompany one of the Foundation-sanctioned research teams.

The Underworld was the undisputed territory of the Guilds, however, and they took their right to police the Alien tunnels very seriously. Not that they actually had any legal rights to the vast network of glowing green tunnels. But tradition was a powerful thing on Harmony—probably because humans had only been on the planet for a couple of centuries. Two hundred years ago traditions of all kinds had taken on new meaning to a bunch of stranded colonists who had found themselves cut off from their home world. The First Generation had established a lot of traditions and their descendants were stuck with them.

Take marriage and family, for instance, Sedona thought glumly. She rolled the brandy glass between her palms. Now, there the colonists had outdone themselves with traditions—traditions they had locked down with mag-steel laws that were only now starting to loosen ever so slightly.

Why in the world was she thinking about the marriage laws tonight? Marriage was the last subject she wanted to contemplate. Her track record in the romance department had been deplorable even before she had metamorphosed into some kind of weird multi-talent. In a culture where family was everything, a person who could not claim strong clan relationships was something of an outcast. In theory, those born of an illicit union were not supposed to pay for the sins of their parents, but the reality was that a bastard faced a very difficult time socially, and that went double when it came to finding a lifetime marriage partner.

And now, of course, she wouldn't dare register with a matchmaker. If being a bastard was a problem when it came to finding a match, being an unstable multi-talent bastard made for impossible odds. She would likely find herself hauled off to a para-rez psych hospital as soon as she completed the questionnaire.

Her phone rang. She picked it up and glanced at the screen. FENWICK NASH REED. She'd lost count of the calls she'd had from the law firm. Her grandfather's lawyers did not give up easily, she reflected. Then again, they were well-paid to follow Robert Snow's orders. She disconnected the call without answering and put the phone down on the end table.

She finished the brandy, got to her feet, and went back into the tiny kitchen where she rinsed out the glass and sct it on the counter.

When she crossed the living room and looked out the windows she saw that the mist had blanketed the entire town of Shadow Bay now. Even the lights of the Halloween lanterns and the Haunted Alien Catacombs attraction near the marina had been swallowed up by the dense fog.

She walked into the short hallway that led to her bedroom, reaching out to rez the light switch.

The light did not come on. She made a note to install a new bulb in the fixture first thing in the morning.

She felt her way into the bedroom doorway and groped around the edge of the door for the light switch. She found it and rezzed it. Nothing happened.

Just her luck that both bulbs had failed at the same time. What were the odds?

The damned wind chimes clashed, loud and discordant.

She felt a small object under the carpet.

"What in the world?"

Her first thought was that Lyle had hidden one of his

toys under the small rug. She bent down, intending to lift one corner to retrieve the object.

Dark energy feathered her senses.

"Crap."

Instinctively she backed away toward the living room, her talent flaring wildly. But by then it was too late. Currents of cold, heavy dreamlight energy exploded in the atmosphere, plunging her into a nightmare.

Terrible images of formless horrors materialized around her. Ghostly, nerve-shattering voices called to her.

She tried to retreat but she was off-balance and already badly disoriented. Strange images from a landscape lit with a freakish, psi-green radiance swirled around her, trapping her.

The dangerous dreamlight worked rapidly. Hallucinations seethed in the shadows. She tripped, staggered, and nearly went down. At the last instant she managed to flatten one hand on the wall to steady herself.

She knew that the only reason she was not already unconscious was because of her powerful talent. But it could not protect her for long. At least, she thought, her old talent could not hold out against the trap energy.

Frantically she groped for the flicker. It took a huge amount of concentration just to get it out of her shirt pocket. But at last she had it clutched in one hand. She rezzed it with a desperation she had not experienced since the night she escaped from the lab.

A paranormal firestorm erupted in the hallway, forming a protective circle of energy around her. The dream images receded. Then she smelled smoke and realized that some of the fire energy in the atmosphere was coming from the normal end of the spectrum. In another second or two she would set fire to the cottage.

She pulled hard on her talent, dampening the flames from the normal end while the paranormal circle of fire continued to burn around her. She did not know what to expect. Most people discovered the nature of their paranormal senses more or less by accident when they first came into them. Until you knew what you could do, you couldn't do it very well.

Still, power was power and control was control, and she had always possessed a lot of both.

She could not halt the flood tide of dreamlight but she could force it to flow around her, just as she did when she controlled the psi-winds of a gate or an energy river. The terrifying images and the currents of eerie lights streamed around her on all sides. The voices faded. The dreamscape was no longer as disorienting as it had been a moment ago but the boundary between the normal and the surreal was murky, at best. It helped to keep one hand on the wall. The tactile sensations were easier for her fractured senses to interpret than the visual and audible kind.

This wasn't the first time she had waded through a sea of bad energy. She could do this.

She concentrated fiercely on navigating out of the darkened hallway. She knew she was in the living room when she lost contact with the wall. The weak glow of the night-light beckoned from a great distance, illuminating the path to the front door. She could not maintain her balance so she went down to her hands and knees and crawled across the room, moving within the eye of the energy storm.

Behind her the ghastly dreamlight subsided but she needed time to recover. The nasty little trap had caught her by surprise. She knew that her senses had taken a serious blow. She was stunned and disoriented. All she wanted to do was collapse on the front porch but the chimes warned her that she had to keep moving.

In situations like this, you went with your intuition, she reminded herself.

She used both hands to open the front door. When she finally succeeded she found herself looking out into a wall of moonlight-infused fog and a muffled stillness. Her senses were still flaring but at least she was no longer generating flames.

Should have brought the flashlight. No, a flashlight would give away my position.

She could not explain why it seemed so important to get out of the cottage. She just knew it had to be done. She fought back the last of the hallucinations as she inched her way across the porch. The front door squeaked as it swung slowly closed behind her. She found one of the wooden posts that marked the steps.

She managed to haul herself upright and limp cautiously down the three steps. When she felt hard ground under her shoes she walked forward slowly, her hands outstretched in front of her face.

She could not see a thing in the absolute darkness, but her senses were no longer disoriented. She knew approximately where she was. She veered left, counting the paces to the woodshed.

When her outstretched fingers found the structure she breathed a ragged sigh of relief. She worked her way around the shed and stopped behind it, utterly exhausted from the effort it had taken to fend off the dreamlight.

She put her back against the rear wall of the shed and slowly sank down until she was sitting on the ground. Her fingers brushed against a fist-sized rock. She gripped it tightly. She still clutched the flicker in her other hand but she was not sure she could count on anything more from her talent tonight. She might need a more traditional weapon.

For a time she sat there, wondering why she had gone to such an effort to escape the cottage. Maybe the intuitive side of her nature had been badly scrambled by the psi-explosion.

But eventually she heard muffled footsteps. She glimpsed the faint, thin beam of a small flashlight slicing like a needle through the mist. The light disappeared when the newcomer went up the front steps.

From where she sat, shielded by the woodshed, she could not see anything. But she heard the footsteps crossing the front porch. The door squeaked again when it was opened.

Someone had gone inside the cottage.

For a moment or two, nothing happened. She held her breath and clutched the rock.

And then the door slammed open. Footsteps sounded

again, moving quickly back across the porch and down the front steps. Soft, muffled thuds. Athletic shoes, Sedona decided.

She tightened her grip on the rock and the flicker. The way her luck was running lately, the intruder would probably come looking for her, and the woodshed was the obvious place to start.

But the footsteps kept going, down the graveled driveway to the road. When Sedona risked a peek around the edge of the shed she could see the beam of a flashlight dancing wildly in the fog but it was impossible to make out the running figure. A moment later the bouncing light vanished, too.

Chapter 7

SHE SAT THERE WITH HER BACK AGAINST THE SHED WALL, trying to calm her abused senses. She hadn't been this rattled since the Disaster. But at least she wasn't sliding into unconsciousness this time. She was pretty sure the psychic side of her nature hadn't been shattered.

Pretty sure. She just needed time to get her act together, she thought.

The auroras started then, the brilliant green lights flooding the night sky, infusing the thick fog with an eerie green glow. It didn't make it any easier to see things in the mist, but at least the world was no longer so oppressively dark.

Maybe she was hallucinating again. No, she had seen the auroras last night and the night before that. Everyone else in Shadow Bay had seen them, too. The locals said they were a common atmospheric event around Halloween. The waves of light were real.

A familiar rumble came out of the fog.

"Lyle," she said. "About time you showed up. Hope you had fun tonight. I had a blast."

Lyle appeared out of the glowing green mist. She wouldn't have been able to see him at all if it were not for the fact that he had all four eyes open. He hopped up onto her knees and made urgent little noises.

"It's okay," she said. She reached out to pat his head. "But I need a minute here."

Lyle rumbled again, jumped down off her knees, and disappeared into the green mist.

"Just when you think you've found the right guy," Sedona said, "he ups and disappears on you."

Damn. Now she was talking to herself. This was not good. Maybe she had hallucinated Lyle. It was a deeply disturbing thought. Maybe the drugs they had given her in Blankenship's lab had done more damage than she had realized. Maybe there had been no psi-trap in the bedroom tonight. Maybe she wasn't seeing aurora light reflected in the fog. Maybe she was permanently lost in a dreamscape.

More footsteps echoed in the mist. She listened closely. Boots, this time, and moving fast. She wondered if she was now having auditory hallucinations. Dreams were strange.

She listened hard, wondering if the boots would go into the house. But they didn't. They came directly toward the woodshed.

Lyle materialized out of the bright fog. All four eyes still open. But this time he chortled reassuringly and bounced up onto her thigh.

Relief flashed through her. She clutched him close.

The boot steps came to a halt. She was suddenly pinned in the beam of a flashlight. When she looked up she saw a large dark shadow looming in the mist.

"What the hell is going on here?" Cyrus said.

"It's sort of complicated," Sedona said.

She put down the rock and struggled to get to her feet.

Cyrus reached down and helped her stand.

The physical contact was a mistake. She knew it instantly but by then it was too late. She was in the midst of a post-burn buzz. The crash would come later, but for now all of her senses were at high-rez and not under full control.

"Wait," she gasped. "You don't want to do this."

But Cyrus had already scooped her up into his arms. "Take the flashlight."

She took the flashlight in her right hand. She was still clutching the flicker in her other hand. She aimed the flashlight at the front porch.

"I'm trying to explain something," she said. "I'm a little jittery at the moment. I'm not in full control of my senses. I think I may have been psi-burned."

Cyrus carried her up the steps. "What are you worried about?"

Small sparks and flames leaped in the atmosphere. One of them nipped at the front of his shirt. She smelled charring fabric and realized that she had accidentally rezzed the flicker. She groaned.

"Well, among other things, I might set your shirt on fire," she said.

He looked down and smiled. She felt a rush of energy—Cyrus's talent, not her own, she realized. The tiny flames that threatened his shirt evaporated. So did the little sparks in the atmosphere. Her frazzled senses seemed to sigh in relief.

"How did you do that?" she whispered.

"Why do you think they call me Dead Zone Jones? I'm a cooler."

Chapter 8

"I DIDN'T THINK THAT COOLERS REALLY EXISTED," Sedona said. "Thought they were a myth."

She was pretty sure she had her senses back under full control. She didn't think there was any danger that she might set fire to the curtains. But who knew?

She sat on the sofa, feet slightly spread. She leaned forward, her elbows braced on her knees. She watched Cyrus pour hot water from the kettle into a cup. He was still dressed as he had been earlier when he had arrived on the island, but it looked like he had used his fingers to comb his dark hair straight back behind his ears.

"For obvious reasons, it's not the sort of talent you advertise," Cyrus said. "As a general rule, most people tend to run in the opposite direction as fast as they can. No one wants to get close to someone who can dampen another person's talent."

She gave that some thought. "Your men know about your talent. Doesn't seem to worry them."

"That's because in our world, power of any kind gets a lot of respect. Why do you think I joined the Guilds in the first place?"

"Oh, I see."

"Socially, however, I run into a few problems."

She nodded in understanding. "Probably not the kind of thing you mention on a first date."

"Or the third or fourth of fifth date. The matchmaking agency gave up on me."

"Geez. Talk about the ultimate rejection."

"Tell me about it."

Coolers were so rare as to be relegated to the category of legend and myth—and not in a good way. It was impossible to measure a cooler-talent. What couldn't be measured was hard to demonstrate in a scientific fashion. And there was no getting around the fear factor, Sedona thought.

When it came to paranormal talents, coolers were considered bad news. Stand too close to a high-rez cooler when he was using his talent and your own psychic senses were temporarily frozen; useless. It was said that really strong talents could permanently ice another person's aura and stop his heart.

There were a lot of names for folks with Cyrus's kind of talent—psi-zombies, flat-liners, and icers—but coolers was the most polite and also the oldest. It derived from Old World casino jargon. Got a player on a hot winning streak? Just send in the cooler. All he or she has to do is walk past the table, get a fix on the way-too-lucky player, and send out a little whisper of energy to neutralize any talent he was using to control the cards.

Back on Earth a lot of successful gamblers had probably never realized they were using a little psi-energy to count cards or influence the dealer. Here on Harmony, where almost everyone had some natural paranormal ability, casino managers had to take precautions to protect the natural house edge. Sedona knew that any of them would have paid a fortune to get the services of a genuine cooler.

Well, at least she wouldn't have to worry about accidentally setting the cottage on fire.

Flat-liner or not, Cyrus looked surprisingly good in her kitchen. What's more, he was acting like he had every right to be there. She was not sure what to make of that, but she was still too frazzled to think about it.

The bad news was that, although she was back under control, she was still in the midst of a serious post-burn buzz. It was a well-documented fact that using a lot of talent had some side effects, one of which was that the adrenaline rush spilled a lot of biochemicals, including some significant sex hormones, into the bloodstream. True, she hadn't ever experienced a rush like the one that had her on edge at the moment. But, then, she'd never had an occasion to share the aftermath with a man as interesting as Cyrus Jones, either.

"So you think that whatever happened to you when you were kidnapped is responsible for this new fire-starting talent you've got now?" Cyrus asked.

"I suspect my new ability is a result of those experiments that damned Blankenship conducted on me. All I know is that when I went on that last contract job I was a gatekeeper. A really strong gatekeeper, but, still, just a gatekeeper." She thought about it. "Now I'm something else, as well."

"Multi-talents are very . . . rare," Cyrus said quietly.

The soft, masculine timbre of his voice sent another frisson of sensual arousal across all of her senses. This was not going well. She made another effort to pull herself together.

"You don't have to tiptoe around it," she said. "I did my research. I'm aware that most multi-talents go crazy while they're still young and end up dead or permanently hospitalized."

"But you feel okay," Cyrus said. It was a statement, not a question.

"Well, yes." She wiggled her fingers. "Except for this little fire-starting talent I seem to have developed."

"Interesting."

He took a pretzel out of a jar and walked toward her across the hardwood floors, the mug of tea gripped easily in one strong hand. There was a very focused gleam of curiosity in his eyes but he did not sound concerned. Most strong talents would have been running for cover about now, she thought.

Then again, there probably wasn't much that could make Cyrus run. Besides, given the nature of his own talent, he didn't have much to fear from someone like her.

She was probably the one who ought to be running for cover.

She realized that Cyrus was still watching her closely. She could almost feel him weighing and judging; making decisions that could affect her new life here on Rainshadow. It occurred to her somewhat belatedly that she should have kept her mouth shut.

"Forget your new talent," Cyrus said. "We'll get to that later."

That sounded ominous.

"We've got other priorities right now," he continued. "Drink some tea and tell me what happened here tonight."

When she took the mug from him she got another little lightning jolt of awareness. She had known from the start that she was attracted to him and that the attraction was dangerous, but she had been in full control until now. Going to bed with a Guild boss was definitely not on her agenda. She had taken care to avoid that sort of complication from the start of her career.

"Before we get to whatever happened here tonight, I'd like to ask a favor," she said. "I would really, really appreciate it if you would not mention the possibility of me having a second talent to anyone."

"No problem," he said easily. "You have my word on it."

She raised her brows. "Just like that?"

Amusement flickered in his eyes. "Is there more to the business of making a promise?"

She thought about that.

"No, I guess not," she said. "I'm not sure why, but I think I believe you." Or maybe she just desperately wanted to believe him.

"Guild bosses are good at keeping secrets," Cyrus said.

"Right."

What they were really good at doing was keeping secrets that they figured would give them an edge. For all she knew, her secret might very well fit into that category as far as Cyrus was concerned. She must not forget that.

There was some hopeful chortling from the back of the sofa.

Cyrus handed the pretzel to Lyle who took it in one paw and fell to crunching with typical enthusiasm.

Cyrus lowered himself onto the sofa and sat a short distance away, not quite touching Sedona. He probably knew that she was still in the grip of the aftermath thing, she thought. He had no doubt been there on a number of occasions himself.

"Don't worry," he said. "You're holding that blackmail material over my head, remember?"

She drank her tea and did not respond. As threats went, her vow to release the file on Blankenship's lab was puny and they both knew it.

"Let's get back to what happened in here tonight," Cyrus said.

"Okay," she said. "How did you know I was in trouble?"

"Lyle showed up at my window. He made a lot of noise. I got the impression he wanted me to follow him."

"Sadly, this is not the first time Lyle has had to rescue me. If this keeps up, he may start looking for someone else to bond with, someone who doesn't need so much help getting out of trouble."

Cyrus gave Lyle a considering look. "Got a feeling that Lyle isn't the kind who would leave a buddy behind."

She smiled and inhaled the aroma of the tea. Something inside her started to relax. The tisane was a special blend of herbs that Rachel Blake, the owner of Shadow Bay Books, had mixed for her the day she had arrived on the island. Rachel was an aura reader with a talent for creating just the right individual blend for each client.

She drank some tea, savoring the warmth, and lowered the mug.

"I walked right into a small psi-trap tonight," she said.

"Here?" Cyrus asked. "Inside the cottage?"

She could not tell if he believed her or not. It would be perfectly reasonable for him to conclude that she had hallucinated the whole thing. It took a special kind of talent to work trap energy. People who could do it were usually referred to as tanglers. Most respectable, reputable tanglers pursued careers in para-archaeology. But there were those who took different paths.

"Someone set it in the hallway." She glanced across the room. "Whoever it was loosened the bulb in the fixture there and in the bedroom as well. I suppose the tangler wanted to make sure I didn't notice anything out of the ordinary before I blundered into the device. It was under the carpet. I stepped right on it."

Cyrus looked at the darkened hallway. There was a hard, assessing expression in his eyes. She could almost feel him running scenarios and calculating odds.

"You think you used your new talent to escape the trap," he said.

"I know I did." She drank some more tea, cradling the mug in both hands. "I nearly set the cottage on fire."

Amusement came and went in his eyes. "That explains the slightly smoky smell. Thought you'd burned something in the oven earlier. All right, tell me the rest, step by step."

He looked intrigued, she decided, not shocked or horrified—just seriously intrigued.

"There's not much to tell," she said, trying to recall the details. "The dreamlight energy was generating a lot of hallucinations. I was totally disoriented. I went on autopilot. You know how it is when your intuition kicks in and all of a sudden you're using your talent without consciously focusing it."

"Been there," he agreed.

She looked at the flicker on the coffee table. "Evidently, all I need is a spark or a flame of some kind to ignite my new talent. I used that flicker. Once I had a kind of shield around me, I got out of the cottage and hid."

"Who were you hiding from?" Cyrus asked in that same neutral voice.

Sedona turned her head to look at him. "I was dazed from the force of the initial blast. But I figured that whoever had set the trap would come back to see if it had worked. I was right."

Cyrus's eyes were chips of ice now. "The tangler came back?"

"Yes. Shortly after I got outside I heard the footsteps and caught a few glimpses of light from a flashlight bouncing in the fog. Whoever it was went into the house, stayed there for a moment or two, and then left in a very big hurry."

Cyrus did not speak for a moment. He just sat quietly, contemplating the fire. She exhaled slowly, deeply. *Should have seen this coming,* she thought.

"You don't believe me," she said. "I don't blame you. Hey, I recently escaped from a secret Guild lab. What can you expect? I probably hallucinated the whole thing. All indications are that I'm an unstable multi-talent who has become a full-blown conspiracy freak. Thanks for making the tea. You can go back to your own cottage now."

"I told you, I'm a Jones," Cyrus said. "Got a long history of conspiracy buffs in my family. Got a few ancestors who were rumored to be multi-talents, as well. I'm not going anywhere, at least not until dawn."

She choked and sputtered on her tea. "What?"

He did not respond. His attention was fixed on the hallway. She was still trying to wrap her mind around the concept of him spending the night when he got to his feet.

He crossed the room and stood looking down the short, dark hallway into the darker bedroom. Experimentally he rezzed the wall switch. When the light didn't come on, he took the small flashlight off his belt and walked slowly, deliberately into the hall.

Ever hopeful of a new game, Lyle hopped down off the back of the couch and scurried after Cyrus.

They both disappeared. A low growl emanated from the hallway. Probably Lyle, Sedona decided. She had a hunch that Cyrus's growl would sound a little different—a whole lot sexier.

She drank some more tea and waited.

Cyrus reappeared a short time later, Lyle bouncing along at his heels.

"Someone was here, all right," Cyrus said. "There are partial footprints on the carpet that don't match yours. Remnants of psi-trap energy in the hallway, too."

She raised her brows. "You can sense that?"

"One of the side effects of being a cooler. Don't worry; the residue isn't strong enough to give you nightmares. But what's really interesting is that there are some traces of the tangler's energy. Fear, I think. Maybe even a little panic. Must have been caught off guard when he didn't find you lying unconscious in the hallway."

Sedona made a face. "Nice to know I may have made him a tad nervous, at least."

"You probably scared the hell out of him. He couldn't be sure that you weren't hiding somewhere waiting to attack whoever came to see if the trap had worked."

She exhaled slowly. "If only. Unfortunately it was all I could do just to get myself out of the cottage without setting fire to the place. I was the one in a panic. Sure you're not picking up my vibes?"

"I can sense some of your energy, too. For the record, it doesn't feel unstable."

She stilled. "You're sure?"

"Positive." Cyrus regarded her with a considering air. "You were fighting for your life but you were in control. I can tell that you're an off-the-charts talent. You're right; I think you could do some actual damage if you tried."

She looked down at the flicker. "I gotta tell you, that's

scary. Who knows what I might do if I got really mad and lost control altogether?"

Cyrus's smile was startlingly sexy. "Excellent question. I think it explains why whoever came after you used a trap to try to catch you instead of a mag-rez pistol."

"That means that, whoever it is, he has some idea of what I've become," she whispered.

"I think so, yes."

"Blankenship."

"Or someone working for him."

"Buzzkill and Hulk," she said. "His so-called assistants. I wouldn't have thought either of them could work trap energy, though. They seemed like traditional hunters who were jacked on steroids. Setting a trap requires a certain finesse, to say the least. One false move and the tangler gets caught in his own trap."

"True." Cyrus waited a beat. "Any idea why Blankenship would go to the trouble of trying to kidnap you? From what you've told me, it sounds like it would be simpler to find himself a new research subject."

In spite of everything, she managed a grim smile. "I've got a pretty good idea of why he wants me back."

"I'm listening."

"Blankenship was using some kind of paranormal radiation to prepare the serum. I don't have a lot of clear memories of the time I was locked in the dreamstate, but I do know that the crystal that he used in his experiments was vitally important to him. He kept it in a steel-and-glass strongbox. I sealed the container with a little fire lock before I escaped from the lab. Sealed the doorway of the lab, as well."

Cyrus's eyes sharpened. "Are you telling me that Blankenship needs you to unlock both his secret lab and the strongbox?"

"Yep." She finished the last of the tisane and set the cup down. "Looks like I may have shot myself in the foot, doesn't it? Now he's out to kidnap me. And he's got Kirk Morgan, the boss of the Gold Creek Guild, to help him."

"You're sure Morgan is his accomplice?"

"All I know is that Morgan left me behind after I diverted the river for him and his men. The kidnapper was waiting at just the right place in the Rainforest to grab me. What are the odds that was a coincidence?"

"I agree the kidnapper had help, but it could have come from someone else who was on that exploration team that day."

Sedona wrinkled her nose. "I suppose so. But I saw Morgan's face just before the gate closed. He knew what he was doing when he left me behind. I'm sure of that much."

"Maybe."

She shook her head. "None of this makes any sense, does it? Everyone knows that the Guild bosses do favors for each other all the time. Why send someone to kidnap me when it would be so much simpler to just ask the new Rainshadow Guild boss to pick me up and transport me back to Blankenship's lab?"

"Another good question."

Sedona went very still, her imagination conjuring a horrible possibility, one she had not even considered until now. Her pulse skittered. Her breath tightened in her chest and her senses flared. Cyrus watched her, waiting calmly for the verdict.

Lyle hopped into her lap and rumbled in concern. She put one hand on his furry body, taking comfort. With an effort of will, she forced herself to think logically.

"You're wondering if I'm the one who set the trap, aren't you?" Cyrus asked. "Or if I arranged to have someone else do it for me."

She did not take her eyes off him. "It wasn't you who set that trap tonight."

"What makes you so sure?"

She moved one shoulder in a small shrug. "Among other things, it doesn't seem like your style, for some reason. I think that if you wanted to take me down and ship me back to the lab you would be a little more direct and discreet about it." She sighed. "I'd probably be on my way there, as we speak, in a private charter plane." She looked down at Lyle. "And then there's Lyle. He's a pretty good judge of character. He seems to like you."

"Good to know I've got him as a reference," Cyrus said. "Getting back to your question, I think the reason that Morgan didn't call on me for any favors—assuming Morgan is involved in this thing—is that he knows I would not be inclined to do one for him."

"Why not?" she asked.

"The short story is that I'm a Jones and I'm Arcane. There's a longer version but it's complicated, and this is not a good time to go into old history. You need to get some sleep."

Sedona got to her feet. She studied the hallway for a moment. "Not much in the way of evidence, is it?"

"No." The corner of Cyrus's mouth kicked up in a cool smile. "But I'm a Guild boss, remember? According to some folks, we don't need much in the way of evidence. We make our own rules."

She looked at him, trying to read his sorcerer's eyes. "Do you really believe my story of what happened here tonight?"

"Yes."

That was all he said but it was enough.

"Thanks." She paused. "I know I need sleep but I'm not sure I will be able to get any tonight. I haven't been sleeping well lately."

"Bad dreams?"

"Nightmares about my time in Blankenship's lab," she said.

"You used a lot of energy tonight fighting off the trap. It won't be long before you crash. You'll sleep and I'll keep watch while you do. You're safe, Sedona."

She wasn't sure where to go with that. She was dreading the deep sleep of the crash that always followed a major psi-drain. She did not like the idea of being vulnerable.

She went to the window and watched the waves of aurora light shift restlessly through the fog.

"Thanks," she said. "I mean it. I appreciate your offer to act as a bodyguard tonight."

He came to stand beside her at the window.

"No problem," he said. "As a contract employee, you're entitled to Guild protection."

She started to remind him that she had not actually signed a contract but at that moment, the aurora flashed especially bright, illuminating the fog with a dazzling brilliance. Another shiver of intense awareness swept through her. The nervy, edgy sensation grew stronger.

Cyrus touched her shoulder. It was a slight, fleeting touch, meant only to calm her, but her senses reacted as if some of the aurora fire had sparked right through her. She went very still.

Cyrus watched her closely in the ghostly light. "Are you all right?"

She took a sharp breath. The fear she was trying to suppress was abruptly swamped by the cleansing fire of anger.

"Yes, damn it, I'm fine," she said through set teeth. "But I sure as hell am not looking forward to crashing, especially not now that I know that Blankenship has found me and that he sent someone to take me back to that lab."

Cyrus cupped her face between his hands.

"Take it easy," he said. "I told you, I'd stay until dawn, remember?"

"I appreciate that but I hardly know you, and Blankenship or one of his people is out there somewhere in the night, waiting to grab me. I was just getting to the point where I could sleep again, thanks to Rachel's tea and the fact that I felt safe here on Rainshadow. Now I'm back to square one."

"I'll deal with Blankenship."

She hesitated, wanting to believe that Cyrus could do exactly what he said he could do.

"But what if Blankenship has the backing of the Chamber?" she said.

"I don't think that's the case but if it is, I'll deal with the Chamber, too."

"Really? And just how do you plan to do that? No offense, Jones, but it's not like you're the head of one of the big city-state Guilds. Rainshadow is a very small territory. Heck, the island itself isn't even on most maps."

Cyrus's mouth curved slightly in a secretive smile. She could have sworn that there was a little more heat in his eyes.

"Trust me," he said. "I can handle the Chamber."

"The weird thing is that I do trust you." She searched his face in the shadows. "Why is that?"

"Maybe because one of your ancestors, a woman named Arizona Snow, and one of my ancestors, Fallon Jones, had some history back on Earth."

"What?"

"It doesn't matter now. The important thing to remember is that the Joneses have a very long memory. You can consider me an old friend of the family, Sedona Snow."

His mouth closed over hers before she could ask any more questions.

And suddenly her senses were on fire.

Chapter 9

ENERGY SPLASHED THROUGH HER. THE RUSH CAUGHT HER and swept her away on a great wave of sensation.

She made a soft, urgent little sound, gripped Cyrus's shoulders, and returned his kiss with all the heat that was burning inside her. His own talent flashed into full-rez mode, challenging her to a reckless paranormal duel. She met the midnight ice of his energy field with the blazing fires of her own psychic senses.

The clash of their auras was the most exhilarating experience she had ever known. For the first time since the Disaster, she felt free to let herself test the limits of her new talent. Thrill after thrill coursed through her. She did not have to be cautious with Cyrus. There was no need for restraint.

"You can handle my aura," she whispered against his mouth.

"Anytime, sweetheart," he said. His mouth shifted a little, deepening the already deep kiss. When he raised his head his eyes were pools of hot ice. "Anytime."

The sexy edge on the word sent more chills of excitement across her senses. She reached up and pulled his mouth back down to hers. A daring recklessness drove her now.

The heat building between them threatened to outdo the fireworks produced by the aurora light. She had never been so thrillingly aroused in her life. She wrapped one jean-clad leg around his thigh. He groaned, caught her around the waist, and lifted her higher so that she could get both of her legs around him. She clung to him, kissing him wildly.

He swung around and braced her against the wall. Flattening one hand on the wooden paneling beside her head, he undid the front of her shirt. Her bra surrendered beneath his touch and then he was cupping one of her breasts in his palm. His thumb teased her nipple. His breathing roughened. She knew that she was pushing him to his limits and she savored the knowledge that she had the power to do it.

"Yes," she whispered into his ear. "Yes. Tonight. Now."

Another burst of aurora light lit up the room. Cyrus abruptly went very still. It was as if the pulse of paranormal energy outside had flipped a switch somewhere inside him. She could literally feel the mag-steel gates of his control slam into place.

"No," he said. His voice was ragged but resolute. "Not tonight. You're about to crash."

"Not yet. Besides, I told you, I probably won't be able to sleep at all tonight."

"You'll sleep. The crash is going to hit you hard."

He eased her away from the wall, cradled her in his arms, and carried her toward the bedroom.

He was right. She knew it. But she did not have to like it. She told herself that after-burn sex was always a bad idea, the kind of sex a woman usually regretted in the morning. She had made it a long-standing rule to avoid it. After-burn sex was all hormones and hot psi; not real emotion.

But after-burn sex with Cyrus would have been different, she thought.

No, probably not.

The bedroom was lit with the same flashing paranormal shadows that blazed in the living room. Closing the drapes wouldn't do much good. Much of the energy came from the paranormal end of the spectrum. It passed easily through fabric. Darkness would come only when her skyrocketing senses finally shut down for some extended rest, assuming they did shut down tonight.

Cyrus set her on her feet and pulled back the covers. The moment his hands left her body she felt the heaviness of the oncoming crash. She yawned and swayed a little. *After-burn sex was always a bad idea.*

"Thanks," she said. "I guess."

She sank down on the edge of the bed and started to remove her shoes.

Cyrus watched her for a moment. "Are you going to be all right?"

"Sure, just peachy. Go on, get out of here. You don't need to keep watch until morning, really."

"I'm staying. Lyle will be my backup. Between the two of us, no one else will bother you tonight."

She wanted to protest, but at the same time logic told her that she could not risk becoming sleep-deprived. Sleep-deprivation had disturbing effects on the paranormal senses. Besides, she didn't think she could ward off the crash for much longer.

She had to rest and recover, and that meant, for now, she would have to trust Cyrus Jones. To her vague astonishment she fell hard into a dreamless sleep.

Chapter 10

ONE KISS WOULD NEVER BE ENOUGH. NOT WITH SEDONA Snow.

Cyrus found a coffee machine on the tiled counter. There was a jar of ground coffee next to it. He set about making a pot of caffeine, his senses, both normal and paranormal, still dazzled by the one kiss.

It was going to be a long night, not because he would have trouble fending off sleep—he could use psi and coffee to take care of that problem—but because he was going to be spending the hours until morning alone in the living room. The fantasies would be murder. He needed to find something to take his mind off the lady he was supposed to be protecting.

Lyle bounded up onto the counter to watch the coffee-making process. He clutched a bright bit of quartz in one paw. The stone had come from a collection of small stones arranged on the windowsill. He gazed at the coffeepot, evidently entranced by the sight of the brewed coffee dripping into the glass carafe.

"You like coffee?" Cyrus said. "Guess we'll both be a little buzzed on caffeine tonight."

His phone rang. He unclipped it from his belt, saw Marlowe's code, and took the call.

"I thought you were going to bed," he said.

"I am but I wanted to let you know that I found something on Blankenship," Marlowe said. Excitement laced her voice. "Not much, but it's a start and it looks promising. Blankenship joined the staff of the Gold Creek Guild's medical division and worked at Amber Crest Hospital for nearly a decade. He did some pioneering work in the field of psi-burn treatment. His career has been nothing short of stellar. He's been a leader in devising new therapies designed to treat ghost hunters and others who have suffered serious trauma to the para-senses."

"What happened to him?"

"He resigned his position nearly a year ago. He didn't exactly disappear but he's been keeping a very low profile ever since he left Amber Crest. He does some consulting and occasionally attends a para-psych conference but mostly he's become something of a recluse as far as I can tell."

"Does it look like he might have the kind of scientific background it would take to re-create the formula?"

"Who knows what it takes to re-create the drug?" Marlowe said. "All I can tell you at this point is that his resume is very strong in the fields of chemistry and something called Extreme Paranormal Radiation Therapy. That last field was his specialty at Amber Crest. It's not considered to be mainstream medicine. Highly experimental."

"Sedona said that Blankenship used a special crystal to irradiate the serum. Does he have any connection to Arcane?"

"You're wondering how he might have discovered the old formula, aren't you? The answer is, I haven't been able to find any link between Blankenship and Arcane but that doesn't mean there isn't one. A lot of the colonists who were members drifted away from the Society after they arrived on Harmony. The thinking was that this would be the land of milk and honey for people with genuine psychic talents. Who needed a secretive, fuddy-duddy, Old World organization that was founded by a freaky alchemist?"

"In other words, the Society has lost track of a lot of its members."

"Right. There's no telling how a version of the formula fell into Blankenship's hands. But one thing's for sure. The old genie is out of the bottle."

"Anything new on Sedona Snow?" he asked.

"Nothing more than what you already know. Both of her parents were married to other people when they had an affair. The birth of Sedona was a massive embarrassment to both sides of her family, blah, blah, blah. Evidently her parents didn't care about the social stigma. They were both academics specializing in para-archaeology. They were killed in an explosion of some kind while excavating one of the ruin sites."

"Sedona was thirteen at the time," Cyrus said. "Just coming into her talent."

"Right. The families of her parents had certain legal obligations, which they dutifully carried out. The Snows and the Callahans packed her off to a fancy boarding school and dumped her out into the world, alone, at eighteen. From what I can tell, Sedona hasn't had much, if any, contact with either of her families since the day she graduated from that boarding school," Marlowe said.

He had only known Sedona for a few hours but he had a hunch it would take a hell of a lot to make her go to her relatives to ask for help with anything—money, a job, or introductions to potential marriage partners.

"The fact that she is so alone in the world might be one of the reasons Blankenship decided to use her in his research experiments," Marlow said.

"He knew that no one would look too hard if she went missing," Cyrus said.

"Anyone who had decided to look for her would have to have been in a position to apply pressure to the Gold Creek Guild or else fund a private search-and-rescue operation," Marlowe said.

"The Snows could have done both."

"So could Brock Prescott, her ex–MC husband," Marlowe said. "But he didn't bother."

"The son-of-a-bitch." Cyrus tightened his grip on the phone. "How did Sedona end up working for the Guilds?"

"She came into her gatekeeping talent in high school. There's not a lot you can do with that talent except open gates and control energy rivers in the Underworld. After she graduated she started taking contracts. She made good money and used it to put herself through a couple of years of college before eventually leaving to work full-time in the Underworld." Marlowe paused.

"How did she meet her ex?"

"In the course of a Guild contract job. Prescott's company does a lot of business in the Rainforest. Prescott was touring one of the company projects and met Sedona. Evidently they hit it off right from the start. Prescott asked her out to dinner. The rest is the usual sort of MC history."

"Anything else?"

"That's it for now," Marlowe said. "I'll pursue the Blankenship and Amber Crest leads in the morning. How's the monster-hunting going?"

"Haven't done any hunting yet. But something interesting did happen tonight."

"What?"

"Someone set a psi-trap for Sedona."

"Good grief. Were you able to get medical attention for her there on the island?"

"She's okay." Cyrus looked toward the bedroom hall. "She's asleep now."

"How can she be okay if she tripped a trap?"

"Her talent saved her. She's strong." No need to mention that it was Sedona's new talent that had protected her. Marlowe would be seriously alarmed if she thought that the experiments on Sedona had been successful.

"Hmm," Marlowe said.

"It was a close call but she's all right," Cyrus said

smoothly. "The point is that it looks like someone—most likely Blankenship—tried to grab her tonight."

There was a taut silence on the other end of the line.

"Are you absolutely certain that she stumbled into a trap?" Marlowe asked. "By all accounts, she must have been badly burned on her last job. It's a wonder she survived whatever Blankenship did to her. She might be suffering some serious side effects. Hallucinations and bad dreams are not uncommon in such situations."

"The trap was real. Trust me."

"Guess that means you've got other problems on Rainshadow besides finding Sedona Snow and hunting monsters."

"Looks like it."

"Where are you now?"

"Playing bodyguard while Sedona sleeps off the post-burn buzz. She used a lot of energy evading the trap tonight."

"Bodyguard? That sounds . . . cozy."

"Got to go now, Marlowe. I'll check in with you tomorrow."

He ended the call before Marlowe could ask any more questions.

The coffee was ready. Cyrus poured a cup for himself and then put some in a shallow bowl for Lyle. He carried the mug and Lyle's bowl into the living room and set the coffees on the table in front of the sofa.

Lyle chortled and hopped up onto the table. He put down the quartz pebble that he had been playing with and headed straight for the bowl of coffee.

"It's hot," Cyrus warned.

He picked up the chunk of quartz. It glittered an attractive shade of yellow and gold, illuminated from the inside by some kind of energy. When he rezzed his senses the quartz went dark. The currents deep within the stone flatlined.

He sent the quartz spinning across the table. The little rock fell over the edge and landed on the hardwood floor.

Distracted from his coffee, Lyle chortled and chased after the quartz. He hopped down, retrieved the rock, and bounded back up onto the table. He gave it to Cyrus who sent it skittering once more across the table, this time with more force. It shot over the side of the table with some momentum.

Gleefully, Lyle charged after the rock.

Cyrus used his phone to go online. He was making notes on the cursory search-and-rescue operation that had been launched by the Gold Creek Guild after Sedona was reported missing when another phone chimed.

He got to his feet and followed the trail of sound until he saw Sedona's phone sitting in a charger on an end table. There was no movement from the bedroom. Sedona had crashed. It would take an earthquake or a volcanic eruption to wake her for the next few hours.

He looked down at the screen of Sedona's phone. The caller ID gave no name, just a phone number. He recognized the Resonance city-state code.

Like the other city-states, Resonance was a large, sprawling region that encompassed the city itself, as well as miles of outlying suburbs and agricultural areas. A lot of people lived in Resonance, including many of the members of the Callahan family, Sedona's mother's clan.

"Could be a coincidence," Cyrus said to Lyle.

Lyle consumed the last of his coffee and bounded off the low table. He fluttered across the room to play with his collection of quartz stones on the windowsill. The phone stopped ringing. After a moment an icon appeared. The caller had left a message.

"According to the file, Sedona has been estranged from both sides of her family for years," Cyrus said quietly to Lyle. "It's entirely possible she has some other connections in Resonance City, but if so they aren't in the file, which is pretty damn complete. I think we have to assume that Sedona's mother's people are trying to get hold of her."

Evidently unconcerned by the question, Lyle continued to arrange and rearrange his quartz collection.

Cyrus went back to his research.

Toward dawn he thought he heard a faint, distant roar. He jacked up his senses. The sound emanated from inside the Preserve. It could have been thunder. But it also could have been the hunting cry of a great beast of prey.

Over on the windowsill, Lyle sleeked out. His second set of eyes opened. He looked hard into the night.

"It's okay," Cyrus said. "The experts from the Foundation are sure the critters can't escape the Preserve. Then again, experts have been known to be wrong."

Lyle continued to stare fixedly out the window. After

a moment Cyrus put down his computer and went across the room to see what had fascinated the dust bunny.

The aurora energy had all but disappeared. The fog was lifting slowly and so was the heavy darkness that presaged dawn. Cyrus could just make out the gates of the Shadow Bay Cemetery.

As he and Lyle watched, the flat gravestone inside the locked cage swung open. The eerie green glow of the Underworld briefly illuminated two shadowy figures as they emerged from the catacombs. Between the lingering fog and the paranormal shadows spilling out of the gravesite, Cyrus could not even be sure if the figures were male or female.

One of the pair quickly lowered the gravestone back into place. Darkness descended again. But a moment later the narrow beam of a flashlight speared the predawn gloom.

Cyrus watched the flashlight change direction as the figures hurried out of the mag-steel cage and disappeared into the trees.

So much for Foundation security at the entrance to the catacombs. The question was, who would want to take the risk of going down into the Underworld alone in the middle of the night?

Chapter 11

SEDONA AWAKENED TO THE AROMA OF FRESHLY BREWED coffee and the sound of loud pounding on her front door.

Coffee. That could only mean that Cyrus was still in the cottage. And now someone was at her front door. Whoever it was would see Cyrus and draw all the wrong conclusions.

Her eyes snapped open. She bolted out of bed, grabbed her robe, belted it, and stepped into her slippers. She headed for the hall.

The knocking sounded again. Booted footsteps echoed in the front room. Lyle zipped down the hallway toward the bedroom, chortling his customary morning greeting. Sedona bent down, scooped him up, plopped him down on her shoulder, and kept going. She arrived in the front room just as Cyrus reached for the doorknob.

"No," she said in a loud whisper.

But it was too late. The door was open. Brock Prescott stood on the porch. He took in the little domestic scene with an expression of stunned disbelief.

"Sedona?" he said. He looked at Cyrus. "Who the hell are you and what are you doing in my wife's house?"

Cyrus raised his brows and looked at Sedona for guidance. And all of a sudden she was not the least bit sorry he had opened the door. *Call me petty,* she thought. As revenge went, it wasn't too bad, all things considered.

"Ex-wife," she corrected in her sweetest tones. "Meet Brock Prescott. And I repeat for the record, we are no longer married. He filed for divorce after he concluded that I wasn't coming back from the last job."

Outrage tightened Brock's nicely chiseled features. "We—everyone—thought you had been killed."

"You only waited four days," she said. "The least you could have done was give me a full week. But that's neither here nor there. We have both moved on, haven't we? Actually, you moved on first with Diana Easton."

"I can explain Diana," Brock said coldly.

"No need. Allow me to introduce Cyrus Jones. He's the new boss of the Rainshadow Guild. No explanations necessary."

Both men exchanged mutually assessing looks in that mysterious way that men did when they were sizing up each other. Lyle growled. Sedona reached up to hold him still.

"It's okay," she said. "You mustn't bite Brock. He might sue and he's got a team of lawyers."

"Prescott," Cyrus said.

Brock nodded once. "Jones."

There was a stark silence. For his part Lyle appeared to lose interest in the proceedings. Maybe he figured Cyrus could handle things, Sedona thought. Aware that it was time for breakfast, he bounced down to the floor and fluttered toward the kitchen counter.

"When did you arrive on the island, Prescott?" Cyrus asked.

The question was deceptively civil and amazingly casual given the rather awkward circumstances.

"Late last night," Brock said. His eyes narrowed. "Came in on a private charter float plane. We were delayed in Thursday Harbor by weather. When we finally got to Rainshadow we had trouble finding a place to stay. The pilot and I managed to get the last two rooms at some low-rent motel called the Bay View Inn."

"Oh, right," Sedona said. She beamed at Cyrus. "That would be the suite that I told my friend at the inn to save for you."

"Looks like she managed to rent out those rooms, after all," Cyrus said. He did not take his attention off Brock. "How did you find Sedona's place so early this morning?"

It finally occurred to Sedona that Cyrus was not going out of his way to make casual conversation. He was interrogating Brock. With a shock she realized there could be only one reason. He was trying to decide if Brock had arrived on the island in time to set the psi-trap last night.

She thought about assuring Cyrus that Brock didn't

possess the kind of talent required to work that sort of Alien psi and then she decided she could do that later.

She was almost certain that what Brock possessed was a talent for charisma. Generally speaking, people *liked* Brock Prescott. They were drawn to him. He would have made it big in politics.

He had a lot of other things going for him, as well. He was a good conversationalist. He was well-mannered. And he was rich. There was nothing at all wrong with Brock Prescott, except that he would never be the faithful type. This morning, for the first time, he also appeared rather boring. Really, what had she seen in him?

News flash, woman: Having met Cyrus Jones, you are doomed to view every other man in a new light.

She gripped the lapels of the collar of her robe and frowned at Brock. "Good question. How *did* you find me? What are you doing on my doorstep at this hour of the morning, and why in the world would you come all the way to Rainshadow to see me?"

Brock relaxed visibly. He gave her his mega-rez smile, the one that made you want to agree with everything he said.

"Lots of questions, honey, and I've got all the answers," he said.

She knew what was going through his head. Cyrus Jones might be a problem but Brock did not anticipate any difficulty dealing with her. Geez. What made him think that she would be so easy to manipulate? Then she remembered that in the two months they had been together they had never argued over anything. Of course, the demands of her career had meant that she was gone a lot. As for Brock, his position as the head of Prescott Industries meant that he also maintained a busy schedule.

When you got right down to it, Sedona thought, their relationship had been superficial, at best. They had never really gotten to know each other. She could not blame Brock, not entirely. She had played it safe for years, never allowing any man to get too close.

"Yes, I'll bet you do have the answers." She returned his brilliant smile with interest. "You always do. But let's start with the one that matters to me at this particular moment. How did you find me?"

Brock shrugged. "That wasn't a problem. I called your friend Brenda. She knew that you had moved to Rainshadow. She said you were working at some cheap, run-down resort."

"Knox's Resort and Tavern is not a cheap, run-down resort," she said. "It is a quaint bed-and-breakfast with tons of atmosphere and excellent cuisine."

Cyrus looked amused. "Haven't tasted the food yet, but I can vouch for the atmosphere."

Brock threw him an annoyed look and then switched back to Sedona. "Honey, we need to talk."

"Do. Not. Call. Me. Honey."

"I have some explaining to do," Brock continued as if he had not heard the warning note in her voice. "I understand that. But there's a lot you don't know."

"And a lot that I am no longer interested in knowing," she said. "You'll have to excuse us now. We're going to eat breakfast. Cyrus and I have to work today."

She caught hold of the door and closed it very deliberately. Brock stepped back automatically to avoid getting slammed in the face.

Sedona quickly locked the door and transferred her bright smile to Cyrus.

"Is that freshly brewed coffee I smell?" she asked.

"I believe it is."

"We'd better get some before Lyle figures out how to pour a cup for himself."

She heard Brock's footsteps on the porch. He must have concluded he wasn't going to get over the threshold. She peeked out the window and saw him go down the steps and walk down the tree-studded drive to the road that led to Main Street.

She was suddenly feeling remarkably invigorated. It had felt very good to shut the door in Brock's face. She crossed the room to the kitchenette and went behind the counter.

"Thanks," she said. "I mean it. I know that you are not involved in this and I know it was a fluke that you happened to be here this morning, but thanks. That little scene couldn't have gone better if I had planned it."

Cyrus watched her pick up the glass carafe.

"Aren't you curious to know why Prescott followed you all the way to Rainshadow?" he asked.

She gave that some thought as she poured two mugs of coffee. "Well, yes, now that I think about it, I guess I am curious." She put the pot back on the hot plate. "You were the one who started interrogating him. You're wondering if he set the trap here last night, aren't you?"

"Finding him on the doorstep first thing this morning does seem a bit of a coincidence."

She handed him one of the mugs and then lounged against the counter to drink her own coffee.

"The thing is, although Brock does have some talent, it's not the kind required to work Alien psi. What he's good at is charming people. I believe that he's got some true charisma talent."

"The experts claim there is no such thing."

"Oh, sure, and the experts are always right, right? People didn't invent the word *charisma* for nothing. We all know folks who have it—the best actors, the most successful politicians, cult leaders, the local neighborhood sociopath."

"I'm not arguing with you," Cyrus said. "Probably some as-yet-unidentified form of hypnosis talent."

"Maybe." She drank some of her coffee. "The thing is, it doesn't always work—not once you know the truth. It sure won't work on me again. Not ever."

"Did it work on you previously?"

She gave that some thought. "Maybe. For a while. No woman likes to feel that she was deceived by a man. In my own defense, I can say that even though I was under the impression that Brock and I had a pretty good relationship, I always knew there was never going to be anything permanent between us. Certainly not a Covenant Marriage. When I showed up on his doorstep the night I escaped from Blankenship's lab, I wasn't all that surprised when his new lover opened the door."

"Still, that had to hurt."

"Oh, yeah." She smiled. "But this morning really took care of that particular pain. Nothing like a little well-timed revenge. I suppose if I were a better person, I would be above that sort of thing but evidently I'm not. So, thanks, again."

Cyrus lowered himself onto one of the bar stools. "Glad I could be of service."

She opened the refrigerator door. "You definitely earned breakfast."

He watched her crack four eggs and whisk them in a bowl. "You're sure that Prescott could not have set the trap last night."

"As certain as I can be." She added a splash of cream and some fresh herbs to the eggs. Then she set a skillet on the stove, put in a pat of butter, and rezzed the heat. "But I suppose anything's possible. I'll be the first to admit I don't have a clue what's going on here."

She busied herself with the toast and juice, taking secret pleasure in the homey little scene. She hadn't had breakfast with anyone, male or female, since she had been kidnapped. People always said that nights were the hardest for singles but she had always found that breakfast and dinner could be the loneliest times of the day.

Holidays were the worst, of course. Luckily, they only came around a few times a year. She had learned to spend those days alone because, although friends usually invited her for a traditional feast, she always felt odd surrounded by the members of someone else's family.

Halloween was the exception. It was a holiday for people like her, she thought, people who had learned to wear masks to conceal their real identities. It was the only holiday she bothered to celebrate with decorations and goodies.

"By the way, you had a phone call last night," Cyrus said.

She had just plunked her plate down on the counter beside his. She came out of the kitchen and glanced uneasily at her phone.

"I did?"

"Don't worry, I didn't answer it," Cyrus said. He picked up his fork. "But I think the caller left a message."

She picked up the phone and glanced at the screen. A cold sensation drifted through her. She did not recognize the number but she knew the area code. She set the phone down with great care and went to sit on the stool next to Cyrus.

"Something very weird is going on in my life," she said. "The Snows' law firm has been hounding me for a couple of weeks. Now, out of the blue, it looks like someone from my mother's family is trying to get hold of me."

"You're not close to either side, I take it?"

"Nope." She forked up a bite of eggs. "I'm an embarrassment to both the Callahans and the Snows."

"Aren't you even a little curious to find out why they're trying to get in touch with you?"

"It makes me nervous. They must want something from me. The question is, what?"

Cyrus ate some toast. "Ever considered the possibility that they might want to reestablish family bonds?"

"Not for more than three seconds." She took a sip of

coffee. "And even if I do allow for that unlikely possibility, it seems way too much of a coincidence that both clans would suddenly decide to rebuild family ties simultaneously."

Cyrus pondered that briefly. "Good point." He looked thoughtful. "Both the Snows and the Callahans started looking for you this past month?"

"Uh-huh."

"*After* you emerged from the Underworld?"

"Uh-huh." She ate some more toast.

"And now your ex is on the island, wanting to have a cozy chat. You know, you're right, that is an interesting coincidence."

"Suddenly I seem to be very popular. Like I said, it makes me nervous."

"I don't blame you." Cyrus finished the last of his coffee and got to his feet. "There's one way to get some answers."

She wrinkled her nose. "Take some of those phone calls?"

"That would be the most efficient approach." Cyrus glanced at the amber face of his watch. "I've got to get moving. I need to go back to my cottage to shower and shave before I meet with Harry Sebastian, the head of the Foundation's security division and the police chief, Slade Attridge. You should be safe enough during the day. There are lots of people around. But try to stay in plain sight. Don't go wandering off."

"I won't. I'll be at the front desk most of the day. Thanks again for hanging around last night."

He watched her with a steady gaze. "About last night—"

She winced and held up one hand, palm out. "Sorry about jumping you the way I did. All I can say is that I was in a serious after-burn and you know what that's like."

He wrapped one hand around the doorknob. "In other words, any man who happened to be handy would have worked for you last night?"

"No." She choked and sputtered on a mouthful of coffee, aware that she was turning a dreadful shade of red. She waved one hand wildly in a negative way. "No, I didn't mean that at all."

"But you will concede that I was useful, both last night and this morning?"

She was mortified. "For pete's sake, stop twisting my words. It wasn't like that. I wasn't trying to use you." She groaned. "Okay, maybe this morning I did use you. A little. I apologize."

"No need to apologize." He let go of the doorknob and walked back across the room. He halted in front of her. "I get the picture."

She stared at him. "Cyrus—"

"I just want to make sure we both understand what's going on here."

Before she could come up with a response to that, he bent his head and kissed her. It was a quick, efficient, proprietary kiss, the kind of kiss that promised more to come at some point in the future. She was too frozen with confusion to even begin to figure out how to react.

Before she could pull herself together he was walking back across the front room and letting himself out the door.

And then he was gone.

She looked at Lyle.

"Damn it, I did not use him last night," she said. "That is a total misreading of the situation. It was just one of those things."

Lyle chortled and deftly hopped from the kitchen counter to the windowsill. He set about rearranging his collection.

She slid off the stool and picked up the dishes. "That's one of the things I admire about you, Lyle. You've got your priorities straight. I think you're onto something. It's risky to trust people. But like the ghost hunters say, good rocks will never let you down."

Chapter 12

"YOUR EX IS ON THE ISLAND?" RACHEL'S EYES WIDENED. "Oh, my. That's bound to make your life a lot more interesting."

"Tell me about it." Sedona collapsed back into the chair and gazed morosely at her friend.

They were sitting at a table in the tea shop at the back of Rachel's bookstore. Rachel was engaged to Harry Sebastian, a member of the powerful Sebastian clan. Harry's family had been guarding the secrets of the Preserve for generations. Lately those secrets had been surfacing in a number of unsettling ways. To deal with them Harry had taken charge of Foundation Security on the island.

"The thing is, why is Brock here on Rainshadow?" Sedona said.

Rachel twitched a lock of red hair behind her ear and studied Sedona with her aura-reader's eyes; eyes that saw beneath the surface. "Obviously he's here because of you."

"That's what's got me worried. He's the one who dumped me, remember? I told you, the SOB cancelled our MC the minute he found out I hadn't returned from my last job."

Rachel shuddered. "That was cold."

"Well, in fairness to him, it's not like our MC was ever going to turn into a Covenant Marriage."

"Still."

"Still. It's the principle of the thing. He could have had the decency to wait a couple of weeks. Maybe even a whole month."

"So a few weeks ago he was in a rush to end the MC and now he's come looking for you." Rachel drummed her fingers on the table and smiled. "He must have received a rather nasty shock when Cyrus opened your door this morning."

Sedona winced. "It's all over town, isn't it?"

"The news that Cyrus was seen leaving your cottage at a very early hour today?" Rachel smiled a commiserating smile. "I'm afraid so. Small towns, you know. That old graveyard is a bit out of the way but it's not exactly remote."

"I don't suppose it helps to say that the situation was not exactly as it appeared?"

"In my experience those sorts of situations are never exactly as they appear—not in small towns."

"Doesn't stop the gossip, though, does it?" Sedona said, resigned.

"No. If anything it makes the gossip more interesting." Rachel sat back in her chair. "So what was the situation at your cottage this morning?"

"Complicated."

"Naturally."

"Okay, here's the short version," Sedona said. "Someone set a psi-trap for me last night, right in the middle of my own cottage. I managed to get outside. Lyle sensed I was in trouble and went for help. He must have concluded that Cyrus Jones was the closest person at hand."

Shock replaced the amusement in Rachel's eyes. "Good grief. You're serious."

"Sadly, yes."

"Wait a minute." Rachel's red-gold brows scrunched. "A psi-trap exploded in your cottage and you got out safely?"

"Thanks to my talent," Sedona said, skating over that part of the story as quickly as possible. "But here's the thing, Rachel—whoever set the trap came back to see if it had worked. I heard the footsteps. The intruder didn't stick around. He was long gone by the time Cyrus arrived."

Rachel squinted a little. "And the following morning your ex shows up at your front door."

"It did occur to both Cyrus and me that those two factoids could be strung together. However, in all honesty, I just can't see any connection."

Rachel reached across the table with one hand and touched Sedona's arm. "Don't worry, we won't let anyone smuggle you off Rainshadow and take you back to that clinic. You're safe here."

Sedona closed her eyes for a moment and then looked straight at Rachel. "Thanks for the reassurance. It means a lot, believe me."

It was so good to have friends who cared, she thought, but not so good to lie to them. She hated not telling them the whole truth about her talent but they already knew she had been psi-burned. She did not want them thinking that she might be an unstable multi-talent on top of everything else. You have a right to your secrets, she reminded herself. She was very sure that Rachel and her fiancé, Harry, had a few of their own.

"Where does Cyrus Jones stand in this?" Rachel asked. "After all, he's a Guild boss."

Sedona shook her head. "He didn't set that trap. Lyle would never have gone to him for help if that had been the case."

"Okay, point taken. And while it's true Cyrus is Guild, he's also Arcane. Not only that, he's a Jones."

Sedona frowned. "That matters?"

"It matters within Arcane. The Jones family *is* the Arcane Society in some ways. One of their ancestors, an old alchemist named Sylvester Jones, founded it back in the 1600s, Old World time. It was a secret society of psychics before the First Generation colonists even arrived on Harmony and discovered that there is such a thing as a latent paranormal sensitivity in humans."

"Not so latent, not here on Harmony," Sedona said.

"True. But that's my point. The Arcane Society families were strong talents before they even got here. And within the Society, the Joneses have always been rumored to be the most powerful. They pretty much control the Society, or at least what's left of it. It's true, Arcane isn't what it used to be back on Earth, but believe me when I tell you that the Joneses can protect you."

"Why should they?"

Rachel smiled knowingly. “Gee, I dunno. Maybe because Cyrus Jones spent the night at your place?”

“I told you, nothing happened. I was sleeping off a bad burn.”

“Doesn’t matter. You’ve got friends here on Rainshadow.”

Sedona drank some tea while she thought about that.

“Rachel, are you still sure that my aura is stable?”

“Positive.”

Sedona’s phone rang. She glanced down, saw the same city-state code and number as the voicemail she had dumped that morning. She reflected on Cyrus’s advice. There was only one way to find out why people from both sides of her family were pursuing her.

Against her better judgment, she took the call.

And regretted it immediately.

“Sedona?” The older woman’s voice had a brittle edge that made it clear that she had not wanted to place the call. “Is that you? This is Margaret Callahan—your aunt.”

The subtle stress on the word *aunt* was interesting, Sedona thought. The Callahans had always taken great care to downplay any familial relationship.

“I know who you are, Margaret.”

“I left a message for you last night. The least you could have done was show me the courtesy of responding.”

“What’s going on?” Sedona asked. “Did someone die?”

There was a startled silence on the other end of the connection.

“No, of course not,” Margaret said. “Why would I call you about a death in the family? Never mind.”

"I'm a little busy at the moment," Sedona said. "If you have something to say, please say it fast."

"There's no need to be rude," Margaret said. "Not after all this family has done for you. I'm calling because the Snow family's lawyers have been trying to get in touch. I'm told that you have not returned their calls."

"Nope. I'm only taking this call because a friend of mine insisted."

"I'll come straight to the point. The reason the Snow lawyers have been attempting to get in touch is because your grandfather wishes you to attend the annual reception that is going to be held in honor of his birthday later this week."

"Good grief." Sedona nearly dropped the phone. "You're kidding. That's what all the phone calls have been about? A birthday invitation?"

"Yes. It seems to me the least you could do is to attend the festivities."

"Why in the world would I want to do that?"

Margaret cleared her throat. "When they were unable to get hold of you, the lawyers contacted us. Your mother's family."

"Yes, Margaret, I am aware of who the Callahans are. But I still don't understand why the Snows would want to get in touch."

"It's very simple. It seems that your grandfather has inserted you into his will."

"Really . . ." Sedona smiled. "I can see it now. Paragraph Five, Clause Number Seventeen: *To my illegitimate granddaughter, one dollar.* How exciting. Of course

I'll travel all the way to Crystal City to thank Granddad for acknowledging me as blood. Who wouldn't?"

"Your juvenile sarcasm is unwarranted," Margaret said. "The lawyers informed me that your grandfather has provided quite generously for you in his will. In addition, he has set up what I'm told is a substantial trust fund. You may begin drawing on it immediately. All he asks in return is that you do him the courtesy of showing up at his birthday party."

"Is this some sort of sick joke?"

"I don't go in for jokes of this sort," Margaret said. She sounded grim and determined, now. "I have been assured that your grandfather is serious. I believe he wants to make up for everything that happened all those years ago when his son seduced your mother and convinced her to humiliate herself and embarrass the entire family by running off with him."

Sedona thought about that for a few seconds.

"I don't believe it," she said finally. "Not for a minute."

"I beg your pardon?"

"Maybe I'd buy that story if I were Bob Snow's only surviving descendant and he was panicked because I was the only one left to carry on the bloodline. But that's not the case. He's got two legitimate sons who have both started to produce lots of legitimate grandsons and granddaughters. Bobby Snow doesn't need me."

"Obviously Robert Snow has had a change of heart."

"Unlikely."

"People change, Sedona."

"Not much," Sedona said. "At least not in my experience."

"The least you can do is give your grandfather the chance to show you that he regrets the way things were handled in the past."

"Why?"

"Why?" For the first time Margaret loosened the tight rein she had been keeping on her temper. "Because like it or not, you're family. Who do you think paid for that expensive boarding school you attended?"

"I thought that the costs of keeping me tucked away out of sight until I turned eighteen were split fifty-fifty between the Callahans and the Snows."

There was another short pause.

"It was agreed that boarding school would be best for you," Margaret finally said. "But the Callahans could not afford to pay the fees. The Snows offered to handle that end of things."

Sedona heard distant chimes clashing.

"Oh, wow," she said. "You pressured the Snows into paying those fees on the grounds that you all wanted me out of the way and boarding school was the most effective way to pretend I didn't exist. Nice work, Margaret. Not a lot of folks can say they got the better of Robert J. Snow in a business deal."

Margaret chose to ignore that. "There is a considerable amount of money at stake. It is not only the compassionate thing to do but also in your best interests to attend your grandfather's birthday celebration."

"Gosh, I don't know. It will be pretty expensive. I'd have to take time off from work. Then there's roundtrip airfare, a rental car, the price of a hotel room. Oh, and I'll need a nice dress."

"I have been told that your expenses will be covered," Margaret said, her cool tones plunging well below zero. "Obviously I did not state the question correctly. I should have said, what will it cost your family to make sure you show this small degree of respect to your grandfather?"

Sedona held the phone away from her ear and stared at it for a few seconds, trying to make sense of the call.

"Sedona?" Margaret's voice was tinny.

Sedona put the phone back to her ear.

"Forget the money," she said. "What I want to know is why you have decided that I should attend this shindig."

"I told you, whether you appreciate it or not, you are a Snow. Your grandfather clearly regrets the animosity of the past. He realizes that your parents' actions were not your fault."

"Gee. That's real broad-minded of him. What about the Callahans? Should I look forward to an invitation to Grandmother Callahan's birthday party? Or, hey, yours, Aunt Meg?"

"I am trying to be patient, Sedona. It's not surprising that you still harbor some immature resentment toward both sides of your family. But you need to understand that what your father and mother did all those years ago was a terrible shock to both the Callahans and the Snows. A lot of people were hurt."

"Including me."

"Yes," Margaret said quietly, "including you. Now Robert Snow is attempting to make amends. The least you can do is be gracious enough to accept this invitation. As I said, it's in your own best interests."

"I'm guessing it must be in your best interests as well or you would not have made this call," Sedona said

"I have no idea what you're talking about," Margaret said.

"Right. Sorry, I've got to go now. I've got a new job, not to mention there have been some recent complications in my life."

"Complications?"

"Nothing out of the ordinary. Awhile back I was kidnapped by a mad scientist who took me to a secret lab and used me in some bizarre experiments. Last night some twit set a psi-trap for me, which I barely survived, and now everyone on Rainshadow seems to think that I'm sleeping with the local Guild boss. Just the usual. Don't worry, nothing I can't handle."

There was a horrified pause on the other end of the connection.

"Sedona, are you . . . having para-psych issues?" Margaret finally asked tentatively.

"Nah. I feel great. I don't suppose you happened to notice that almost two months ago I went missing for about three weeks?"

"Missing?"

"Like I said, it's complicated. But I appreciate the call, Margaret. I think you have cleared up a few questions for me."

"You will go to your grandfather's reception? It will mean so much to him."

"You haven't told me exactly how much this call was worth to old Bob," Sedona said.

"You are the one who will benefit. I thought I made it clear, not only is Snow putting you back into his will, there is a generous trust fund that you can access immediately."

"I'm not talking about what's in it for me," Sedona said. "I'm asking what's in it for you. How much did old Bob's lawyers pay you to make this call? A quarter of a million? Half? Oh, and let's not forget that you plan to squeeze me for more money if I do start drawing on that trust fund. After all, I'm family, right, Margaret? And the Callahans have another generation to put through college, right?"

Margaret made an outraged sound that was not quite a hiss. "You are the most ungrateful little bitch I have ever met in my life."

Sedona was suddenly exhausted by the skirmish. "Does Ethel know you're making this call?"

"Yes."

"Did she approve of it?"

"Like everyone else in the family, your grandmother thinks it is in your own best interests," Margaret said very steadily.

"Why would she care about my best interests? She hates me."

"Ethel has some unresolved anger and resentment issues," Margaret allowed in stiff accents.

"There's nothing unresolved about Ethel. She's resolved to hate me because she thinks that if I hadn't come along Mom would never have run off with Dad."

"Don't you understand?" Margaret snapped. "This is about family, Sedona. You are being handed a golden opportunity to put some closure on the past and reunite with your blood kin. It is up to you to do the right thing. You know what that is."

"You had to pull the take-the-higher-path card, didn't you?" Sedona said. "Here's what I will do. I will consider attending Bob Snow's birthday celebration but I'm not making any commitments. Is that understood?"

"Yes, absolutely." Margaret sounded almost pathetically relieved. "As I told you, all expenses will be covered. I'll have your uncle Mark's administrative assistant make all the travel arrangements for you."

"Don't bother. If I decide to attend I'll make my own travel arrangements. I really do have to go now. Good-bye, Margaret."

"Sedona—"

"What?"

"Thanks for at least considering this invitation," Margaret said. "I know how hard it must be for you."

"I don't think so. Good-bye, Margaret."

Sedona ended the connection and looked at Rachel.

"My life has just gotten even more complicated," Sedona said.

"Anyone can tell you that when it comes to complicating a person's life, there is nothing like family," Rachel said.

Chapter 13

"THIS MORNING A FEW FOLKS WHO LIVE OUT NEAR THE fence reported hearing what may have been some very large critters deep inside the Preserve last night," Slade Attridge said. "The sound was described as a muffled roar. Could have been thunder, but given that we've found a couple of large carcasses in the past few weeks, I think we'd better assume there was another kill last night."

"I'll put a Foundation team together this morning and see if we can find the new carcass." Harry Sebastian looked up from the maps. "I've got to tell you that our research people are loving this stuff. They're like kids with big bags of Halloween candy."

"I know," Cyrus said. "I had a chat with Dr. Knutson this morning. He says the two carcasses you've found thus far match descriptions of fossils that date back a few million years. He's beyond thrilled with the possibility that the Aliens may have managed to reverse-engineer some living dinosaurs."

"Knutson isn't the one in charge of containing those critters," Harry said.

"Or the one in charge of making sure they don't decide to stampede down the Main Street of Shadow Bay," Slade added.

"No," Cyrus said. "That would be us."

The three of them were in the makeshift office that had been set up for Guild operations. The furnishings were spare. They consisted of a battered desk and a couple of folding chairs. Maps of the island and charts of the surrounding seas—some dating back to the Colonial Era—were stacked on the top of the desk.

The most prominent feature on each map of Rainshadow was the large swath of the island that was designated as the Rainshadow Preserve. The powerful psi-fence that surrounded the mysterious region was indicated with a forbidding red line on the newer maps. The thickly wooded interior behind the fence was labeled UNCHARTED, and Cyrus figured that it was likely to remain that way for some time. The heavy paranormal forces that swirled like the tides and currents of an invisible ocean inside the fence rendered even the most basic navigation and charting equipment useless. Aerial photographs were always wildly distorted by the clouds of psi that covered the interior of the island.

HERE THERE BE MONSTERS was clearly printed in large, bold letters on all of the historic maps of Rainshadow. The newer maps took the legal approach to discourage trespassers: PRIVATE PROPERTY. DANGER. KEEP OUT.

Maybe they should add TRESPASSERS WILL BE EATEN, Cyrus thought.

He was well aware that he had lucked out when it came to his counterparts among the local authorities. He had recognized kindred spirits in Slade and Harry. It wasn't just the auras of strong talent that whispered in the atmosphere around them. He had met a lot of high-rez talents in his time—some of them very dangerous.

He knew that Slade and Harry could be dangerous, too. He was good with that. When you went monster hunting, you needed folks who could deal with monsters. As soon as he had shaken hands with Sebastian and Attridge, he had understood that he could not only work well with them—he could also rely on them to have his back if there was real trouble. You didn't meet a lot of people like that in a lifetime, he thought. He was fortunate to find two of them on Rainshadow.

He put down the pen he had been using to make notes. "The monsters may be the big problem but the more immediate concerns are treasure hunters and thrill seekers. Saw a couple of them come out of the graveyard entrance site last night. I'm going to station a guard there starting this evening."

Harry shook his head. "We installed the latest in security fencing but no barrier is perfect."

"*Keep Out* signs are magnets," Cyrus said. He leaned back in the chair. "You know, other new Guild bosses get territories that contain lucrative amber mining operations and Alien ruins," he observed. "Their clients are big government agencies, corporate R-and-D divisions, and academic exploration teams with unlimited budgets. I get a territory with dinosaurs and one client—the Foundation."

"Don't forget the crystal pyramid down below," Harry said. "My brother, Drake, says it's some kind of ancient Alien storehouse of knowledge—a paranormal library. The value is incalculable."

"Right," Cyrus said. "And it's already been claimed by your family firm."

"Look on the bright side," Harry said. "The research teams we send into the pyramid will be paying high fees for Guild protection."

Cyrus smiled. "We like to think our services are worth every penny."

Slade looked amused. "No one ever said that Guild bosses don't have a talent for making the most of the business opportunities that come their way."

"It's a job requirement," Cyrus admitted. "But at the moment no one is going to be making any money down below in the catacombs—not until we get those tunnels cleared and charted."

"All right, looks like we've got something resembling a plan," Harry said. "You'll oversee the Underworld operations, Cyrus. I'll control activities inside the Preserve. Slade will handle his usual police duties in Shadow Bay and try to control the thrill seekers who have been trickling into town ever since the rumors about the weirdness on the island started to leak out awhile back."

"I'll take a dinosaur trotting down Main Street any day

over a dumbass thrill seeker," Slade said. "And things aren't going to be easy this week, what with the Halloween tourism promotion the new mayor has been running. Every time a ferry docks, another bunch of strangers walks off."

"Which brings me to the problem that Sedona encountered last night," Cyrus said.

Both men looked at him with speculative expressions and some amusement.

"There was a problem last night?" Slade asked rather blandly.

"We had the impression that things had gotten quite cozy between you and Sedona," Harry said.

Cyrus ignored the innuendoes. He gave them a quick rundown of the psi-trap episode. By the time he had finished all of the male humor in the room had dissipated.

Slade walked over to the window and looked out onto Main Street with its crowds of tourists and garish decorations.

"A few weeks ago, after Sedona arrived on the island, she told Rachel and my wife, Charlotte, that she was afraid Blankenship might try to track her down," he said. "I've had someone at the dock every time the ferry arrives. But so far we haven't spotted anyone matching the descriptions of Blankenship or the two assistants."

"Rachel is watching for unstable or dangerous auras, but when you've got this many strangers on the island, it's impossible to check out everyone," Harry added.

Cyrus looked at him and then he switched his attention to Slade. "You believed Sedona's story from the start?"

"This is Rainshadow," Slade said. "No one ends up

here without a really good story. In my experience, most of those stories turn out to be true."

"Sedona is one of us now," Harry said. "It's a small town. We look out for each other."

"Thanks," Cyrus said.

Chapter 14

CYRUS GLANCED AT HIS WATCH AND THEN LOOKED AT Brock Prescott. "You've got five minutes. What do you want?"

"I want to know why you're hanging around my wife," Brock said.

"Two points. First, she's not your wife, not anymore. Second, regarding my relationship with her—I don't owe you any explanations."

Prescott had shown up just as Cyrus was finishing a briefing with his lieutenants. Cyrus had considered ignoring him, but in the end he had concluded it made more sense to try to get a handle on what Prescott wanted. Once you knew an opponent's priorities, you could usually predict his actions with a fair degree of accuracy. Motive was all.

Brock's face tightened with an expression of Serious

Concern. "I'm sure you're aware that my wife is believed to have suffered a bad psi-burn in the course of her last Guild job. She is probably in a very fragile condition."

"She's not your wife," Cyrus repeated. "You filed the papers, remember?"

"Damn it, I thought I had no choice. The Gold Creek Guild authorities informed me she was missing and presumed dead." Brock shoved his fingers through his hair and went to stand at the window. "It seemed clear that she was not coming back. What the hell was I supposed to do?"

"Look for her," Cyrus said.

Brock spun around. "That's easy for you to say. You're a Guild exec. And you're a Jones. You could afford to mount a private search-and-rescue operation."

"You're the head of Prescott Industries. You could have paid for your own private search-and-rescue op."

"They told me she had been lost in an energy river. No one comes out of a river."

"Almost no one," Cyrus said. There was a loud, protesting squeak when he leaned back in the old office chair. "You still haven't explained why you're here on the island."

"Isn't it obvious? I care about her. She's my wife, damn it."

"She was your wife. And it was just an MC. What's more, you had every intention of keeping it that way, didn't you?"

"Our relationship started out as an MC," Brock said through his teeth. "But after she disappeared, I realized that what I felt for her was something much deeper and more profound."

"So deep and profound that you decided to start sleeping with your administrative assistant?"

Brock's face creased in grim lines. "It was all a misunderstanding. Sedona never gave me a chance to explain."

Cyrus raised his brows. "Now you're thinking Covenant Marriage?"

"Absolutely." Brock walked forward and planted both hands, palms down, on the surface of the desk. "Not that my relationship with Sedona is any of your damn business."

"Actually it is my business. She has agreed to take gatekeeping contracts with the Rainshadow Guild on an ad hoc basis. As far as I'm concerned, that makes her a member of my team. I have every right to look out for her welfare."

"Is that so? Do you make a habit of sleeping with all your female team members?"

Cyrus stood and confronted Brock across the depth of the old desk. "If you make one move to take Sedona away from this island without her clear, informed consent, I will make sure that Prescott Industries never gets access to the Underworld again."

"That's bullshit." Fury came and went in Brock's eyes. "You can't threaten me like that. You may be a Jones, but we both know you're just a low-rent Guild boss with a small, unimportant territory on an island in the middle of the Amber Sea. It's not like you're the head of one of the big city-state Guilds."

"This may not be Crystal City or Resonance City. But the Underworld here on Rainshadow is my territory."

Brock's eyes narrowed. "Is that a threat?"

"If you know anything about the members of the Chamber, you know they don't assign any territory, large or small, to someone unless they think he can control it. Believe me when I tell you that I can and will protect what's mine. We're done here, Prescott. It's true, I don't have the power to order you off the island—just out of the Underworld. But if you aren't very careful I will make sure that you disappear from Rainshadow, one way or another. Now get out of here. I've got work to do."

Prescott looked as if he was going to refuse to be hustled out of the office. But in the end, he evidently concluded that there was no benefit to pushing the issue.

He yanked open the door and strode outside as if it were his idea to leave. On the sidewalk he paused briefly to look back at Cyrus.

"Who the hell do you think you are, Jones?"

"The man they sent to take care of the monsters on Rainshadow," Cyrus said.

Chapter 15

IT WAS JUST AFTER EIGHT O'CLOCK BUT THE NOISE LEVEL in the tavern was climbing rapidly. Lyle had vanished into the darkened interior twenty minutes earlier. There had been no sign of him since, but the rez-rock music and the roars of masculine laughter booming out of the doorway that separated the bar from the lobby did not bode well in Sedona's opinion.

She was about to leave her post behind the front desk to check on the situation when a six-foot-tall Amazon with endless waves of blond hair and a bust that would have done credit to a lingerie model came through the lobby doors. Hannah Holbrook was dressed in her trademark head-to-toe leather and all of it—jacket, vest, and trousers—clung to her centerfold-worthy figure like a hand-tailored glove. High-heeled boots and a leather computer bag completed the look.

"Hey, Sedona." She flashed her camera-ready smile. "Sounds like you've got a crowd in the tavern tonight."

"Hi, Hannah. Knox is getting rich but I'm getting a little worried about Lyle."

"I've always heard that dust bunnies can take care of themselves." Hannah glanced toward the doorway. "I could really use a drink but it looks like I'm going to have to wade through a bunch of drunken ghost hunters to get it."

"I'll be happy to have Knox bring one out to you."

Hannah chuckled. "Thanks, but I'll take my chances in the bar. I am in desperate need of information and who better to get it from than a crowd of inebriated hunters?"

Hannah might look like Miss July but she had a reporter's eyes. She had arrived on the island a few days earlier and it had immediately become clear that she was determined to use all of her impressive assets and her journalist's savvy to get her story.

"I'm not so sure you'll get anything out of them, even if they are drunk," Sedona said. "I hear they've been given strict orders not to talk to the press. The local authorities are trying to keep a lid on the rumors that are circulating about the Preserve."

"Fat chance."

Sedona smiled. "True."

Hannah gave her a suspiciously sweet smile. "The new Guild boss seems to be determined to run a tight operation. I caught Jones on the street today, but all I got from him was the same thing I got from Harry Sebastian and the police chief. 'No comment.' "

"As I'm sure you're aware, the Foundation controls

most of Rainshadow," Sedona said. "It doesn't want any publicity. Neither do the local residents."

"In that case, they shouldn't have announced Halloween Week."

"I'll give you that. All I can say is that when the new mayor proposed the idea, the town council thought it was a good idea at the time."

Hannah narrowed her eyes. "There's a story here, I can feel it. Sooner or later it will be covered in the media."

"Not if the Rainshadow Foundation and the Guild have anything to say about it."

Hannah groaned. "That's becoming more obvious by the minute. All I've got are rumors of monsters running around in the Preserve. But according to the local legends, that's not exactly news on Rainshadow."

"Nope, it's not."

Hannah got a crafty look. "I heard that Brock Prescott is on the island."

"Mmm."

"I find that rather interesting under the circumstances." Hannah crossed the lobby to lounge against the front desk. She winked in a conspiratorial fashion. "Not like his family's company has any interests here on Rainshadow. Most of this island, and anything found inside the Preserve, belong to Sebastian, Inc."

"Don't look at me," Sedona said. "I have no idea what he's doing here."

"According to my research, you and Prescott were in an MC not so long ago."

"That's old history," Sedona said, going for casual.

"Men like Prescott don't usually follow an ex to a remote island in the Amber Sea if they believe that the relationship is actually over," Hannah said.

Sedona folded her arms on the counter. "It's over."

The truth was, she'd been expecting Brock to show up at the inn ever since she had arrived at work that morning. Each time the front door of the lobby opened she braced herself for the confrontation. But there had been no sign of him all day. She had begun to hope that he had left the island.

Another wave of shouts and laughter rolled through the doorway. Hannah looked in that direction.

"Sounds like a real party going on in there," she said.

"Yes, it does, doesn't it?" Sedona straightened, rounded the end of the counter, and started toward the tavern door. "And I'll bet I know who is wearing the lampshade."

Hannah perked up. "Yeah?"

Sedona went through the doorway.

"Look out," a hunter shouted. "Incoming dust bunny."

A man's hand closed around Sedona's upper arm and hauled her aside just as a small, makeshift trapeze sailed past her. She caught a glimpse of Lyle riding the wooden platform.

He chortled exuberantly. When the trapeze reached the end of its arc he leaped nimbly off the platform and onto the bar.

A cheer went up around the room. Lyle bounced up and down and chortled wildly.

"I knew it," Sedona said, resigned. "Always the life of the party."

"Doesn't take much to entertain a bunch of ghost hunters," Hannah said.

"Or a dust bunny," Sedona said.

The hunter who had whisked Sedona aside released her as if he'd been burned.

"Sorry, ma'am," he said. "Didn't mean to grab you like that. I was afraid you would get hit by the trapeze we built for the little guy."

"It's okay," Sedona said. "You probably saved me from getting clunked on the head."

The hunter looked relieved. "Just having a little fun with the dust bunny." He raised his voice. "Let's lower the rez level, people. The boss's lady is here."

The reaction from the crowd was almost as jolting as the hunter's description of her. The noise level immediately dropped several decibels.

The boss's lady.

Crap, Sedona thought. The word that Cyrus had spent the night at her place had spread far and wide. She had worked with ghost hunters long enough to know there was no stuffing the toothpaste back into the tube. As far as Cyrus's men were concerned she was now officially the boss's lady.

"If you don't mind, I'll take Lyle and leave now," she said politely. "He needs his rest."

A path through the throng of hunters opened up as if by magic. She went to the bar and collected Lyle.

Knox frowned, his bushy brows bobbing up and down over his sun-faded eyes. "You're going home now?"

"Yes, I am. Call the police department if things get out of hand."

Knox leaned forward and lowered his voice. "I'm not worried about these hunters. After what happened last night I'm worried about you going back to your place alone."

"I'll be fine," Sedona said.

"You should wait until Jones gets here to walk you home and keep an eye on you."

The boss's lady.

"I know you mean well, Knox, however, Cyrus is very busy these days."

Knox glanced toward the door and looked relieved. "There he is now. Jones will take care of you. Off you go."

Sedona turned her head and saw Cyrus filling the tavern doorway. Everyone else in the room noticed him at the same time. There was an abrupt silence. Chairs scraped and hunters got to their feet.

"Good evening, gentlemen," Cyrus said. "Go back to your burgers and drinks. Report to headquarters in the morning at oh-seven-hundred. We'll be clearing Sector One tomorrow. I will expect everyone to be at full rez."

There was a chorus of *"Yes, sir."*

Cyrus looked at Sedona. "Ready to go home?"

She considered the options and concluded that all but one of them would make her look foolish or, worse yet, like a sulky teenager. She went with the only remaining alternative.

"Yes," she said.

With Lyle under one arm, she walked through the

gauntlet of hunters to where Cyrus waited in the doorway. He stood aside for her. She did not pause, but kept moving across the lobby. Cyrus followed her.

"Don't know about you, but I'm hungry," he said when he caught up with her. "What do you say we get some dinner over at the Marina Café?"

Well, she did need to eat, Sedona thought. And really, how much more damage could it do to have dinner with Cyrus?

The boss's lady.

"Okay," she said.

Hannah surveyed the crowded tavern with a sparkling smile.

"I know the boss probably told you all not to talk to me about your work in the tunnels," she said cheerfully. "But would anyone like to buy me a drink?"

Chairs scraped again and every man in the room shot to his feet. There was a great deal of pushing and shoving.

"Over here, Miss Holbrook."

"Be my pleasure, ma'am."

Hannah laughed a throaty, sexy laugh and headed toward the bar. "No need to fight over me, gentlemen. I plan to be here for a while. Not like there's anything else to do on this rock at night."

Someone cranked up the music.

Sedona went out into the night with Cyrus.

"I know what you're thinking," Cyrus said.

"I'm thinking I'm hungry."

Chapter 16

IT WAS GOING ON TEN O'CLOCK WHEN THEY LEFT THE restaurant. The taverns and bars in Shadow Bay were staying open late again so that the locals could vacuum up as much cash as possible from the tourists as well as the ghost hunters and the members of the various Foundation research teams. The Halloween lanterns glowed in the evening fog, illuminating Main Street in a ghostly radiance.

"There is absolutely no need for you to spend the night at my place," Sedona said. But she didn't bother to put any energy into the statement.

"You're right," Cyrus said. "We could spend the night at my place, instead. But I haven't had a chance to stock the refrigerator. Come morning, we'd have to go to your cottage for breakfast."

No getting around it, Sedona thought, given recent

events, she was glad to have Cyrus as well as Lyle with her for the dark trek back to her cottage. But the thought of Cyrus spending another night at her place made her uneasy. Not quite as uneasy as the possibility of running into another psi-trap, though.

The boss's lady.

"Fine, my place," she said, aware that she sounded gruff.

"Okay," he said. "But let's stop by my cottage first. I want to grab a few things."

A few things. She knew that as far as the residents of Shadow Bay were concerned it was going to look like the new boss had moved in with her.

"Think of me as a roommate," Cyrus said, as if he had read her mind.

"More like a bodyguard," she said, determined to be mature about the situation.

"Or a bodyguard," he agreed.

When they reached the end of the street Cyrus rezzed his flashlight.

"While we're on the subject of my personal life, there's a rumor going around that Brock Prescott went to your office today," Sedona said.

"I can confirm that rumor."

"Damn. I was afraid of that." She halted and turned to face Cyrus. "What did you two talk about?"

Cyrus stopped. "Take a wild guess."

She winced. "Me."

"Yes, you."

"What did you tell him?"

"I told him to stay away from you or else I would see to it that he disappeared from Rainshadow."

She thought about that. "You used the word *disappear*?"

"I believe I did."

In spite of the many complications that had cropped up in her life recently, she could not help but feel touched.

"Wow," she marveled. "That was cold."

"Do you think so?"

"Very old school." Historically speaking, when a Guild boss made someone disappear, the individual in question wound up taking a long walk in the catacombs without tuned amber. "I'll bet your threat gave Brock some second thoughts. Not that you would actually do something like that."

"Don't be so sure of that," Cyrus said. "I'm a great believer in tradition."

She paused. "You really told Brock Prescott that you would make him disappear if he came near me again?"

"What do you think?"

"I've only known you for about twenty-four hours but I'm inclined to believe you did, indeed, threaten Brock Prescott." Sedona started walking again. "I probably shouldn't say this, but thanks."

Cyrus fell into step beside her. "You're welcome."

She glanced sharply at him. In the heavy darkness it was impossible to read his face, but she thought she detected sincerity in his tone. Possibly a little too much sincerity.

"Look, I really appreciate the gesture, but promise

me you won't actually send him into the tunnels without amber, okay?" she said.

"You still care for him?"

"No. But I got my revenge this morning when he arrived at my place and found you there. That's good enough for me. I don't want to be responsible for his disappearance."

"I'll tell you what. I'll give you my word that I won't make him disappear into the Underworld but I reserve the option to ask Slade Attridge to kick him off the island. Fair enough?"

"Fair enough." She smiled. "Slade would do it, too, if you asked him."

"Yes, I know. He'd do it to protect you. You've got friends here, Sedona."

"Yes." She hugged the knowledge close.

When they neared the gates of the Shadow Bay Cemetery, Lyle chortled and bounded down from Cyrus's shoulder. He vanished into the fog and the darkness.

"Have fun," Sedona called out softly. "Try to stay out of trouble."

They went up the front steps of Graveyard Cottage. Cyrus rezzed the lock and opened the door. He found the wall switch and rezzed it, too. Then he stood back to allow Sedona to enter first.

Old school when it came to his manners, as well, she thought.

He followed her into the small space and kept going into the darkened bedroom. The lights came on. She listened to him rustling around and knew that he was packing shaving gear as well as a change of clothes. Think of him as a roommate. Or a bodyguard. Yeah, right.

"One thing I don't understand," she said.

Cyrus emerged from the bedroom with his leather pack slung over one shoulder.

"What's that?" he asked.

"I keep wondering, why is Brock Prescott here on Rainshadow in the first place? I mean, it's not like he suddenly realized he was madly in love with me."

"You're sure of that? He indicated otherwise."

"Give me a break. The man commands the resources of a very impressive corporation that specializes in Underworld exploration. Prescott Industries has had a lot of experience in the Rainforest and it even has its own security division. But Brock never even bothered to send out a search-and-rescue team after he heard that I was missing. It was as if once I was out of his sight, I was out of his life."

"And now it seems he's changed his mind."

"The only thing I've ever seen Brock get really obsessed with is his family's business." Sedona led the way back out onto the front porch. "So why did he follow me here to Rainshadow?"

"Good question," Cyrus said.

Chapter 17

SHORTLY BEFORE MIDNIGHT SHE HEARD THE FRONT DOOR of the cottage open and close. Cool night air wafted down the hallway into the bedroom.

"Have a good time tonight?" Cyrus asked in low tones.

Lyle chortled a cheery reply. Sedona heard his little claws clicking on the hardwood floor in the hall. A moment later he bounded up onto the bed, a small rock clutched in one paw. He dropped the chunk of amber onto the quilt near her hand. Her senses pinged in recognition. She smiled.

"Where did you find this?" She picked up the amber. "It's lovely, thank you. I'll have Charlotte tune it in the morning. A woman can't have too much good amber."

She placed the chunk of amber on the bedside table. Satisfied, Lyle rumbled contentedly and settled down. She reached out and gave him a couple of pats.

Out in the front room the sofa creaked beneath Cyrus's weight. It occurred to her that she could get used to the notion of having him close by at night if not for the frustration factor. The attraction between them was definitely not diminishing with proximity. It was only growing more intense—at least on her end.

But she was deeply wary of allowing the sparks to flash into a full-blown flame. Some relationships a woman could walk away from relatively unscathed—the relationship with Brock Prescott, for example. Sure, she had not been above taking some satisfaction from the unexpected shot at revenge that had come her way. She was only human, she thought. But her heart had not been broken. She had been pissed off when Diana Easton had opened the door of Brock's town house but not heartbroken. There was a difference. Singed but not burned.

Her intuition told her that things would be different if she allowed herself to get drawn into a more intimate relationship with Cyrus.

She heard the sofa springs creak once more. Cyrus was up again. She could hear him moving around in the front room. Alarm shot through her when she heard his boots on the floor, heading toward the door.

Lyle woke up, too. All four eyes snapped open. He sleeked out, leaped off the bed, and shot down the hallway.

"What in the world?" Sedona said.

There was no response. The front door opened and closed.

She tossed back the covers, grabbed her robe, and shoved her feet into her slippers.

The *thud-thud-thud* of running footsteps echoed in the night just as she went outside onto the porch. In the orange and green lighting of the Halloween decorations she could see Cyrus silhouetted against the dense fog. He gripped the railing and watched the cemetery. Lyle, still sleeked out and ready to rumble, was perched nearby.

A portable light had been rigged up to illuminate the cage around the gravesite, and a guard had been posted to prevent unauthorized entry into the Underworld.

To Sedona's ears, the pounding footsteps sounded unnaturally loud in the fog-muted night. A flashlight beam bobbed frantically in the mist. She thought she could hear ragged breathing now. Then she caught the sound of a second set of running footsteps and saw another flashlight beam.

"Stop," a man shouted. "Orders of the new Guild boss."

The first set of footsteps did not slow.

"Got to get help," the first runner gasped.

Sedona moved to stand next to Cyrus.

"What's going on?" she asked in low tones.

"I'm not sure," Cyrus said. He, too, kept his voice pitched low. "Treasure hunter, maybe."

"Coming up from the catacombs?"

"Probably. I saw two people emerge last night. Figured they were locals who were using the gravesite entrance to do some treasure hunting. That's why I stationed a guard there tonight."

"Sounds like your guard scared off an intruder," Sedona said.

"Maybe."

The ragged breathing and the pounding footsteps got

louder. A figure burst out of the fog and scrambled to a halt at the foot of the porch steps, chest heaving with exertion. Sedona recognized him immediately.

"Joe," she said. "What's going on?"

Joe Furnell was most likely in his midforties but there was a tough, hard-bitten quality about him that made it impossible to guess his true age. He lived alone in a cabin located near the psi-fence that surrounded the Preserve. Like many on Rainshadow, he kept to himself for the most part. He drove into town in a battered truck once a week to pick up groceries and a fresh supply of the herbal tisane that Rachel brewed for him. Joe was grouchy even on his good days and he did not have much use for people in general, but Sedona had always felt a certain sympathy for him.

"This is Joe Furnell," Sedona said quietly to Cyrus. "Retired hunter."

A second man appeared out of the fog. He stopped when he saw Cyrus.

"Sorry, boss," he said. "He took me by surprise. I was watching for intruders attempting to go down into the tunnels. Wasn't expecting one to pop out like this guy did."

"It's all right, Montrose," Cyrus said. He switched his attention to Joe. "What's going on here?"

Joe aimed the flashlight at Cyrus.

"You're the new Guild boss, right?" Joe said. "Heard you had taken up with Miss Snow, here. You gotta do something, sir. My boy's down there."

Cyrus released his grip on the railing, went down the

steps, and snapped the flashlight out of Joe's hand. Joe did not seem to notice. Sedona could see that he was dazed and disoriented.

"Joe Furnell," Cyrus said in a cold voice that carried the bracing edge of a command. "Report."

Joe responded immediately. He straightened and seemed to pull himself together.

"Yes, sir," he wheezed. "Henderson and I went down into the catacombs tonight."

"That was an unauthorized entry into the Underworld."

"Yes, sir. I know, sir. I apologize, sir."

"Did you use the cemetery entrance?"

"No, sir. Used another one that I found awhile back just outside the Preserve. It's farther out but we switched to that one after you put a guard on the cemetery entrance today."

"What happened tonight?"

"Henderson and I are working a site," Joe said. "Awhile back we found a cache of Alien artifacts. Worth a fortune."

"Go on," Cyrus ordered.

"We were clearing out the last of the relics. But something happened when Henderson touched one of the artifacts. He said he was pretty sure he could resonate with it. Next thing we know, a gate opened up in the tunnel wall. Thought we'd find ourselves looking into the Rainforest but it wasn't like that at all. Everything on the other side of the gate seemed like it was made of crystal and quartz and it was all loaded with hot psi. Dazzled our senses. Henderson got real excited. He said he wanted to take a look around. I tried to stop him but he wouldn't listen."

"Something went wrong, I assume," Cyrus said.

"Yes, sir. Henderson went through the portal. And then the damned gate started to slam shut. That's when I heard it, sir."

"What, exactly, did you hear?" Cyrus asked.

Joe appeared to be on the verge of losing his control. His mouth opened and closed. His face crumpled. Sedona realized he was starting to cry. Impulsively, she went down the steps and touched his arm.

He looked at her, as if he had forgotten she was there.

"Miss Snow," he rasped. "Tell the boss here that he's gotta help me."

"You said you heard something just as the gate started to close," Sedona said quietly. "What was it?"

"Henderson," Joe whispered in an agonized voice. He turned back to Cyrus. "I heard Henderson screaming. He started running toward the gate. But . . . but he didn't make it. The gate closed up solid."

"Who is Henderson?" Cyrus asked.

"He's my son," Joe said. "He found me a few months ago. They told him I was dead, you see. But when he grew up, he came looking for me. Henderson is the only family I got left in the world. You gotta help him, Mr. Jones."

Sedona looked at Cyrus.

"You'll need me to open the gate," she said.

Cyrus did not look thrilled but he didn't argue. "Yes, I will."

His lack of enthusiasm hurt a lot more than it should have, she thought. What had she expected? He was a Guild boss who was going to have to lead a dicey search-and-rescue mission with a gatekeeper who might be an unstable multi-talent.

"Don't worry," she said. "I won't crash and burn on you."

He looked at her. "No, you won't."

She suddenly felt a whole lot better.

Chapter 18

SEDONA STOOD WITH CYRUS, JOE, AND A SMALL, HAND-picked group of ghost hunters that included Duke and Tanaka, the hunters who had recently engaged in a game of dust bunny tossing.

But no one was playing games now, not even Lyle. He was crouched on Sedona's shoulder, alert and energized.

She was dressed for fieldwork in jeans, a long-sleeved pullover, and boots. Her hair was in a no-nonsense knot at the back of her head. Like everyone else on the team, she wore a small day pack filled with emergency supplies.

They all looked at the solid wall of gently radiant green quartz. There was no sign of a gate. But then, there rarely was any outward indication of one. Gates got discovered either by accident or by gatekeepers—those with a talent for working gate energy.

"You're sure this is the place, Joe?" Cyrus asked.

"Yes, sir," Joe said. He nodded toward a small pile of green quartz objects. "I marked it with those artifacts before I went aboveground to get help."

Cyrus glanced at Sedona. "Well?"

She pulsed some energy through the tuned amber that she wore in her ring and got a whisper of heat in response. The green quartz wall shimmered faintly.

"There's a gate here," she said.

"Can you open it?" Joe demanded anxiously.

"Yes, I think so." Sedona looked at Cyrus for direction.

"Go for it," Cyrus said. He glanced at his team. "Flamers on standby until we know what we're dealing with here."

The flamers were simple, amber-fueled devices that fired short bursts of flame. They were new in the Underworld, an invention that had come out of the Sebastian labs. The range was limited to about fifteen or twenty feet at most, depending on the talent of the person rezzing the trigger. But they were one of the few weapons that worked in the catacombs besides knives. Even bows and arrows were undependable underground.

Not every ghost hunter had adopted the new technology with enthusiasm. Everyone knew that the real weapons in the tunnels were the energy ghosts that strong hunters could forge out of the ambient psi in the atmosphere. But when facing the unknown—a daily event underground—everyone liked to have some backup. Flamers were the latest experiment in defense weaponry.

Sedona set to work, trying to ignore the little rush of energy she had experienced when they had descended into the catacombs. It was good to be back, she thought; good to be working again. She had Cyrus to thank for that.

She pulsed more energy through the amber in her ring and got a clear, sharp focus. Charlotte Attridge, Slade's wife and the owner of Looking Glass Antiques had done a beautifully nuanced job of tuning the currents of the stone to Sedona's personal aura.

The section of the wall that had shimmered a moment ago quickly dissolved as Sedona applied more power. The green quartz gave way to reveal the gate—a raging storm of glacial blue psi.

One of the men whistled in astonishment. "Never saw anything like that before."

The energy gate was large enough to accommodate a truck but Sedona knew that no vehicle designed and built by humans would be able to crash through the violent currents.

"I spent fifteen years in the tunnels and never saw anything like this," Tanaka said.

"Same here." Duke studied the portal. "This doesn't look anything like the gates into the Rainforest. I'm thinking that there's probably a damned good reason why this one is so hot."

Joe stared at the gate and then he looked at Sedona. "My boy's in there."

"I understand," she said.

Cyrus looked at Sedona. "Recognize the energy?"

"No, it's new to me, too, but I'm sure I can unlock it. Piece of cake." She smiled. "Okay, maybe not exactly a piece of cake, still, I can handle it."

They were all watching her now.

This was it, she thought. The time had come to prove to herself and everyone else that she could still control gate energy.

She heightened her senses, slowly at first—getting a feel for the hot psi churning in the portal. The currents were unfamiliar but it did not take long to find the frequencies.

She got a fix and gently sent out pulses of counterpoint energy. The secret to handling the most powerful gate was to employ a delicate touch. It was an intuitive skill, one she had honed over the course of her career. She had met some gatekeepers who used raw power to break through a locked gate. That approach worked on less formidable portals. But when it came to dealing with Category Five gates, nuance was the key. Too much blunt force and the gate might literally explode, creating a lethal vortex that sucked in everything and everyone within range.

She went closer to the portal, probing cautiously with her talent. Lyle chortled and bounced a little. She understood. The sensation of controlling gate energy was always exhilarating, and this particular gate was the most powerful she had ever encountered.

She did not try to fight the currents. Instead, she allowed them to draw her deeper and deeper into the heart of the storm.

. . . And then she was there and in control. She went to work adjusting some of the frequencies.

A moment later the gate winked out of existence. The portal was open. Sedona stood on the threshold and looked into a dazzling crystal-and-quartz landscape. The energy in the atmosphere was strong enough to send shivers across her senses. The sensation wasn't unpleasant, just disorienting. She had to concentrate to stay focused.

"Son of a ghost," Duke said. "Thought I'd seen everything down here."

"Welcome to Wonderland," Cyrus said.

It took a lot to stun a team of experienced ghost hunters, Sedona thought. Heck, it took a lot to dazzle her. She and the others had seen many strange marvels in the course of their work in the Underworld. But she had never encountered anything like the scene on the other side of the portal. Judging by the low-voiced expressions of awe and amazement behind her, none of the others had ever seen anything like it, either.

The hidden world on the other side of the portal was a vast realm of glacial blue and mirror-bright quartz and crystal. It was a landscape illuminated by an eerie azure radiance that came from the ultralight end of the spectrum.

A stream of what looked like frozen mirror-quartz—the surface flashing sparks of blue sunlight—wound through a forest of glittering crystal blue trees studded with sapphire leaves.

Cyrus moved to stand beside Sedona in the opening. The others crowded closer.

"What in green hell is this place?" one of the men asked.

"It's another underground world constructed by the Aliens," Sedona said. "But unlike the Rainforest, which is alive with a thriving, balanced ecosystem, this place feels as if it's frozen."

"But it's not cold," Tanaka said. He came to stand in the opening and extended one arm over the threshold. "The temperature feels the same as it does everywhere else in the catacombs."

"This place isn't frozen," Cyrus said. "Not literally. It just looks that way because everything seems to be made of quartz and crystal." Experimentally he kicked at the glittering pebbles that covered the ground. The blue gems scattered, revealing hard blue rock. "There will be time enough to study it later. We're here on an S-and-R job." He looked at Joe. "You said your son is wearing an amber locator?"

"Right." Joe moved forward, stiffening a little when the hot atmosphere hit him. "A Sebastian model seven-point-oh. The latest on the market."

Cyrus unclipped his own locater. "Give me Henderson's code."

Joe rattled off a string of digits. Cyrus plugged them into the device and nodded once, satisfied.

"Got a location," he said. "He's not far away. Looks like he was smart enough to stay near his entry point."

For the first time, Joe's expression lightened with something that might have been hope.

"He's still alive," he said.

Cyrus glanced at Sedona. Neither of them spoke. Everyone on the small team knew that all the signal meant was that the locator was still functioning. It did not mean the person it belonged to was still alive. Joe knew that, too, Sedona thought. But he had a right to nourish his hopes.

"Try calling him," Cyrus said to Joe.

Joe cupped his mouth with one hand and shouted into the unnatural silence.

"Henderson."

The name rang from the crystal trees and echoed for seemingly endless moments. But finally there was silence.

Then they heard the answering shout.

"Pa. I'm here. Hurt my leg. Trapped. Can't get out."

Joe's face glowed. "He's alive."

"Tell him we're coming to get him," Cyrus said.

Joe relayed the message. When the crystal forest finally stopped ringing, Cyrus turned to one of the hunters.

"Dinkins, run a ghost check."

"Yes, sir."

Dinkins, a burly man who looked like he'd seen plenty of action in the catacombs, moved through the doorway. Like Joe, he winced a little when the currents of psi hit him. But he got himself under control immediately.

He concentrated for a moment. Sedona's senses were sparking in response to the high levels of energy so she was aware of the subtle tension building in Dinkins's aura. She knew that he had heightened his talent in an effort to pull a ghost.

Dinkins lowered his talent and looked at Cyrus. "No luck, sir. The energy in this place isn't the same as the stuff in the catacombs and the Rainforest."

"No surprise there," Cyrus said. "Everyone back into the tunnel."

Sedona and the others obeyed. Cyrus waited until they were safe on the other side of the gate before aiming his flamer through the portal at the nearest crystal rock and rezzing the trigger. Flame leaped in a long, narrow beam. The blue stone was undamaged but there was no explosion.

"All right, we know the flamers work in this atmosphere," Cyrus said. "Keep them out and in your hands. Duke, Tanaka, and Gibbons, you'll come with me. Everyone else will stay inside the tunnel. When we find Henderson we'll assess the situation."

"I'm coming with you," Joe said. "You got to let me come, too."

Cyrus hesitated and then nodded once. "All right."

No one argued. The boss had spoken. Sedona got the underlying message. Cyrus was not about to risk any more of his team than necessary. But she could hear chimes clashing in some other dimension.

"Cyrus," she said, "I think I should go with you. I can sense energy building in the atmosphere. Feels a little like a river. You might need someone with my kind of talent."

Tanaka squinted into the glittering forest. "She's right, boss, something's happening in here. Feels like a storm brewing."

Cyrus looked grim. "I can feel it, too. Come on in, Sedona. Stay close. Visual contact at all times."

She went back through the portal, into the crystal forest. Lyle rumbled softly and opened all four eyes.

The small group moved cautiously into the shimmering, glittering blue forest. Quartz pebbles and crystals in a million shades of ultralight blue crunched and skittered beneath their boots.

"Watch your footing," Cyrus said. "We don't want anyone going down in this sea of quartz."

"Be a real hard landing," Duke said.

Lyle got distracted by a small, glowing blue gem. He bounded down from Sedona's shoulder, retrieved his find, and offered it to Sedona with a cheery chortle. The stone looked like all of the others scattered about the floor of the strange forest but she bent down to take it. A little murky energy sparkled through her when her fingers came in contact with the rock.

"It's amber," she said, amazed. "Blue amber. It's beautiful."

She tucked the gem into a side pocket on her pack. Lyle appeared much gratified with the reception of his gift. He sped on ahead, pausing here and there to examine other small pebbles. Sedona watched him for a moment, wondering what qualified some of the stones as gift-worthy.

When he disappeared from view behind the blue trunks of a stand of trees, she reached out to touch one of the sapphire leaves on a low-hanging branch. The leaf was perfect in every detail but it was solid stone. Experimentally, she tried to snap it off the branch. The stem looked as fragile as the stem of a champagne flute but she discovered that she could not break it.

"Hard as a rock," she said. She looked around, fascinated. "What happened here?"

"I don't know," Cyrus said. "But I'm starting to wonder if this was the Aliens' first attempt at bioengineering a world they could comfortably inhabit."

"If so, I'd say that something went horribly awry,"

Sedona said. "Nothing we've seen is alive. It's like everything has been turned to stone." She caught her breath. "Petrified."

"Yeah, petrified," Tanaka said. He looked around. "That fits."

"One thing we've learned is that when it comes to Alien science and technology, there's a hell of a lot we don't know," Cyrus warned.

He stopped and turned in a slow arc. When he halted again he was looking toward a jumble of glacial-blue, boulder-sized crystals in front of the entrance of a cave. The interior of the cavern glowed with a strange blue radiance.

"Got him," he said. "He's inside that cave."

Joe lurched forward, skidding recklessly on blue stones. *"Henderson."*

"I'm here, Pa."

Tanaka, Duke, and Gibbons followed Joe through the tumbled boulders.

A moment later Duke emerged.

"The kid's okay, sir. Scared half out of his wits and his leg is broken but he'll live."

"Rig up a sling and let's get him out of there," Cyrus said. "I don't want to hang around here any longer than necessary."

He clipped the locator to his belt and went toward the entrance of the cave. Sedona started to follow but a subtle shift in the atmosphere stopped her.

Ominous energy whispered across the nape of her neck. Not gate energy or the familiar currents of a psi river, she thought. An ancient, Old World quote from a play she had watched when she was in boarding school flitted through her mind. *Something wicked this way comes.*

She had worked in the Underworld long enough to pay attention to her intuition. Automatically she looked at Lyle.

He hopped up onto a nearby rock and made the low, rumbling sound that she had learned to interpret as a growl of warning. But he was still fully fluffed and only his blue eyes were open.

She went to stand closer to him and jacked up her senses a little.

"What is it?" she asked softly.

She did not get an answer from Lyle but there was no need for one because her own senses were registering another shift in the atmosphere. This time she recognized what was happening.

She went to the tumble of blue quartz boulders and saw that the men had rigged a sling to carry the victim. Henderson was a thin, gawky young man of about eighteen or nineteen. His narrow features were twisted in pain and fear. His eyes were closed and he was mumbling.

". . . Monsters. Hurry. They may come back. . . ."

"He's hallucinating," Joe said. "I think it's the pain or maybe he's been psi-burned. We've gotta get him out of here."

Duke looked at Cyrus. "He's ready to transport, sir."

"Good," Cyrus said. "You four handle the sling. We don't know what we're dealing with here. Henderson may or may not be hallucinating. I'll walk point. Sedona will cover our backs."

It took some willpower, but Sedona managed to conceal her astonishment. Cyrus had just tasked her with a crucial responsibility. She was supposed to cover the rescuers' cxit.

There was no time to contemplate the fact that he trusted her to such an extent. She had a mission to execute. Henderson had used the word *monsters*. She was not at all certain that he was hallucinating.

She readied her flamer and took up a position at the rear of the small procession. Lyle bounded up onto her shoulder and sleeked out. It occurred to her that the dust bunny might not believe that Henderson was hallucinating, either.

Her senses were already jacked but she kicked them up another notch. The atmosphere stirred around her and brightened with ice-blue psi. The trees became a more intense shade of blue. The sapphire leaves glittered and flashed in the strange light. Every pebble beneath her foot glowed like the rarest of gems.

Joe, Tanaka, Gibbons, and Duke hoisted the sling with Henderson on board and hauled it out of the cave, carefully negotiating the heap of quartz boulders at the entrance. With Cyrus in the lead, the small procession wound a path back through the forest toward the gate.

It started as a faint flutelike tingle along her senses; fairy music played on exquisite, delicate instruments. Sedona's first instinct was to stop and listen. But the chimes of her intuition overrode the gentle music. They clashed loudly, discordantly, forcing her to pay attention.

"Does anyone else hear the music?" she asked. She kept her voice very soft, but contrasted with the delicate psi music, the words sounded harsh and off-key to her ears.

Lyle hissed softly.

The four men carrying the sling glanced back at her. She saw the uncertainty in their eyes. She knew her question had alarmed them. They were wondering if she was starting to lose it.

"I don't hear any music," Duke announced a little too forcefully. He looked over his shoulder. "Creepy place, though."

Cyrus looked back at Sedona. "I hear music. Where is it coming from?"

Henderson stirred in the blanket sling. His eyes fluttered open and then closed. "The monsters sensed you. They're coming back."

Joe tightened his grip on the blanket. "We gotta hurry."

No one argued. Sedona knew that Cyrus was moving as swiftly as possible, his attention shifting between the locator screen and his surroundings.

The sweet, gentle music grew louder, tugging at Sedona's senses, urging her to stop and listen more closely.

Up ahead, Duke stopped, forcing Joe, Gibbons, and Tanaka to halt also.

"What in green hell?" Duke rasped. "I'm hearing it, too. Where is that music coming from?"

"Auditory hallucination?" Tanaka suggested, looking around.

Sedona felt energy shift in the atmosphere and knew that Duke was pushing his talent higher. The others were doing the same. It was a natural response in a crisis. All of the senses—normal and paranormal—responded automatically by rezzing swiftly to high alert.

"Duke," Cyrus snapped. "Move, man."

"Yes, sir," Duke said.

He shook his head, as if trying to get rid of the music and lumbered forward with dogged determination. The others were forced to move with him.

Joe clapped his free hand over one ear.

Cyrus managed to keep the small group moving forward but his face was a mask of grim determination. He was employing raw willpower to make himself and the others stumble on toward the gate and the safety of the catacombs.

The glorious, thrilling fairy music fascinated and enthralled, summoning the listeners with irresistible currents.

Experimentally, Sedona lowered her talent a couple of notches. The fragile, elegant sound faded a little.

"Everyone, lower your talent," she said. "Hurry. It's using our para-senses to track us."

"She's right," Cyrus said. "Go normal. Now."

Duke opened his mouth to protest the order.

"Do it," Cyrus said.

Duke obeyed. The others did the same. Sedona was close enough to feel the energy around the men shift to a lower level as they fell back into their normal senses.

There was a moment of silence. Then Joe nodded.

"Sedona is right," he said. "I can still hear that damn music but it's not as loud now."

Duke shot Sedona a quick, searching look. "Yeah, it's a little better this way."

"The thing is," Sedona said, "I think that whatever is tracking us got a fix on our location. It may not need to hypnotize us to find us now."

Joe flinched. "Shit. Is that what it was doing? Hypnotizing us with that damn music?"

"Your son is right," Sedona said. "There are predators in this place and they're hunting us."

"With *music*?" Gibbons said. "That doesn't make sense."

"I don't think it's actually making music, at least not the way we think of doing that," Sedona said. "Our minds are interpreting its psychic lures that way. Probably similar to how certain kinds of deepwater fish use bio-phosphorescence to draw prey."

"Monsters," Henderson gasped through gritted teeth. "Try to sing you to your death. Only reason they didn't get me was the energy in that cave. Once I got inside, I couldn't hear the music."

"I read about some creatures that can do that," Cyrus said. "The story was in a book on Old World mythology. I think the singing monsters were called Sirens. The trick for evading them was to plug your ears. But since this music has a paranormal vibe, all we can do is shut down our senses."

"I can still hear it a little and it's getting louder again," Joe said. "They're closing in on us. How much farther?"

"Twenty yards," Cyrus said. "Use the flamers if anything so much as moves."

Sedona followed the others, casting frequent glances over her shoulder. Joe was right. The music was starting to grow louder. She hated operating in extreme conditions without her senses at full throttle. She felt half-blind. Lyle hunkered down on her shoulder, rumbling a continuous warning.

A few steps later she realized that the sense of oppressive energy in the atmosphere had become stronger. It reminded her of the dark weight of an impending thunderstorm. She could have sworn that the atmosphere was getting hazy.

The ice-blue sunlight started to dim.

"Now what?" Tanaka muttered.

"There's a storm coming," Duke said. "Not like any energy storm I've ever seen."

Before anyone could respond, they emerged from the crystal forest and found themselves confronting a wall of dazzling white energy.

"Son of a bitch," Joe said. "The damn gate closed."

The locked gate was nothing compared to the paranormal hurricane that was closing in on them but Sedona did not see any reason to point that out. The only thing she could do for the team was open the gate and that meant rezzing her talent again.

She hurried around the men and stopped in front of the blank wall of energy. Lyle muttered.

"Yes, I know," she whispered. "I'm working as fast as I can."

She jacked up her talent.

. . . And the storm exploded around her. Glacial-blue

psi raged in the atmosphere, swirling like a blizzard amid the crystal trees.

She realized the terrible, beautiful music had stopped.

One good thing had come out of the coalescing energy storm, she thought. Evidently the predators were no match for it, either. But the hurricane-force winds of paranormal ice were so strong it would not be long before they overwhelmed all of their senses. She had to get the gate open and she had to do it fast.

She fought her way through the turbulent currents. The interference from the storm was so intense now that she had to put one hand on the gate and establish physical contact in order to find the frequencies. The amber in her ring burned in the dazzling blue light.

Relief slammed through her when she got the focus. She pulled hard on her talent, seeking the delicate counterpoint currents that would unlock the gate.

The wall of blue quartz started to shimmer. Slowly it became transparent. She caught a glimpse of the men waiting on the other side. She pushed her talent higher, concentrating fiercely as the currents of the storm threatened to disrupt the gate mechanism. If she lost control, the gate would slam shut. She could not let that happen. She was rapidly exhausting her psychic senses. She knew she would not be able to open the gate again.

A narrow opening appeared. She pulled on the last of her reserves, fighting the storm as well as the seething gate energy.

"Go," she shouted.

Joe, Duke, Gibbons, and Tanaka needed no urging.

They rushed through the slim opening and carried Henderson into the safety of the tunnel. Grimly, Sedona kept one palm flattened on the gate, holding it open with sheer determination and the last of her energy reserves. The shock of physical contact with the gate scorched her senses. She knew that she was taking a bad psi-burn but there was no other option.

Cyrus looked at Sedona.

"Inside," he ordered.

"I can't," she said. "It will close as soon as I lose contact and I'm not going to be able to hold it open any longer. Get through while you can."

Another blast of hurricane psi struck with blinding force, searing her senses. She could no longer see Cyrus or the others inside the portal. She lost contact with the gate. It slammed closed and locked into a solid wall of stone, trapping her in a world of ice-blue energy.

She could barely make out her hand in front of her face. She was vaguely aware of Lyle hunkered down on her shoulder, claws dug into her leather jacket.

There was nowhere to run, nowhere to hide from the monster psi-storm. All she could do was huddle in on herself and try to survive the onslaught.

She was about to sink to the ground when she felt a strong hand close around her arm.

"I've got you," Cyrus said.

Despair shafted through her. He had not made it through the gate. She had failed to save the whole team.

"No," she whispered. "You were supposed to go through with the others."

"I don't leave people behind."

There was no time to contemplate the disaster. The raging psi-storm overwhelmed her. She knew that if she lived, she would be badly burned—again—probably permanently this time. And Cyrus would likely suffer the same fate. No talent could stand against such violent energy.

Cyrus's arms closed around her, lifting her. She was dimly aware of Lyle hopping from her shoulder to Cyrus's. But in the next instant an eerie silence fell. The acid fire of panic seared her.

"Damn it," she gasped.

"It's okay," Cyrus said. "It's just me."

The strange hush grew more intense. Unnerved, she opened her eyes. She realized that Cyrus was carrying her forward into the jaws of the storm but it was as if they were enveloped in a protected sphere, a murky, gray ghost world that extended for a radius of about ten feet around them.

The sphere of unnatural silence moved with them. It dawned on her that Cyrus was using his talent to shield them.

"Now you know why they call me Dead Zone Jones," he said.

Chapter 19

HE REZZED HIS TALENT STILL HIGHER AND CARRIED Sedona through the eerie silence of the ghost zone that he created around them. He held his locater in one hand and the flamer in the other. He struggled to read the nav screen as he cradled Sedona and kept the sphere in place. Lyle rode his shoulder.

Everything that entered the spectral dimension created by his talent, including the storm psi, flatlined until he had passed out of range.

"You're good," Sedona whispered. "Very good."

"I can't maintain the zone for long," he said. "I'm using too much energy."

"Because you're protecting all three of us. I understand. We're aiming for the cave, I assume?"

"Yes."

In spite of the dire circumstances, or perhaps because

of them, the realization that she didn't fear him lifted his spirits as nothing else except the reopening of the gate could have done. He glanced at the compass and changed direction slightly.

"Give me the locater and the flamer," she said. She plucked both from his fingers. "I may be psi-burned but I can still read an amber compass and rez a flamer." She hesitated. "Assuming both will work if I'm the one who's holding them?"

"They'll work as long as you're in physical contact with me."

"Okay, I'll keep us on course while you concentrate on maintaining this ghost world thing you've got going."

He did not argue. She was right. They needed each other if there was any hope of surviving the storm and the night to come.

With the blazing energy quiescent within the dead zone he could see clearly inside the radius of the energy field that he was generating. When he drew close, the eerie blue trees with their sapphire leaves lost their inner psi-glow as if they had been turned into clear glass. The gemstone pebbles beneath his boots became a dull, lifeless gray.

If the forest had been a living ecosystem, all of the plant life would have wilted. Any creatures—human or otherwise—that fell within the zone would slide into an unconscious state. If he kept up the pressure for too long, everything he touched with his talent would die.

But he was moving quickly through the crystal forest. As soon as he was out of range the inner light returned to the world. The blue glow once again infused the trees and the leaves and the stones. The silently howling winds of the psi-storm returned as well.

"Left one degree," Sedona said. "We're less than twenty yards away now."

"Are you sure?" he asked.

"Of course, I'm sure."

"Okay, okay, just checking."

She concentrated on the compass, reading off directions as if they were driving down an ordinary highway. For some inexplicable reason he smiled, even as his spectral touch drained the colors out of another stand of trees.

Sedona squinted up at him. "Something funny that I should know about?"

"Road trip," he said.

She got it immediately, flashing him a weak but real smile. "And we all know men have a problem when it comes to following directions."

"That's just a myth."

"Good to know. Right one degree. About fifteen feet. The entrance to the cave should appear any second now."

"It *should* appear?"

The last of her smile vanished. "It did occur to me that the storm might have messed up the compass."

"Not within the zone," he said.

"What zone? Oh, you mean the area covered by your talent?"

"The dead zone," he said.

She moved the hand holding the compass in a vague gesture that looked to be the equivalent of a shrug. "But things aren't dead inside the radius of your aura. They just sort of go to sleep."

"If I kept up this level of heat for long and if this forest was alive, I would kill everything I touched within a matter of minutes."

"Oh, yeah? Then why am I still breathing? And what about Lyle? He looks quite perky to me."

The question irritated him. "The reason you and Lyle are okay is because I'm not focusing on your auras."

"You know what they say when it comes to talent. Focus is everything." Sedona stiffened. "Look, there's the cave. I can see the boulders in front. You did it, Cyrus. We made it. Wow, you really *are* good."

He was about to tell her that no one, including the members of his own family, considered his talent a good thing but Lyle suddenly became active. He rose on his hind paws and chortled.

"You can put me down now," Sedona said. "I can stand on my own two feet long enough to get past those big rocks."

"You're sure?"

"I'm sure."

He set her down carefully. She scrambled over the boulders and into the glowing blue cave. Lyle bounded down to the nearest quartz rock and bounced after Sedona, disappearing into the hot blue shadows.

Cyrus lowered his talent and followed Sedona and Lyle into the cave. He was relieved to discover that the interior was free of storm energy. The blue psi locked in the quartz walls glowed softly but steadily, impervious to the heavy psi that surged and churned outside.

"Henderson was right about the energy levels in here," Sedona said. "The para-radiation from the quartz seems to be suppressing the psi outside."

Experimentally Cyrus rezzed his talent again. The glowing blue walls started to dim. He shut it down quickly.

"But it doesn't shut down human psi," he said. "I can still use my senses in here."

Sedona surveyed the radiant cave walls. "It's similar to being inside the tunnels or in the Rainforest, except that all of the energy is coming from the blue ultralight end of the spectrum."

"Henderson survived for a couple of hours in this cave so with luck that means there won't be any nasty surprises." He took the flamer from Sedona. "But I'm going to do a walk-through, just in case."

Flamer in hand, he moved through the cavern. Sedona trailed after him. Lyle dashed on ahead. The dust bunny appeared curious but there was no indication that he was alarmed. He still had all four eyes open but he was fully fluffed.

The cave was littered with glowing rocks of various sizes but there were no signs of plant or animal life. There was, however, a whisper of humidity in the atmosphere.

"Feels a little damp," he said.

"Yes, it does." Sedona looked around. "I wonder if there's water nearby?"

The question was answered by Lyle. Chortling enthusiastically, he dashed around a corner and vanished from sight. A few seconds later there was the unmistakable sound of a small splash.

"Trust Lyle to find a swimming hole in the middle of a frozen forest," Sedona said.

When they rounded the twist in the cavern they saw Lyle. He was paddling in circles around a pool of water that glowed as blue as the rocks.

Sedona went forward, crouched on the rim of the pool, and dipped one hand in the water.

"It's warm," she announced, straightening. "Must be a hot spring somewhere underground."

Cyrus went to the edge and looked down into the depths of the water. The water was crystal clear and the view of the blue stone sides of the pool was laser-sharp. But the bottom curved off and away, making it impossible to see the source of the spring.

"It's probably being fed by a deep aquifer heated by volcanic activity," he said.

He reached into his pack and took out the packet of test strips that he carried. Crouching, he dipped one of the strips into the pool and glanced at the reading.

"Well?" Sedona asked.

"It's safe to drink or swim in but Lyle is the only one who is going to take a bath in it."

"Don't worry, I don't intend go into the water," Sedona said. "I've heard Charlotte and Rachel and the others talk about the creatures that escaped from that ancient Alien aquarium awhile back. They say some of them made it into the flooded caves here on the island.

Rachel's little pal, Darwina, almost got eaten by one. I'd better get Lyle out of there."

"Good luck," Cyrus said. "Looks like he's having a fine time."

Lyle splashed happily, unperturbed by the mysterious blue depths of the pool.

Sedona crouched beside the spring again and held out her hand. "Come out of there, Lyle. Please."

As far as Cyrus could tell, Lyle wasn't the least bit concerned but he seemed to get the message that Sedona was worried. He scrambled out of the pool and shook the water from his fur. Then he scurried over to her and made reassuring noises.

Sedona straightened again and looked around. "Who would have guessed there was a hot pool here? Evidently not everything in this place has been frozen into crystal or quartz."

"If the monsters inhabit Wonderland, they would need fresh water to survive."

Sedona shuddered. "And something to eat."

"The food supply may be running low," Cyrus said. "That could be why the predators have been driven to hunt aboveground in the Preserve."

Sedona glanced thoughtfully at the blue pool. "Whatever was hunting us may decide to come here for a drink."

"Maybe, but I don't think so. There's nothing to indicate that any living creature has been inside here for a very long time. Regardless, we don't have much choice. We need shelter from that psi-storm and this is the only place that's available."

"Understood." Sedona glanced at Lyle who was now engrossed with some of the glowing pebbles. "The good news is that my pal over there makes a good early-warning system. I'm sure he'll alert us if anything dangerous tries to enter the cave."

"Sounds like a plan. Time for you to crash."

She searched his face. "What about you? I'm not the only one who burned a lot of energy a short time ago. You must need some rest."

"I'll be okay," he said. "Putting up an umbrella doesn't take as much energy as . . . some things."

Her lips twitched. "An umbrella?"

He started back toward the front of the cave. "That's what it feels like when I crank up my talent the way I did to get us through the storm."

"A psi-umbrella. Interesting concept."

"That's me, the guy with the umbrella." He stopped when he realized that she was not following him. "I thought you decided you weren't going to take a swim in that pool."

"I'm not but if you don't mind, I'd like to take advantage of the facilities. I'll be along in a minute."

"The facilities?" He went blank. Then he realized what she meant. The larger rocks offered some measure of privacy. "Right. I'll wait here. I don't want either of us to get too far out of visual range of the other."

"Don't worry. Same protocol as working the tunnels or the Rainforest. Partners aren't supposed to lose track of one another."

Partners. Well, that's what they were, he thought. For now at any rate. It wasn't nearly as good as being lovers, but it was a big step up from being Guild boss and contract employee.

"That's the rule," he said. "Partner."

By the time they both finished using the facilities, it was obvious that Sedona was having a tough time staying awake. Cyrus knew that she was barely hanging on but she was fighting the deep sleep she needed so desperately.

"You're afraid to go under, aren't you?" he asked.

"Well, yes. We're in an unknown place with unknown energy and unknown predators."

"Listen to me, Sedona. You'll be fine," he said. "Lyle and I will watch over you. Go to sleep."

She searched his face for a long moment and then she seemed to come to a decision.

"Not like I can stop it, anyway," she said.

"Nope. Let go, Sedona. You've got friends to watch your back."

She finally managed a shaky smile. "Yes, I do. And I signed on with a Guild boss who never leaves a member of the team behind."

"You got that right."

It all came down to whether or not she trusted him, he thought. He did not realize he was holding his breath until she nodded once and patted a yawn.

"Okay," she said.

He spread an emergency blanket on the stone floor. She sank down onto it, her back to the wall, her legs straight out in front of her. He lowered himself beside her.

She leaned her head on his shoulder and closed her eyes. "Wake me if the monsters show up."

"I'll do that."

She was asleep in the next breath. Gingerly he put an arm around her. When she did not flinch away he settled her more comfortably against his side and leaned back against the wall of the cave.

Lyle scooted across the glowing stone floor and settled down next to Sedona's denim-clad thigh. He closed all four eyes and promptly went off into dust bunny dreamland.

"Life's simple for you, isn't it?" Cyrus said very softly. "Any day is a good day so long as you survive to play another day."

Lyle twitched one ear.

"As mottos go, that one's not bad," Cyrus said. "But we humans have a penchant for complicating stuff that probably shouldn't be all that complicated."

Like the fierce mix of emotions that he was feeling for the woman who was sleeping so soundly, so trustingly, at his side. He tried to come up with a description of their current relationship.

For now Sedona was his responsibility. His contract employee. A member of the team. His partner in surviving this strange new country in the Underworld.

All of the labels were correct but none of them felt right.

He sat quietly for a time, watching the blizzard of psi flash and burn across the entrance of the cave. It reminded him of the static that sometimes showed up on a vintage rez-screen. But unlike the snow on the old screens the stuff blowing outside the cavern looked potentially lethal.

He was not at all certain that he and Sedona would have survived the storm if they had not found shelter.

But they were reasonably safe for now, he decided. With luck the storm would blow itself out in the next few hours. There was no reason Sedona would not be able to open the gate again. The only trick would be getting out of the crystal forest without running into the predators that hunted with music.

Sedona stirred a little in her sleep and leaned more heavily against him.

He looked down at her. Several locks of her witchy black hair had come free of the clip she had used to secure it in a knot. In sleep, the wariness and the subtle tension that sharpened her features and burned in her eyes receded. He knew that what lay beneath the cautious, sometimes brittle surface was a resilient spirit and a surprising streak of optimism.

There were other qualities, as well. It was courage and a sense of responsibility that had been on display today when she had stood her ground, holding the gate open, as he got his men to safety. She must have known in that moment that she would not make it through, herself.

He eased her down into a more comfortable position with her head pillowed on his thigh. She was too deep into the crash now to be awakened by such a small shift in position. It was possible to drag someone out of a deep post-burn sleep, but you never knew for sure how the individual would respond. The person was likely to awaken dazed and disoriented—trapped in the no-man's-land between the dreamstate and the waking state.

He assessed his own status and concluded that he had told Sedona the truth when he said he wasn't going to crash.

Like most hunters he carried some "hot shots," an artificial stimulant in pill form. The meds were for use only in cases of emergencies in which conditions were too dangerous to allow for the luxury of sleep.

The effects of the hot shots were short-lived and, as with all things related to the paranormal, there was a price to be paid for using the crap. The crash that followed was inevitably even deeper and more profound than the original version. He rarely used the shots.

Cyrus reached down and touched Sedona's hair.

"You're wrong," he said very softly. "I didn't come back for you just because it was my job to protect you. I came back for you because I need you."

Chapter 20

A SOFT LITTLE CHORTLE WOKE HER SOMETIME LATER. Her first thought was that she was home in her cozy little cottage near the graveyard. But for some reason her pillow was much too solid. And too warm. She opened her eyes and marveled at the blue glow that enveloped her.

Memories slammed back. With a start she realized she was no longer propped against Cyrus's shoulder. Her head was in his lap. Embarrassed, she sat up so quickly that she very nearly clipped him under his chin.

"Sorry," she said. She fumbled with her clothing and raked her fingers through her hair. When she realized she had lost the clip she glanced around the stone floor, looking for it. "Didn't mean to fall asleep on top of you like that."

Cyrus smiled a slow smile of pure masculine invitation. "You're welcome to fall asleep on any part of me you choose."

She flushed. She saw the clip, seized it, and yanked her hair back into a knot. When she looked up she realized Cyrus was still watching her. There was a little heat in his eyes.

She decided the best course of action was to ignore him. "Where is Lyle?"

"He just took off."

"Hunting, no doubt." She frowned. "But there's nothing to hunt in this place."

"That we know of," Cyrus said. "There are predators out there somewhere, remember? Predators can't survive without prey."

"Good grief, do you think he went outside? Lyle is so little. He won't stand a chance."

"He's got good instincts. Don't worry, he'll be fine. How are you feeling?"

She thought about that while she cautiously opened her senses a couple of notches. Relief flooded through her when she realized the paranormal side of her nature felt normal again.

"Good," she said. "I'm okay."

Cyrus looked amused. "You sound surprised."

"I am surprised."

"Told you that you'd be fine."

She smiled. "Yes, you did." She glanced out the front of the cavern. The view was still blocked by the blizzard of psi. "Looks like it's still snowing out there. What are we going to do if it doesn't let up?"

"We'll think of something."

"Guess we'll have to." She leaned back against the

wall and looked around. "You know, in its own spooky way, it's really quite beautiful in here."

"Yes," he said. "Very beautiful. Unique. Unlike anything else I've ever experienced."

She realized that he was not looking at the glacial-blue chiaroscuro that surrounded them. He was watching her as if she were the truly rare, exotic element in the cavern. Energy shifted in the atmosphere and she knew that Cyrus's talent was stirring, but not in the fast, sweeping way it had when he had carried her safely through the storm. This time his talent was a seductive whisper of heat that lightly stroked all of her senses. Everything inside her was riveted by the subtle masculine lure.

"Stop that," she said. But it took a lot of willpower to say it.

"Stop what?"

"You know what you're doing."

He looked thoughtful for a moment. Then he leaned his head against the wall.

"I want you," he said. "I have from the first time I saw you. It's not something I can turn on and off at will. It runs too deep. But if it helps, I can promise you that I can control myself. You're in no danger from me."

She felt parts of her clench in ways that only heightened her awareness of the heat they were both generating.

"I know," she said. "I've never met a man who is as much in control of himself as you are. I suppose that you had to develop that kind of self-mastery to handle your talent."

He looked out toward the storm. "Are you afraid that

if we had sex I might accidentally lose control of my psychic side and destroy your own senses?"

"No." Shocked, she leaned forward, seized his chin in her left hand and turned his head so that he had to meet her eyes. "I'm not afraid of you, Cyrus Jones. I'm just not sure that it would be a good idea for us to get involved, that's all."

"Involved." He moved one hand to indicate the glowing blue walls of quartz and the psi-hot storm at the entrance of the cave. "I'd say it's a bit late to avoid getting involved. We're in this mess together, in case you hadn't noticed."

"I'm aware of that," she said stiffly. "I am referring to our personal relationship."

"Let's see, a few hours ago you saved the lives of several of my men and a dumbass kid who got into more trouble than he could handle. Now we're sitting out an Underworld psi-storm and wondering how the hell we're going to get back to the surface without becoming a snack for some monsters we haven't even seen yet. I'd say that our personal relationship is pretty damn well cemented in stone. Whatever happens after we get out of here, one thing's for sure, I'm never going to forget you, Sedona Snow. What about you? Think you'll forget me?"

The heat in his eyes was so scorching hot it stole her breath. She had to focus to think clearly.

"No, of course I'm not going to forget you," she said. "Everyone knows that sharing danger and . . . and hardship together can produce a bond of sorts between two people."

"Got news for you. I wanted to take you to bed before

we came down here and got this shared danger-bond thing going."

Breathe, she told herself. Just breathe. But it was definitely getting harder to stay on track.

"Did you?" she said.

His mouth quirked faintly. "Oh, yeah."

"I see." She swallowed hard. "I'm not saying that, perhaps, in time, we might not find that there's something between us."

"But for now we should be cautious, sensible, and restrained."

She glowered. "Well, yes. What's wrong with that?"

"Nothing." He smiled a slow, wicked smile. This time the glint in his eyes was laced with pure male amusement, as well as sexual heat. "It's just that, given our current situation, it seems a little ridiculous to be overly concerned about our future relationship."

"Why?"

"Let's face it, we're stuck in a psi-hot cave with limited supplies in the Underworld version of a desert island with singing predators hanging around the front door. Our only backup is a dust bunny that just left to find a hot date or grab takeout or maybe go back to the surface without us."

Anger flashed through her. "Lyle would never abandon me." She paused. "Us."

"That's a relief. For a while, there, I was a little worried. But now that I know that we can count on Lyle, I'm going to scratch that concern off my agenda."

He was teasing her. She couldn't believe it. For some

reason that was all it took to push her over the edge. Now she was mad. And hot. She rose to her knees and clamped her hands on either side of his face.

"You bet," she said. "What else could possibly go wrong? Has it occurred to you that we might end up spending the rest of our lives in this damn cave?"

"I don't think it will come to that." But his voice was suddenly a whole lot rougher than it had been a moment ago.

"Even if we do get out of here we might be so psi-fried that we'll both wind up in a para-psych ward."

"I'm okay with that so long as they let us share the same room," Cyrus said.

"You're not going to take this situation seriously, are you?"

"The situation, yes." He watched her very steadily. "You, yes. But your fears about us getting too deeply involved in a relationship? Nope. I'm blowing those off."

"Are you?"

"I've got bigger problems to worry about. Judging by that kiss last night, I'd say that at least some of the attraction between us is mutual. As far as I can tell, the only thing standing in the way of us having a relationship is the possibility that you might be afraid of me and what I can do with my talent. If that's true, I'd rather we didn't go down that road. I already tried that route with a couple of agency dates—nice women, strong talents—who thought they could overlook that aspect of my nature. Things did not go well."

Inexplicable emotions raced through her in a rush of heat.

"This has nothing to do with your talent," she said. "I'm trying to explain something here."

"Are you afraid of me?" he asked.

"No," she said. "Are you afraid of my . . . other talent?"

"Honey, you are welcome to set fire to my sheets anytimc."

She gripped the collar of his khaki shirt and kissed him—hard. At the same time she rezzed her senses.

. . . And discovered that in the psi-hot environment, she did not need a spark from the flicker to start a fire. Paranormal flames flashed and danced in the blue shadows, winking out as quickly as they appeared. At once everything around her became more intense.

"Oh, damn," she whispered. "I didn't mean to do that."

"Don't worry." Cyrus caught her shoulders with both hands and pulled her down on top of him. "I've always wanted to play with fire."

His eyes burned and she felt the fierce shadows leap in his own aura. The currents of ice that he generated clashed with the fires of her own psi-field. Sapphire lightning danced in the charged atmosphere.

He kissed her again and the lightning became a sizzling storm around them. But they were safe inside the sphere of dampening energy that Cyrus created.

She started to protest. She had trust issues, after all. She specifically did not trust Guild bosses. But Cyrus had come back for her when the gate slammed closed today.

"Don't worry," he said. "I've got you."

It was the second time he had said that to her, she

realized. She had trusted him the first time. She could trust him now.

He used his grip to bring her mouth back down to his. More energy exploded in the atmosphere, blazing up and down the spectrum.

"Good grief," she whispered.

"Don't worry about it."

She let herself sink back into the blazing kiss. He folded her close and tight, his lcgs tangling with hers. His breath roughened. When she moved one hand lower, she felt the rigid length of his erection thrusting relentlessly against his khaki trousers.

The charged atmosphere was intoxicating.

"Like having sex in the middle of a lightning storm," she whispered.

"Oh, yeah," Cyrus said. "Can't wait to try this at home."

She drew her fingertips along the side of his jaw. "Probably indicates that there's something a little abnormal about both of us."

"We already knew that."

She felt his hands slide up under her pullover. His palms were warm and exciting on her bare skin. He tugged the garment off over her head and freed her arms. For the first time she wished she was not wearing a sports bra. It was about as sexy as an elastic support bandage.

"Wow." Cyrus ran a finger under the snug lower hem of the bra. "So this is what women wear into the field. Is it a corset?"

"It's a sports bra," she said, on the defensive now. "It's practical. Get over it."

"It's cute in a way."

"Yeah, right."

He laughed, shoved both hands under the lower edge of the bra, and hauled it up and off in one long sweeping motion. The garment landed somewhere on the far side of the cave.

"Comes off okay," he observed. "That's all that matters."

He cupped one of her small breasts in his palm.

"Nice," he breathed. "Perfect."

He bent his head and kissed a tight little nipple.

She shivered and started to unbutton the front of his shirt. But her fingers were shaking. Frustrated, she yanked on the front of the garment. Buttons flew every which way.

"Oh, geez," she said, genuinely shocked by her own passion.

"They don't make field gear like they used to, do they?"

"That's not what I meant."

She forced herself to take her time getting the rest of the buttons undone.

"Could you hurry things up a bit?" he pleaded. "I'm going crazy here."

"You and me, both." An alarming thought struck her. She stopped work on the buttons and took another look around. "This doesn't actually feel normal. Not for me. Maybe it's something about the energy in this place."

"It's not the damn cave energy." He kissed her throat. "It's us. You and me. To quote you, get over it."

She was beyond arguing now. His mouth was hot and seductive on her skin. The touch of his hands on her sensitive breasts was almost too much.

With a fierce effort of will she got the last of the shirt buttons undone. He was wearing a khaki green T-shirt underneath. She pushed up the hem and spread her palms across his skin. He was warm to the touch and his skin was damp with perspiration.

"You feel like you're running a fever," she marveled.

"I am. You're the cause." He ran one hand down to the waistband of her jeans. "And the cure."

He got her pants undone and then his fingers were inside her panties and she was suddenly very wet.

"Cyrus," she got out in a soft gasp.

He shoved the denim down over her rear and then past her thighs. The panties went with the denim. The garments got tangled up around her knees, trapping her. She was so frustrated, she wanted to scream.

"Damn," she whispered.

"I've got this," Cyrus said.

He levered himself up to a sitting position and rolled her onto her back. With swift, efficient movements of his hands he worked the jeans and panties down her thighs and off her ankles. He flipped the garments aside. Clearly he had only one thing in mind at the moment. But she could hardly complain because she was consumed by the same objective.

Cyrus paused just long enough to strip off his own khakis and briefs, revealing the fierce erection she had detected earlier. She noticed that he was careful to set his gear-studded belt and the flamer within easy reach. Sex might be his immediate goal but he was still a Guild boss, after all.

He stretched out beside her and gathered her close. She

inhaled the heady, sexy scent of him and made a small, choked sound that she feared sounded a bit like a growl.

If Cyrus noticed, he didn't seem to find it alarming. He slipped one hand between her legs and groaned when he found the wet heat there. He stroked her until she was certain she would go mad, until everything deep inside her was clenched tight.

"Yes." She caught his hand in a desperate attempt to force the rhythm. "Now."

"Soon," he said against her throat. "I swear it. Very, very soon."

He did something with his fingers, something that took her to another level. The all-consuming tension inside her broke free in small, pulsing waves. It was too much. She wanted to scream with the wonder of it all but she could not find the breath to do so. She closed her eyes against the shattering sensations and clutched at him, her nails digging into the muscles of his shoulders.

"Sedona," Cyrus whispered in a tight, ragged voice. "My sweet, hot Sedona."

He shifted onto his back and pulled her down astride him. Gripping her hips, he fit himself to her and drove deep, filling her and stretching her in ways that she had never before experienced. Too much. She was too sensitive down there now. *Too much.*

Without warning a second climax rippled through her. This time she was left gasping in disbelief.

Cyrus thrust upward one last time. He roared with the force of his own release.

Blue lightning danced in the shadows.

Chapter 21

HE RETURNED FROM THE POOL ROOM, BUTTONING HIS shirt.

"Your turn," he said. "Still don't see any monsters in the water, but don't try to take a real bath."

"Don't worry." Sedona brushed past him, clutching her clothes. "I won't."

He turned to watch her backside as she hurried into the inner chamber. She had a very nice backside, he decided. He was a man who appreciated nice backsides.

He finished fastening his shirt and stuffed the tails into the waistband of his trousers. He buckled the belt around his waist and checked the flamer to make sure it still worked.

It occurred to him that he was feeling remarkably good for a man who still had a serious to-do list—a list that started with Avoid Singing Monsters While Getting Sedona Safely Out of Wonderland.

"Sex is weird that way," he said.

He didn't realize he had spoken aloud until Sedona appeared. She was back in her jeans and in the process of pulling on thc black pullover.

Her head popped out of the neck opening of the garment.

"What did you say?" she asked.

Masculine intuition kicked in fast.

"Nothing," he said. "Not important."

She did not appear convinced but she let it go. She glanced around, studying the interior of the cave with a thoughtful frown. "It's a lot quieter in here now."

"No kidding."

She contemplated the blue walls and shook her head. "Hard to believe that you and I generated all that energy."

Irritation crackled through him. He reached down to open the pack.

"Not really," he said. "You interested in coffee? I've got some in the pack. We can use water from the thermal pool to make it."

"Sounds good." She watched him take the instant coffee out of the pack. "What makes you so sure that the para-radiation in here wasn't responsible for what just happened between us?"

A man could only be expected to take just so much. He dropped the coffee and moved to stand directly in front of her.

"Trust me," he said, spacing each word with great

care. "It was the other way around. You and me, we're good together. Very, very good." He brushed his mouth across hers. "We're hot together. We were the source of the lightning, not the damn cave."

She flushed and quickly turned away to study the nearest glowing boulder, as if she had never noticed it. "Well, it certainly was an unusual . . . experience."

"Unusual? Is that the best you can do? Damn, woman, you don't leave a man with much pride, do you?"

She turned back quickly, eyes widening in horror. "I didn't mean that there was anything unpleasant about the experience."

"Wonderful." He started toward the thermal-pool room, the packet of coffee and two collapsible cups in one hand. "Now we've moved from unusual to unpleasant."

She hurried after him. "Stop twisting my words."

"I'll try but it's hard not to twist them. Could you at least tell me that it was all right or maybe even *nice* for you?"

"I'm not complaining."

"Damn." He turned the corner into the pool room. "That's something I can hold close to comfort my bruised ego."

"Stop teasing me." She followed him around the twist in the cave. "I'm merely trying to explain that what just happened between us was definitely out of the ordinary, at least for me, and I can't help but wonder how much the energy in here affected things, that's all."

He swung around so quickly she bumped into him. He wrapped one arm around her shoulders, pulled her close, and kissed her—hard—to silence her. When she finally stopped trying to talk, he released her.

"Don't go there," he said. "Please. You'll ruin the glow."

"What glow?" She frowned. "You mean, the paranormal glow?"

"No, the damned afterglow. I was enjoying it until you started analyzing the whole thing."

"Oh. Sorry."

She cleared her throat.

"Gotta tell you that our experience during the psi-storm certainly answers one question," she said.

"What's that?"

"I've been wondering why the Chamber sent you to handle the monsters here on Rainshadow."

A sense of grim despair settled on him like a dark fog of psi. He turned away and crouched to fill the cups with warm water.

"Send a monster to hunt the monsters?" he said. "Yeah, that was pretty much how I got this cool assignment."

"Don't be ridiculous. You're not a monster. You're an off-the-charts talent. Which, when you think about it, is precisely the skill-set required to figure out what is going on here."

Cyrus decided that he felt a little better. Not as great as he had been feeling a few minutes ago but better.

"I'll see what we have to eat," Sedona said.

She turned around and went back into the outer chamber.

He filled the cups with warm water from the pool, ripped open the individual serving packets of coffee, and dumped the contents into the cups. Then he unclipped the flamer and gave the coffee a couple of short blasts.

He carried the cups into the outer chamber and found Sedona sitting on the emergency blanket. She had a couple of energy bars that she must have taken from her own pack. She was contemplating the stormy psi at the cave entrance.

It was time to have the conversation, he decided. Maybe past time.

He gave her one of the cups and lowered himself onto the blanket beside her. She did not shrink away. Baby steps, he told himself. Think positive.

She handed him one of the energy bars. They munched on the bars and drank some of the coffee in silence.

"Field coffee is lousy coffee but it's better than no coffee," he offered.

"This isn't the first time I've had coffee in the Underworld," she reminded him. "It tastes fine to me."

She swallowed some more.

He watched the psi-snow. "There is something you should know about me. About us."

"Is this the part where you tell me that, although you're okay with an affair or an MC, you can't make any long-term commitments because you're a Jones and you're a Guild boss and you're rich and you're a member of a powerful, well-connected family? If so, don't bother. I already know all that."

"That was not what I was going to say."

"Oh." She eyed him warily. "What, then?"

"It's not a total coincidence that I took the Rainshadow job. It came up at a very convenient moment but I pulled a lot of strings to get it."

"Why?"

"Because you were here. Because of what happened to you when you disappeared."

She stilled. "I don't understand. Are you telling me you're working with Blankenship? I don't believe it."

"I'm not working with Blankenship. I'm hunting him."

Her eyes widened. "What do you mean?"

"My family—the Joneses—have been searching for him for months. That private investigation firm I told you about—"

"Jones and Jones?"

He nodded. "It's run by my cousin Marlowe. She's been overseeing the search. You're the first real lead we've had."

Sedona did not say anything. She just stared at him.

"I should have told you sooner what I'm going to tell you now," he said. "But there hasn't been an opportunity. And to be honest, I wasn't sure what the hell was going on. Our biggest concern at the start was that you were one of Blankenship's success stories."

"What are you talking about?"

"Marlowe and others in the family were afraid you might be a very dangerous multi-talent."

"I *am* a dangerous multi-talent."

"You're a multi-talent but you're not unstable. The next shock was discovering that you were alive and sane."

Sedona tipped her head back against the wall. "I feel like I'm falling down the dust bunny hole here."

"I'm starting to piece it together. I'll tell you everything I know. But first, I need to give you a short history lesson."

"About?"

"Arcane."

"Which, I have been told, is more or less the Jones family firm," she said.

"That's one way of looking at it. Arcane was founded by an Old World alchemist named Sylvester Jones."

"I think Rachel mentioned him."

"He was an ancestor of mine, a powerful talent who wanted even more power. Back in the 1600s, Old World Time, he came up with a drug designed to stimulate and enhance the paranormal senses. The idea was that it would not only make him stronger but it would give him additional talents."

"He wanted to become a multi-talent?" Sedona asked.

"Yes, and he was sure his wonder drug would have a lot of additional terrific side effects. He believed it would make him healthier and maybe add a decade or two on to the natural life-span. In short, he was the poster boy for the Mad Scientist in those old horror flicks."

She shuddered. "I think I know where this is going."

"Stay with me here. It gets a little complicated. Sylvester Jones died in his hidden laboratory, which wasn't discovered and excavated until the late 1800s by a couple of his descendants."

"More Joneses?"

"Right. When they found Sylvester's body, they also discovered the formula. Soon afterward it was stolen. The damned drug has been causing trouble ever since."

"Explain," she ordered.

"Historically speaking, every once in a while some fool stumbles across a version of the formula and tries to re-create it. The problem is that nobody has been able to do that without also re-creating some very nasty side effects."

"Such as?"

"Addiction is the biggest drawback—and not just psychological addiction. The drug must be taken on a regular and frequent basis. Miss even a dose or two and you start to deteriorate rapidly. According to the old files, users who are deprived of the drug go insane within a couple of days. They are almost always dead within forty-eight hours. Suicide is the usual cause of death."

Sedona took a deep breath. "You think Blankenship is fooling around with a version of the formula, don't you? That he used it on me?"

"My cousin Marlowe started picking up rumors of hunters who were using some kind of new drug to enhance their talents. Rumors of that sort circulate all the time, of course, but these rumors were different. They implied a connection to Arcane."

"So Jones and Jones opened an investigation?"

"Yes, but it went nowhere. Until you showed up after having disappeared for three weeks with stories about having been held captive in a secret Guild lab."

"Well, I didn't tell a lot of people," Sedona pointed out. "Mostly because it became clear that everyone thought I was crazy."

"You're not crazy." He looked at her. "You're stable and you're not using the drug."

"How can you be sure of that?"

"Marlowe sent an aura reader to Rainshadow disguised as a tourist to take a close look at you a few weeks ago. She reported that your aura was rock steady. An unstable aura is a telltale indicator of the formula."

Sedona's eyes tightened at the outer corners. "Jones and Jones spied on me?"

"I knew you weren't going to like this part. But I'm hoping you'll understand our position—my position."

She exhaled deeply. "Yeah, yeah, I get it. You were worried that I was using the drug and that your aura reader hadn't been able to detect it."

"Yes." He picked up a glowing blue pebble and sent it flashing and skittering across the floor. "But I've spent enough time with you now to be very certain that you aren't using the drug. The really interesting part is that you are still alive."

"I beg your pardon?"

"Theoretically, if you were on the formula for any length of time at all and then deprived of it, you should either be insane or dead by now. We—the Jones family—needed an explanation for that."

Understanding dawned in her eyes. "You ruled out the possibility that I was still on the drug so you're left with only one other answer. You're afraid that Blankenship has finally perfected the formula—that his version works without the bad side effects."

"It may have worked on you," Cyrus said. "That would account for your new talent. But I don't think that it has worked for anyone else, at least not without producing the terrible side effects."

"How can you be so sure of that?"

"Because all indications are that Blankenship is desperate to get you back to his lab."

"I told you, I locked up his lab and the strongbox with the crystal inside."

"He needs access to both, evidently."

Sedona drew up her knees and wrapped her arms around them. "I think the crystal is the important thing. Blankenship was trying to tune it so that it would stabilize the serum."

Cyrus sent another little blue pebble skipping across the floor into the deep sapphire shadows. "So his version of the drug has the same side effects as all the previous versions."

Sedona frowned. "But why would the drug work on me without problems and not on other people?"

Cyrus smiled slowly. "We can't prove it yet, but we have a theory. Marlowe and I are convinced that the reason you were able to tolerate the drug without any problems and developed a second talent with no sign of instability is simple—you're a descendant of Arizona Snow."

"Yes, I know. The Snows consider her an example of the crazy gene that shows up every so often in the bloodline. Why does my connection to her matter?"

"Here's another little bit of Arcane history. A few

centuries ago, back on Earth, the directors of Jones and Jones—Fallon Jones and his wife, Isabella—decided to take on a cold case at the request of their friend Arizona Snow."

Sedona looked at him, eyes wide. "They really did know her?"

He smiled. "I told you to think of me as an old friend of the family. To continue, Fallon and Isabella learned that in her younger days Arizona Snow worked for a clandestine government agency."

"Wow. She was some kind of secret agent?"

"Evidently."

"That's . . . exciting. I mean, to think that I'm related to a woman who was a genuine secret agent. Who did she work for?"

"The good guys, of course."

"Excellent." Sedona nodded, satisfied.

"Anyhow, after Snow retired she became something of a conspiracy theorist and a full-blown eccentric but she and Fallon Jones got along well. Some say it's because they understood each other. She actually consulted with Fallon on a few cases."

"Even though she was a big conspiracy theorist?"

Cyrus shrugged. "Takes one to know one. Like I said, she and Fallon collaborated a few times."

"So what happened to the investigation into her case?"

Cyrus picked up another blue pebble and sent it sailing into the dark aqua shadows on the far side of the cave. "Fallon Jones wrote in his private journal that he and Isabella eventually concluded that Arizona Snow had been used as a research subject in a secret government experiment."

Sedona froze. "*No*. Good grief. Like me, you mean?"

"At this point we have no indication that anyone in the government is involved with Blankenship, but, yes, Arizona was a test subject like you. She was selected for the experiment because the researchers had determined that she had some natural, measureable degree of talent."

"They wanted to see if they could enhance her para-senses?"

"Right. That kind of research was still very controversial in those days because no legitimate scientists would risk their careers by claiming to believe in the paranormal."

"Go on," Sedona said.

"Arizona was not the only subject in the experiment. Fallon was never able to determine if the research was successful because the entire project was shut down for some reason before it was concluded. Supposedly all of the files were destroyed. But Fallon Jones was a damn tenacious investigator. He found the lab notes of one of the researchers, a scientist who was obsessed with the results of the experiments and could not bear to see his work destroyed."

"What was in the notes?" Sedona asked.

"A copy of the scientist's version of the old Jones formula. There was another note, as well, and it concerned Arizona Snow."

Sedona watched him. She was very still now. "What did it say about her?"

"According to the notes, all of the subjects who were

subjected to the drug later died from the usual side effects once the drug was withdrawn. Except Snow."

"Why didn't she die?"

"The scientist who left the journal was convinced that Arizona Snow had some natural immunity to the bad side effects of the formula." Cyrus paused. "He theorized that the ability to tolerate the drug without succumbing to the side effects might be an inherited trait linked to Snow's unique psychic genetics."

Sedona took a long breath and let it out slowly. "In other words, Blankenship grabbed me for his experiment because he hoped that I would be immune to the side effects of the drug."

"I think so, yes."

"I was the perfect research subject. He wanted to find out how I could tolerate the drug."

Cyrus sent another blue gem skimming along the floor of the cave. "Most of what I've given you is speculation mixed with old legends with a few actual facts tossed in for spice."

"But if you're right, Blankenship thinks I hold the key for tolerating the downside of the drug. He's desperate to get his hands on me so that he can continue his experiments."

"That's my theory at this point. One other thing you should know, Sedona."

"What?"

"You told me, yourself, your talent is stronger than ever. In addition you've developed the ability to work fire energy."

She closed her eyes briefly. When she opened them there was grim understanding in her gaze.

"In other words, I'm not just immune to the downside of the formula," she said. "The stuff actually worked on me."

"Without creating addiction or withdrawal issues."

"Arizona Snow and I can't be the only people in history who were able to tolerate the drug. There must be others out there who are also immune."

"We know of at least one other familial bloodline that we strongly suspect carries a similar genetic twist," Cyrus said. "A bloodline that may, in fact, have been affected by an ancestor who took the drug."

"Really? Who?"

"The descendants of the crazy alchemist who invented the damned formula."

She stared at him. "Your family?"

He smiled. "I can't wait for you to meet the rest of the Joneses."

Chapter 22

LYLE'S CHEERFUL CHORTLING ECHOED FROM THE INNER chamber of the cave. He dashed out of the blue shadows just as Cyrus sent another blue stone skipping across the floor.

Lyle changed course immediately and sped after the bouncing stone. He caught it when it hit the wall of the cave.

Euphoric with his success, he scurried toward Sedona and Cyrus, the pebble in one paw.

"About time you showed up," Sedona said.

Lyle graciously gave her the pebble and made excited noises.

"Thanks," she said. She examined the small rock carefully. "More blue amber. It's really beautiful."

Cyrus watched her tuck the amber into her pack. He

shook his head, amazed and a little awed by her cool composure.

"You seem pretty damn calm about everything I just told you," he said.

"Actually, your story about those experiments on my multi-great-aunt Arizona Snow come as something of a relief," Sedona said. "At least it explains a few things. I've been going in circles, even starting to wonder if I had hallucinated the whole prisoner-in-a-lab scenario."

"You prefer that it was the real deal?"

"Yes, because it means I don't have to doubt my memories."

Cyrus nodded. "I understand."

Lyle, evidently satisfied with the reception of his latest gift, hustled closer to Cyrus and chortled expectantly.

Cyrus examined the assortment of blue stones in the vicinity and found another piece of blue amber. He sent it skittering across the cave. Lyle dashed after it and trotted back to give it to Sedona.

"Nice," she said. She patted Lyle. "Thanks."

Cyrus looked out the entrance of the cave. The heavy psi-snow did not look nearly as intense as it had a few minutes ago.

"I think the weather is lifting," he said. He rolled to his feet and started toward his pack. "We need to be prepared to move out in a hurry."

"One more question before we try to leave this place," Sedona said quietly.

"Only one?"

"Did you come to Rainshadow prepared to kill me if you discovered that I was an unstable multi-talent?"

The shock of the question hit him like a blow. For a moment he could not move. When he finally had himself back under control he crossed the room to where she sat, gripped her arms, and brought her to her feet.

"No," he said. "I came here to give you the antidote, if it proved necessary."

She blinked. "There's an antidote?"

"It was discovered in the twenty-first century back on Earth but there hasn't been much experience with it."

"Why not?"

"No one has ever had any need of it here on Harmony," Cyrus said. "Arcane doesn't keep a stockpile on hand. There was only time to brew a single dose before I left for Rainshadow. I brought it with me."

"In case you needed to use it on me?"

"Yes."

She thought about that for a minute and then managed a decidedly misty smile. "So you were never actually planning to kill me."

"I told you, Fallon Jones was a friend of Arizona Snow. In our family we take that kind of history seriously."

"You came here to try to save me."

"That was the general idea. Turned out you didn't need saving."

Tears sparkled in her eyes. "Thanks. No one ever did anything like that for me before—at least not since my parents died."

"You saved my team yesterday. We're more than even." He kissed her forehead and then he released her. When he glanced toward the mouth of the cave he saw that the storm had definitely lessened. "Let's move."

She walked to where her pack sat on the ground. Hefting it with the ease of long practice, she slipped it over her shoulders.

"Ready." She glanced around. "Lyle? Time to stop playing with the pretty rocks. We're leaving now."

Lyle chortled and scurried over to her. She picked him up and set him on her shoulder.

Cyrus went cautiously outside, raising his senses a little to get a better feel for the psi levels. The storm was waning rapidly.

He glanced back at Sedona. "One more precaution."

"What's that?"

He took a thin, coiled length of line off his pack, snapped one end to his belt, and clipped the other end to Sedona's belt. At full length the cord stretched about ten feet between them.

"We don't want to take the risk of running into another freak storm and getting separated," he said.

"Got it."

They walked out into a landscape that was rapidly clearing. The blue sunlight sparked and glittered on the quartz and crystal forest.

"It would be beautiful," Sedona said. "If the whole place didn't feel sort of dead."

Chapter 23

THEY WERE WELL INTO THE TREES BEFORE THE MUSIC started. Sedona knew that Lyle must have sensed the predators, as well, because he growled a low, urgent warning in her ear. The shatteringly beautiful strains of a song that had no words whispered to her; summoning, beseeching, and luring with unspoken promises. It echoed in the stillness of the forest like the sweet, unconditional love of a mother's lullaby and grew gradually into a glorious celebration of the senses.

"Damn," she whispered. "They're here, Cyrus. I can sense the singing."

"They must have holed up somewhere nearby, waiting for the storm to end," he said. "They're hunting us again. Go cold."

She fought the instinct to remain in her heightened

senses but it wasn't easy. With grim determination she managed to lower her talent a few notches.

Some of the heat and glitter evaporated from the landscape. Twilight blue shadows lengthened in the trees, darkening the forest. The music grew fainter but it did not disappear.

"This may buy us some time," she said, "but I don't think going cold will work for long. We'd have to shut down our auras in order to go completely dark. No way to do that."

"Not an option," he agreed.

The human aura gave off a lot of natural paranormal energy. Even those who possessed little or no measurable talent radiated psi whether or not they were aware of it. The bottom line was that all life gave off energy from across the spectrum. The only folks who didn't emit para-radiation were those who were dead.

Cyrus glanced at his locator. "We're closer to the gate than we are to the cave. We'll have to make a run for it. I'll try to give us some cover with a dead zone. Theoretically it should work. Give me your hand. Keep a good hold on Lyle."

His fingers closed tightly around hers. She tucked Lyle under her arm. Energy shifted in the atmosphere and then a chill of icy awareness raised small goose bumps on her skin. She knew that Cyrus had jacked up his talent. The otherworldly sensation enveloped them in a protective sphere, just as it had yesterday when he had swept her up in his arms and carried her through the storm to safety.

She heard Lyle muttering but he did not freak out. She had no way of knowing what the experience was like for him but she got the impression that he didn't like it any more than she did. He seemed to comprehend that the three of them were in this together, though, and that Cyrus was offering protection.

They ran, zigzagging through the trees. The cold, ghostly dead zone moved with them, briefly altering the atmosphere around them until they moved on. Sedona watched as the beautiful quartz trees lost their glow and turned dull and lifeless when she and Cyrus got close; brightening once more when they passed out of range. The ground under their boots was temporarily rendered a cloudy gray color.

It was as if they were ghosts, Sedona thought—real ghosts. The last time she had been too preoccupied with taking readings from the locator to pay much attention to the effects of Cyrus's talent on their surroundings, but now she thought she understood why the matchmakers had been unable to come up with a good match for him. It would take a very strong talent, indeed, not to feel nervous around someone who could drain the energy out of everything and everyone within a fifteen-foot radius.

Lyle hissed. She realized he was watching a thick cluster of sparkling foliage on the right. The jeweled leaves shivered.

But there was no wind, she realized, not even a faint breeze to rustle the leaves.

"Cyrus." She tried to pitch her voice as low as possible and discovered that was not easy to do when you were running with a pack on your back and a dust bunny under one arm. "Over there, to your right. About twenty feet."

"I see it. Keep moving. I think it's confused. It can probably sense our movement but it must be getting conflicting messages because of the dead zone."

The thing in the bushes prowled alongside, keeping its distance. Sedona could not make out a shape but every so often she thought she caught a glimpse of reptilian scales that glinted like a million tiny mirrors in the glacial light.

"Gate's just ahead," Cyrus said. "Get ready to do your thing."

"I'll have to be able to go fully into my senses to open the gate," she warned. "You'll have to dissolve the zone."

"I know. I'll cover you with the flamer while you work."

She caught a glimpse of the glacial-blue-quartz wall. A moment later they burst out of the trees a few feet away from the energy gate.

"Give me your flamer," Cyrus said.

She handed it to him and then went to stand in front of the gate. Cyrus turned his back to her and stood facing the woods, a flamer in each hand.

"Ready?" he asked.

"Ready."

She felt the cold of the dead zone evaporate in a heartbeat. Immediately she raised her senses. The crystal world shimmered back to gemstone brilliance.

She reached for the focus. Lyle scrambled out from

under her arm and bounced up onto her shoulder. From there he leaped to Cyrus's shoulder.

"Here they come," Cyrus said.

She did not turn around to look at the threat. It would do neither of them any good. She would have to depend on Cyrus to watch her back while she did her job.

She heard the *snap-snap-snap* of the flamers followed by a low, keening howl that was unlike that of any animal she had ever heard. It was the roar of a savage beast, and it awakened primordial fears long buried in the most primitive part of her brain.

The flamers snapped and crackled again. Lyle growled.

Every instinct was urging Sedona to turn around to confront the monsters but she had the focus now. She had to hang on to it for all their sakes. She reached out delicately, seeking the core currents that sealed the gate. The hot energy shifted and churned at the touch of her talent.

Behind her the terrible roaring continued. So did the zapping of the flamers.

The gate opened, revealing the green quartz corridor on the other side. She had time to register the sight of a small crowd gathered inside the tunnel. There were several hunters armed with flamers. Rachel and Harry, along with Charlotte and Slade appeared. Joe and his son were with them. Henderson, she saw, was wearing a walking cast. A rescue team, she realized.

"Gate's open," she shouted at Cyrus.

"Go," Cyrus ordered. "I'm right behind you."

She whirled around and saw him fire the flamer one

last time at a monstrous lizard the size of an SUV. It had small, reptile-cold eyes and a mouth full of teeth. The creature was covered in strange, silvery scales that reflected the blue energy of the artificial sunlight—natural camouflage that would make it difficult to detect in the glittering forest.

As she watched, a second monster shimmered into view.

"Sedona," Rachel called. "Get in here."

"Get your ass through the damn gate," Cyrus said. He backed steadily toward the opening, Lyle still hunkered on his shoulder.

"I'm going, I'm going," Sedona muttered.

She ran through the gate, concentrating on holding it open long enough for Cyrus and Lyle to get through.

Slade and Harry joined the hunters at the entrance of the gate. They fired into the glittering world, laying down a blanket of flames to provide cover for Cyrus.

He fired one last shot as he raced through the gate with Lyle clinging for dear life.

"Close it," he said.

Sedona released the gate. It slammed shut with a senses-dazzling rush of energy. The last thing she saw in Wonderland was a mirror-scaled monster shrieking its frustration as its prey escaped.

Chapter 24

KIRK MORGAN WAITED IN THE DARKENED BOATHOUSE. HE lit a cigarette to steady his nerves and listened to the restless slap of the dark water. It was nearly midnight. There were Halloween lanterns strung up along the main drag of Shadow Bay, and someone had turned the nearby warehouse into some kind of stupid theme park attraction. But no one had bothered to decorate the old boathouse. The waterside end of the structure was open to the night. Moonlight illuminated the floating dock and a couple of battered rowboats inside.

He hated boats. Hated water. Hated Rainshadow, come to that. He hadn't wanted to make the trip to the island but the fixer hadn't given him any choice in the matter.

Not that he had seen much of Rainshadow because he and Griff had made the journey from Thursday Harbor by night. But what little he had viewed did not inspire him to book a vacation on the rock. In the light of a big Halloween moon, Rainshadow had loomed like an ancient, mysterious fortress. Most of the island had appeared darker than midnight. The only visible illumination had come from the scattering of lights in the cove that marked the town of Shadow Bay.

No visible illumination, Kirk thought, but he could feel the faint vibes of Alien psi in the atmosphere. Creepy.

He knew from creepy. Hell, he'd worked in the Underworld since the day he turned sixteen and lied about his age to get his first job in the Guild. He'd seen a lot of weird shit down below but from what he could tell, Rainshadow Island was as weird as it got anywhere in the tunnels.

Kirk checked his watch again and then looked at Griff, who was lounging at the end of one of the floating docks. There were only the two of them here tonight. From the start the goal had been to keep the number of people involved in the operation to an absolute minimum. Griff had been with him from the old days. They had come from the same tough neighborhood and joined the same branch of the Guild.

They had made a good team in the tunnels, watching each other's back. Socked away some good money, too, with their off-the-books operations. Everyone knew that corporate exploration work was dangerous business. The disappearance of the occasional high-value amber or quartz shipment on the way out of the catacombs or the rainforest was just part of the price of doing business down in the Underworld.

From the start it had been clear to both men that Kirk was the strategic thinker, the one who was going to make it to the top ranks of the Gold Creek operation. He had been determined to control his own territory and he had achieved his goal. Griff had stuck with him at every step along the way.

"Five more minutes," Kirk said. "If the fixer doesn't show up by then, we're leaving."

"You won't get any argument from me, boss." Griff took a long drag on his cigarette and looked out at the moon. "This island gives me that feeling you get on the back of your neck just before you run into a ghost down in the tunnels."

"You can say that again."

"Probably doesn't help that it's Halloween."

"Afraid of real ghosts, Griff?"

"Nah. I just don't like Rainshadow."

"I'm with you there."

"Hard to believe there's an actual town here." Griff sucked on his cigarette. "Who would want to live on this rock?"

"Misfits and freaks," Kirk said.

Which was what the Snow woman was now, he thought, some kind of freak. Maybe that explained why she had come to Rainshadow after she escaped from the lab.

According to Blankenship, they were all damn lucky she was still alive because she was the only one who could get them back into the lab. The side effects of the drug were rapidly becoming more apparent. The edgy sensation and the nightmares were getting worse. Although his paranormal senses had been strengthened, there was no indication that he or the others had developed a second talent. The damn drug hadn't worked as Blankenship had promised and now they were all addicted. Their supplies were running low.

He hated knowing that he was now dependent on a daily dose of the formula just to stay sane. Worse, yet, Blankenship was concerned that they might all start to disintegrate mentally even with regular doses if they didn't get back into the lab to retrieve the stone. He kept saying he needed to tweak the formula with the para-radiation from the crystal.

Sedona Snow was their only hope. But things had been going wrong since the night she escaped. It had taken weeks to track her down to Rainshadow. And when they finally located her it had become clear that grabbing her was not going to be easy. It was so much simpler to make someone disappear in a big city than it was in a small town—especially a town in which the powerful Sebastian family exercised a lot of muscle and the police chief was a former FBPI agent.

To make matters worse, the Chamber had established a new territory on the island. Under most circumstances that would not have been a major problem, Kirk told himself. He had been a Guild man most of his life and he had connections throughout the organization. Favors were owed. But the new boss wasn't one of his buddies from the old days. The Chamber had appointed someone from the elite ranks of the security division.

There wasn't a lot of information about Cyrus Jones in

the files but the very lack of intel made Kirk uneasy. And now the word was that Jones was sleeping with the Snow woman. That was way too much of a coincidence. Jones was yet another problem.

Reluctantly, he and Blankenship had turned to the fixer, the one who had arranged the kidnapping in the first place. The fixer was also using the drug now and therefore had a personal stake in the operation. But Kirk didn't trust the killer.

"When this is over," he said, "we're going to have to get rid of the fixer."

Griff thought about that for a moment. "Might be hard to do. Don't have an ID on the guy. No one's ever seen his face and lived to tell about it."

"We'll figure it out."

"We always do," Griff said.

Kirk glanced at his watch. "Three more minutes. That's it. If the fixer doesn't deliver the Snow woman we will have to come up with another plan."

"Sure." Griff flicked the cigarette into the black water. He looked toward the side door of the boathouse. "Someone's coming."

Kirk heard the squeak of the dock boards outside and took a deep breath. It was going to be all right. The fixer was here.

The door opened. A figure dressed in a voluminous black cloak and a skeleton mask appeared.

"What's with the Halloween getup?" Kirk asked. Then he remembered what Griff had said. No one ever saw the fixer's face and lived to tell about it. "Never mind. About time you showed up. Where's the Snow woman? You're supposed to deliver her tonight."

Instead of answering, the fixer took out a mag-rez pistol and fired once. The shot took Kirk in the chest. For a few seconds he was too stunned to realize what had happened. He sank to his knees and stared at the fixer's masked face.

"Why?" he said.

Why bother with the mask if you came here to kill us? he wanted to ask. But he couldn't get the words out.

Understanding struck just as the fixer raised the mag-rez for the head shot.

"Griff?" he whispered.

"Sorry, pal," Griff said. "It's been a good run. But like you always said, a man's got to make his own luck. We're getting low on the formula. We need your stash."

Chapter 25

"WHAT THE HELL DID THE ALIENS CONSTRUCT DOWN there?" Slade asked.

"Another biolab, from the looks of it," Cyrus said.

"Or maybe some sort of living natural history museum?" Sedona offered tentatively. She powered up her computer and clicked on the images she had discovered in her research. "I knew those creatures appeared familiar. Take a look at what I found."

They were gathered in Cyrus's makeshift office. She was aware of the tension in the room. In addition to Cyrus and herself, Harry, Rachel, Slade, and Charlotte had joined them.

They gathered around Sedona and looked at her computer screen. She clicked on one image after another.

"These pictures are all computer-generated models of prehistoric animals—dinosaurs and reptiles," she explained.

"They were created from fossils that have been dug up at various excavation sites on Harmony. The experts gave them names based on the similarity to Old World dinosaurs." She aimed a pen at an image of a large, two-footed creature with massive, tooth-filled jaws and short arms that ended in sharp claws. "This one is called an Allosaurus. I think it looks a lot like the predators that we encountered."

"Except for the mirrored scales," Cyrus added.

Rachel frowned. "It's entirely possible that the experts got that aspect wrong when they did their reconstruction. They work from fossils and impressions in rocks. There wouldn't be much, if anything, left to tell them about the psi-reflecting qualities of the scales."

"That makes sense," Charlotte said. "When you think about it, it's logical that creatures adapted to a heavy-psi environment and therefore developed various forms of camouflage and other hunting strategies."

"Those critters were definitely using some kind of psychic lure to hunt us," Cyrus said.

"But how could prehistoric creatures know how to trigger music in the human mind?" Rachel asked.

"I'm sure they weren't doing it intentionally," Sedona said. "They have obviously evolved some paranormal mechanism for attracting their prey. It just so happens that in human brains the psychic lure is interpreted as music. In other creatures it's probably translated as a mating call or the smell of food."

Rachel raised her brows. "Guess we can all be glad it doesn't translate as sexual attraction for humans. That could certainly complicate the research and exploration work."

"Imagine a team of techs and scientists and a bunch of hunters suddenly overwhelmed by the conviction that they had just entered the world's most outstanding pickup bar," Harry added. "Sort of boggles the mind."

Charlotte winced. "Thanks for that visual. I won't be able to get it out of my head for days."

Sedona knew she was turning pink. She glanced up and found Cyrus watching her, dark amusement gleaming in his eyes. She didn't have to be able to read minds to know that he was remembering her desperate effort to attribute their mutual passion to the effects of the psi in the cave. Hurriedly she returned her attention to the image of the Harmony version of an Allosaurus.

"What doesn't make sense is how those creatures could have survived and reproduced for maybe millions of years in a world where, as far as we could tell, all the vegetation has been turned into crystal and quartz," Cyrus said.

"You only saw a small sector of that place you're calling Wonderland," Slade reminded him. "If it's like the Rainforest or the catacombs it could extend for hundreds or maybe thousands of square miles underground. There could well be sectors that are capable of sustaining life."

"I'm not so sure about that," Cyrus said. "It wasn't like the Rainforest. That has the feel of a vast, sprawling jungle. This place had a more contained, closed-in feeling—like a wild-game park or a zoo."

Sedona hesitated. "I'm no expert, but here's a scenario. Let's say Cyrus is right—the Aliens did some serious bioengineering in an attempt to re-create a heavy-psi landscape. Maybe they actually produced a few dinosaurs."

"The Aliens vanished from Harmony centuries ago," Slade reminded her. "What have their pet dinosaurs been doing down there in Wonderland all this time?"

"Everything down there that we saw had a frozen-in-time feeling," Cyrus said. "Maybe the dinosaurs were in a state of hibernation or suspended animation until recently."

Charlotte's eyes widened behind the frames of her glasses. "Frozen in psi like everything else you found down there and then awakened by the recent violent storm activity on the island? That makes sense in a bizarre way."

"One thing's for sure," Harry said. "We need to get a Foundation team in there to find out what we're dealing with."

Cyrus looked at him. "I don't want any research teams going down below until we've figured out how to provide adequate security."

"Agreed," Harry said. "But it might be easier to locate the entrance up into the Preserve that the monsters are using from down there. We're not having any luck finding it on the surface. The deeper we go inside the fence, the weirder things get. Sounds like Wonderland is at least navigable."

"We've all got work to do," Cyrus said. He went back behind his desk. "Meanwhile, I don't want to lose any more stray treasure hunters. Sedona locked the gate into Wonderland. It stays that way until we get something resembling a plan."

Slade nodded. "Plans are good."

Chapter 26

IT SEEMED ODD TO GO BACK TO WORK AT THE FRONT DESK of Knox's as if nothing extraordinary had occurred in the past twenty-four hours, but Sedona was grateful for the comforting sense of normalcy. Always assuming that you could call riding herd on an inn full of ghost hunters normal, she thought. She did have one big advantage now. As irritating as it was to know that Cyrus's men called her the boss's lady, it did result in instant obedience to any request she made.

Shortly after three that afternoon she went across the lobby and into the tavern to get a cup of coffee. The place was empty because Cyrus was keeping his men busy.

Knox was behind the bar polishing glassware.

"Coffee?" he asked, reaching for the pot.

"Yes, please." She took a seat on one of the bar stools.

Knox eyed her over the rims of his glasses. "You've

been through a lot, from the sound of it. How're you doin'?"

"Surprisingly enough, I feel fine," she said. "Good to be back on the surface, though."

"I'll bet. Where's your little buddy?"

"Lyle took off to play with some of the kids," Sedona said. "Rachel and Slade said their pals vanished at about the same time. We suspect a dust bunny–kid conspiracy."

"Well, it is Halloween Week."

"I'm sure Lyle will be back by dinnertime. He won't want to miss any of the action in here when the hunters get off work and show up for their beer and pizza and hamburgers."

Knox chuckled. "Looks like Lyle has become the Rainshadow Guild's mascot."

"Tell me about it. I can see the T-shirts now: *By the Time You See the Teeth, It's Too Late* with a picture of Lyle. He'll love that." She brightened. "You know, maybe we should have some made up. Might be a hit with the tourists."

"Good idea." Knox set the mug on the counter in front of Sedona. "Assuming we ever get any more visitors to the island. Word going around town is that Foundation Security and the new Guild boss are trying to restrict visitors to residents and authorized personnel only."

"Good luck to 'em, is all I can say. The more *Danger, Keep Out* signs they put up, the more the thrill seekers and treasure hunters will show up."

"Can't stop the locals from doing a little exploring down below, either." Knox slipped the polished glass into a rack and folded his arms on the bar. "So, are the rumors true? Did you and Jones run into a couple of real dinosaurs down below?"

"They sure looked like dinosaurs, but who knows?" Sedona said.

Knox started to ask another question but he glanced toward the door of the tavern and paused.

"Looks like you've got visitors," he said.

Sedona heard a familiar chortle and swung around on the bar stool. Three kids hovered in the doorway. Each of them had a dust bunny tucked under one arm. She recognized the girl holding Lyle as Annie Bell. Devin Reed, the grandson of Myrna Reed, a member of the tiny Shadow Bay police force, clutched Slade's dust bunny, Rex. Rex, in turn, clutched a small, elegant evening bag. The tiny purse looked expensive. He had no doubt shoplifted it from Charlotte's collection of exquisite antique clutches. Devin's buddy Nate had Darwina under his arm. Darwina had her Amberella doll in one paw. She rarely went anywhere without the small doll dressed in its crystal-studded evening gown.

"I knew it," Sedona said. "A conspiracy. What's up?"

Devin frowned. "What's a conspiracy?"

"Never mind." Sedona smiled. "What's the plan?"

Annie patted Lyle. "We want to ask you if we could use Lyle to go trick-or-treating on Halloween night."

"Please, Miss Snow," Devin pleaded. "The chief said we could take Rex."

"And Miss Rachel over at the bookshop said Darwina can go with us, too," Nate added quickly.

"Why?" Sedona asked.

"Because we figure that we'll get a lot more candy if we have the dust bunnies with us," Annie explained. "Everyone thinks they're so cute."

"Huh." Knox looked impressed. "Not a bad plan."

"I told you," Sedona said. "It's a conspiracy." She studied the kids. "I agree with Knox. It is a cunning plan. Go for it and good luck to you all."

"Yay," Devin said. He exchanged high fives with Nate. "Told you, she'd say yes."

Annie cheered gleefully. Caught up in the moment, Lyle, Rex, and Darwina chortled.

"We have to go make their costumes now," Annie said.

The gang disappeared from the doorway before Sedona could change her mind.

"Should make for an interesting Halloween night," Knox observed.

Sedona spun back around to face the bar and picked up her mug. "Can't wait to see what costumes they come up with for the dust bunnies."

Knox gave her a sharp glance and cleared his throat. "So," he said, "you and the new Guild boss."

Sedona paused her mug in midair. "Me and the new Guild boss—what?"

"I know it's none of my business, but you work for me and you don't have any family on the island—"

Sedona shuddered. "Thank goodness."

"Yeah, well, given that you don't have anyone to look after you, I sort of feel like I need to make sure you're okay with being, you know, real friendly with Jones."

"Real friendly. That's one way to put it."

Knox winced. "You know what I mean."

She reached across the bar and patted his arm. "It's okay. I do know what you mean and I appreciate your concern. But I'm a big girl now, Knox. I've been taking care of myself for a long time."

"That's what you keep saying but there's times when everybody needs someone to watch out for 'em." Knox stopped talking. He angled his jaw toward the doorway. "Speaking of which."

Sedona twirled around on the bar stool a second time. Irritation crackled through her when she saw who loomed in the opening.

"Hello, Brock," she said.

"I need to talk to you." Brock looked at Knox and then turned back to Sedona. "In private, if you don't mind. It's important, Sedona. You owe me a conversation, at least."

She reached behind herself, picked up the mug, and took a sip of coffee while she considered her options. She'd had her moment of petty revenge. She could afford to be civil. It was obvious Brock was not going to leave the island until he'd had his say. She might as well get the conversation over with.

She set the mug down on the bar and slipped off the stool. "We can talk in my office."

Knox leaned over the bar and lowered his voice to a conspiratorial whisper. "Want me to call Jones?"

"No." She said it clearly and with great emphasis. She could handle her own problems. "This won't take long."

She crossed the empty tavern.

"I'm on duty," she said to Brock. "So we don't have a lot of time."

Brock did not look thrilled with that but after a second glance at Knox he evidently concluded he didn't have much room to argue.

"Fine," he said. His jaw tensed. "Thanks."

Sedona slipped past him, rounded the front counter, and led the way into her tiny office. She propped one hip on the corner of her desk, crossed her arms, and looked at Brock.

"What is it that you feel you need to tell me?" she said.

Brock shoved his fingers through his hair. "I want to explain a few things, that's all. You owe me that much."

"You keep saying that but I don't owe you anything, Brock. You're the one who filed for divorce, remember?"

He fixed her with a haunted look. "I explained that. I was told you were missing and presumed dead. What the hell else was I supposed to think?"

"Gee, I don't know. Maybe you could have used some of your money to finance a private search-and-rescue operation? We've already been over this."

Brock flushed. "I was informed by the authorities that it would be a waste of time."

"And you took that at face value. Well, there you have it. You made an executive decision." She gave him her most vivacious smile. "We both know how good you are when it comes to executive decisions, right? You told me, you always go with your gut and you're almost never wrong. But once in a while you screw up, just like everyone else."

"Damn it, you've got to give me another chance. We had something good together."

"Maybe. But we both knew that it wouldn't last. Sooner or later you would have come under pressure from your family to marry someone from your own social class, and while I have several very admirable qualities, I definitely don't have the sort of family connections you need in a wife. Your relatives would never approve of me."

"You're wrong," Brock said, very earnest now. "That's one of the things I'm trying to explain. My family will approve of your people. You're a Snow."

"An illegitimate Snow."

"That doesn't matter," Brock said. He crossed the small space in two long strides and gripped her shoulders. "Not now."

She went very still. "Not now?"

"Hear me out. After they told me that you had vanished into the tunnels I realized how much you meant to me. You may not believe it, but I was heartbroken. I started drinking too much in the evenings. Diana was worried about me. That's why she was at my place that night. She was concerned that I would do myself some harm."

"You? Drinking yourself into a stupor because of me? Give me a break. We had some fun together but I don't believe for one minute that you were pining away just because I dropped out of your life."

Brock tightened his hands on her shoulders. "This is about what you think you've got going with Jones, isn't it? I know he's a Guild boss, but do you really believe for one minute that he will offer you a Covenant Marriage? Don't be naïve. Everyone knows the heads of the Guilds are notorious when it comes to women. Sure, he'll probably agree to an MC for a while. Why not? You're convenient and for now, at any rate, he's stuck with a territory that is nothing more than a large chunk of rock in the middle of the Amber Sea."

Sedona looked down at his left hand.

"Let go of me," she said, her voice very even.

But Brock didn't seem to get the message. There was a vibe of desperation about him that she did not understand.

"You have to listen to me," Brock said.

"I can't believe that you have suddenly concluded that I am the love of your life," she said. "What is going on here? And before you even try to explain, take your hands off me."

Brock ignored her.

"Please, Sedona—"

She reached into her pocket, took out the flicker, and snapped out a spark. At the same time she rezzed a little energy. Flames flashed in the atmosphere.

Brock released her and scrambled backward. He looked stunned.

"What the hell?" he said.

She lowered her talent. The sparks disappeared.

"What did you just do?" he demanded. "What kind of talent are you?"

"Never mind," she said. "Tell me the real reason why you followed me all the way to Rainshadow."

"I told you the reason," he said. But he sounded less certain now.

A dark shadow filled the doorway of the office. Sedona turned and saw Cyrus. He looked at her.

"Is Prescott bothering you?" he asked.

"Nothing I can't handle," she assured him. "I'm just waiting for a believable answer to my question."

Cyrus switched his attention to Brock. "Right. You want to know why he's stalking you."

Brock flushed a dark red. "I'm not stalking her."

Cyrus turned back to Sedona. "I just got word from my cousin, who runs that private investigation firm I mentioned. I asked her to take a close look at Prescott. She did a little checking around and discovered that Prescott Industries is in trouble."

"That's bullshit," Brock said.

"And with the company in trouble, it follows that the entire Prescott family is facing some serious financial problems," Cyrus continued. "Problems that could conveniently be resolved if the head of Prescott Industries were to marry a woman who happened to be in line to inherit a portion of the Snow family fortune. A woman who also had access to a sizeable trust fund. A woman who could bring Prescott a direct connection to the head of another powerful business empire."

"Well, there you go," Sedona said. She unfolded her arms and straightened away from the desk. "That explains everything. So long, Brock."

"Don't believe a word Jones says," Brock snarled. "He's lying."

Sedona looked at him. "I guess the only question left is, how did you find out that the Snows have invited me to join the family?"

Brock shook his head. "That's not what this is about, I swear it."

"Never mind," Sedona said. She held up a hand, palm out, to silence him. "I can piece together what happened. At some point a Snow family lawyer contacted you, right? Perfectly logical. Our MC was a matter of public record. It must have come as a terrible shock to you to realize that I was related to *those* Snows and that the family is trying to bring me into the fold. No wonder you needed consoling that night I showed up on your doorstep. You had let a valuable asset slip away without even bothering to send out a search party."

Brock looked sadly disappointed in her. "After all we meant to each other, I can't believe that you would take the word of a Guild boss over mine."

"Here's the one thing I know to be true about this particular Guild boss," Sedona said. "When stuff goes wrong down in the Underworld, he doesn't leave any of his team behind. He came back for me yesterday. He saved my life."

"And you think he did that because he loves you? You're out of your mind. He's not just any Guild boss, he's a Jones—one of the Arcane Joneses. Ask him what that means. It's a clan with a lot of secrets. Rumor has it that there are some real psi-freaks on the family tree. Trust me, you have no idea what you're dealing with here."

"Maybe not," she said. "But I do know what I'm dealing with when it comes to you, Brock. And it's not very attractive; not anymore. Please go away and leave me alone."

Brock hesitated. For a moment she thought he was going to argue. But he took one look at Cyrus and evidently changed his mind.

He went toward the door, silently challenging Cyrus to get out of the way. Cyrus gave him a cold smile and did not move aside.

"Thought I told you not to go near Sedona again," he said.

"You can't threaten me, Jones."

Something hard and dark glittered in Cyrus's eyes. Sedona felt icy energy shift in the atmosphere. Belatedly, she realized that Cyrus was raising his talent. Her pulse kicked up in fresh alarm.

"Cyrus, no," she said. She put out a hand as if she could stop him physically.

He looked at her, his eyes brilliant with cold fire.

"Please," she whispered. For a couple of heartbeats she was afraid he would not stop. But the ice in the atmosphere evaporated.

For his part, Brock seemed unaware that he had ever been in any serious danger. He had already turned away and was walking off through the lobby. He slammed the front door on his way outside.

Cyrus lowered his talent and looked at Sedona. "You only know one thing about me?"

She relaxed, more relieved than she wanted to admit. "That was not entirely accurate. I do know a couple of other things about you."

"Are any of those other things that you know about me matters of concern?"

"Nope. Should they cause me some concern?"

"No." Cyrus propped one shoulder against the doorframe and folded his arms. "Prescott was right about some stuff, though. My family has kept a lot of secrets over the centuries and there are rumors of the occasional whackjob in the bloodline."

She shrugged. "Wouldn't be a family if it didn't have some secrets."

Chapter 27

IT WAS THE KNOWLEDGE THAT HE WAS LOSING OUT TO A low-rent Guild boss that rankled the most, Brock concluded.

Then again, Jones was no ordinary Guild exec. Nor was he low-rent. The Jones family was very private and very powerful. Rumor had it that the Joneses made dangerous enemies. Yet here was one of them taking on a no-name Guild territory on a no-name island in the middle of the Amber Sea. Brock's intuition was pinging him. It was not a coincidence that Cyrus Jones had tracked down Sedona and seduced her.

Something big was going on here. He could sense it. A couple of months ago, Sedona had been just another gatekeeper taking contract jobs with the Guilds. True, she was a very high-rez gatekeeper but that didn't alter the facts. She had been born out of wedlock, the product of an illicit union, and both sides of her family had disowned her as soon as it had become legally possible to do so. What was wrong with this picture?

He reached the marina and stopped. He needed to put the pieces of the puzzle together. He stood in the shade cast by the overhanging roof of a small boathouse and gazed unseeingly at the assortment of boats moored in the harbor.

Back at the start Sedona had been no one special, just an amusing companion. Their relationship had been destined to be short-lived and they had both known it.

But now it seemed that a lot of folks were after Sedona—important, influential folks, including the Arcane Joneses and the Snows. Sedona's mother's family, the Callahans, had contacted him recently, too, trying to find her. There had also been a call from someone who had identified himself as a Guild para-psych doctor who claimed to be worried about Sedona's mental state.

He knew why he wanted Sedona, but why did the others want her? Clearly she had some serious value. He had to find a way to use that fact to his advantage. The future of Prescott Industries depended on it. And the future of the sprawling Prescott family depended on Prescott Industries.

No pressure, Brock thought.

"I saw you leave Knox's Resort a few minutes ago."

The woman spoke from behind him. He turned and saw a striking blonde with smart, savvy eyes. He liked her on sight.

"Have we met?" he asked.

She smiled. "We have now. I'm Hannah Holbrook. Full disclosure, I'm a freelance reporter and I'm here to cover whatever the hell is going down here on Rainshadow."

"Aside from the Halloween crap, you mean?"

"I've been in this business long enough to know that the Chamber doesn't usually send one of its best security people—a man who just happens to be connected to a powerful family—to take over a low-rent territory like Rainshadow."

"Funny you should mention that," Brock said. "I was just thinking along the same lines."

"It occurs to me that we each have an agenda here and that we might be able to accomplish more working together than alone."

"What's in this for me?" Brock asked automatically.

"Just taking a wild guess here, but it looks like you want Sedona Snow. Right now Cyrus Jones has her. I have some information that might give you an edge."

"Maybe I should ask what's in this for you?"

"Deep background. Something big is going on here and Sedona seems to be at the center of it. You were in an MC with her for a while. I think you might know a few things that would be of interest to me. Why don't you buy me a beer and we'll talk about what we can do for each other?"

He thought about that for a minute. "Fine. I'll buy you the beer. But we should probably go somewhere other than Knox's Resort."

"Definitely."

Chapter 28

"I'M NOT SURE LYLE AND THE OTHER DUST BUNNIES WILL ever recover from the excitement of Halloween night," Sedona said. "You should have seen him when little Annie Bell arrived to dress him in the costume she made for him. He was ecstatic. He may never take it off."

"The kids should be here soon," Cyrus said. "It's not like there are that many houses to hit on the island. Expect a horde. Slade and Harry are taking them around in one big group."

Sedona glanced out the window. A full moon shone down on the graveyard, illuminating the headstones in a ghostly glow. She had added extra lanterns to her front porch to draw the kids but she wasn't sure what to expect. It was her first Halloween on the island.

"What if they don't come here because they're afraid of the cemetery?" she asked.

"In that case we are going to be left to eat a lot of candy all by ourselves." Cyrus glanced toward the door where a large basket sat on the floor. The basket was heaped high with what amounted to a mountain of treats.

Sedona followed his gaze. "I may have overdone the candy."

A knowing smile flickered at the edges of Cyrus's mouth. "Don't worry, got a hunch you'll get rid of it all tonight. The kids won't be able to resist calling on a house near a graveyard."

"I hope you're right."

"It's okay, Sedona," he said. "You're a member of the community now. The kids will show up sooner or later."

"Right."

But she wasn't entirely certain of that, and she didn't have to ask herself why that mattered. She knew why it was important. She wanted to be accepted by the good people of Rainshadow. For the first time in her life she felt as if she had a home where she belonged. Some part of her was convinced that having the local kids show up on Halloween would help her lock herself into the tightly knit little community.

She opened the refrigerator and took out the Amber River salmon that had been marinating in olive oil, ginger, and soy sauce. The salmon was a splurge but Hank, the proprietor of Hank's Seafood, had given her a deal on it. According to him, he was awash in Amber River salmon and had to unload it fast. But she had a hunch that he had done her the favor because, like everyone else in town, he knew she was cooking for the new Guild boss. Everyone liked to be on the right side of a Guild CEO.

Sedona rezzed the stove. "Any updates from your cousin Marlowe?"

"Yes, as a matter of fact." Cyrus studied his screen. "She sent an agent sensitive to catacomb energy to Amber Crest disguised as a visiting para-psych consultant. Thc agcnt was able to get a good look around the place. He didn't find any obvious traces of Alien psi but that doesn't mean there isn't a secret entrance to the tunnels inside the building or the grounds."

"What about the ruins I told you about?"

"They weren't hard to find. Marlowe sent a team down below through that entrance but no luck so far. They're still looking, though. Turns out that sector hasn't been charted. No surprise that's why Blankenship picked it."

"It's ridiculously easy to hide something like a lab in an unmapped sector. Drug dealers do it all the time."

"We'll find it, Sedona. Wherever Blankenship and his two assistants are, we know one thing for certain—they have to come back to the surface, at least occasionally, for supplies."

She thought about that. "Good point."

"Speaking of problem people, Brock Prescott did not leave on the afternoon ferry."

Sedona picked up her wineglass and leaned back against the edge of the counter. "You checked?"

"Slade has one of his officers, a young guy named Willis, watching the ferries. Prescott is still on the island. That fact is of some concern."

"He wasn't the one who tried to kidnap me," she said quickly. "It's just not his style. He relies on his charm to get what he wants." She took a sip of wine. "Not that he was at his most charming today."

"He could have hired someone with the right kind of talent to grab you. Now that we know that he's desperate to save the family company, we have to assume that he's willing to take extreme measures."

She nodded. "There is the family pressure thing." She set the glass down, and turned around to pick up a pair of tongs. "While we're on the subject of weirdness, did you come up with a strategy for exploring Wonderland?"

Cyrus eased the computer aside, leaned back in his chair, and picked up his beer. "Still working on it."

"How are you going to deal with the music issue?"

"The first step is to find a specialist, an expert in paranormal music, who can assess the situation."

"Music is complicated. It operates on both the normal as well as the paranormal end of the spectrum."

"Music isn't the only phenomenon that crosses the spectrum," Cyrus said. "It's not like the Guilds haven't had some experience in that regard. We'll figure out a way to deal with the singing monsters."

She smiled, amused by his confidence and enthusiasm. "You like this job, don't you?"

He shrugged and drank some more beer. "It's interesting."

"A challenge."

"That, too."

"Think you'll stick around after you get the problems under control?"

"Maybe. Depends." He looked at her. "What about you? Going to stay on the island?"

She hesitated. "Maybe. Depends. But I like it here."

He smiled. "Rainshadow is unique, I'll say that for it."

"I've been thinking," she said quietly. "Maybe I will go to my grandfather's birthday reception."

Cyrus said nothing. He waited.

"Someday, if I'm lucky, I may have children of my own," she continued. "Maybe a little girl with Arizona Snow's genetics. I would want her to know her family history. I would want her to know her cousins and her aunts and uncles. If my grandfather is serious about acknowledging me—"

The sound of excited laughter interrupted her before she could say anything else.

"I think our trick-or-treaters have arrived," Cyrus said.

Sedona's spirits leaped much higher than the occasion probably warranted.

"Great," she said. She turned off the stove and quickly washed her hands. "I can't wait to see the costumes."

There was a great deal of clattering on the front porch. It was accompanied by more giggles, laughter, and a lot of excited chortling. A few seconds later the doorbell chimed.

Sedona dried her hands on a towel and hurried across the living room. Cyrus got to his feet and followed.

Sedona opened the door to a throng of small ghosts, skeletons, Aliens, fairies, superheroes, vampires, and assorted creatures of the night. Most of them were armed with glow sticks and illuminated sabers.

She saw Harry and Slade hanging back in the shadows.

Not every troop of trick-or-treaters traveled with such high-end security on Halloween, Sedona thought. But on Rainshadow things were done a little differently.

There was a loud chorus of *"Trick-or-treat."*

Cyrus made a path through the crowd and went down the steps to talk to the two men.

Sedona admired the costumes and masks of her visitors.

"You all look very scary," she said.

"I'm Amber Man," Nate informed her. He held up Darwina, who was quite fetching in a blue ball gown studded with sequins. "This is Amberella."

"I'm a police officer," Devin announced. He hoisted Rex, who was bedecked in an odd-looking hat and a cloak decorated with strange symbols. "This is Sylvester Jones. He's an old alchemist from Earth."

"I'm an Alien," Annie announced from behind her neon-green mask. "And Lyle is a vampire."

Lyle's dashing black cape was lined with bloodred satin. He looked adorable.

Sedona smiled at the kids and hoisted the basket of candy. "Don't worry, there's no need for tricks. I've got plenty of treats."

At the sight of the candy mountain there was a great deal of excited shouting and mad chortling. Several pairs of small hands dove into the basket. Sedona spotted a few dust bunny paws reaching in as well. Lyle and the others had definitely gotten the hang of Halloween.

The mountain of candy vanished in a surprisingly short period of time. The kids trooped back down the steps, gloating.

"Told you the dust bunnies would work," Annie said to the others.

Harry and Slade raised their hands in a friendly good-bye to Sedona and then set about gathering their charges together. The forest of glow sticks and light sabers headed back toward Main Street.

Cyrus came back up the steps and stood with Sedona, watching the departure.

"Harry told me that this was the last house on the list," he said. "They're all headed to the Haunted Alien Catacombs where they will scare themselves silly and then gorge on candy."

Sedona smiled. "It's such a charming tradition."

"Told you they'd show up."

"Yes, you did," she said.

THE SCREAMING STARTED JUST AS SEDONA WAS PREPARing to serve the chilled, chocolate-cookie-and-whipped-cream dessert she had made that afternoon.

The high-pitched shrieks of terror echoed in the night. Chills flashed down her spine. She dropped the serving spoon and it clattered on the kitchen floor.

"Good grief," she whispered. "I didn't think the kids would be *that* frightened by the exhibits in the Haunted Catacombs."

"No." Cyrus was already on his feet. He paused long enough to take the mag-rez out of the lockbox and check his flamer.

Sedona followed him outside, into the night.

Chapter 29

THE YOUNGSTERS WERE GATHERED TOGETHER IN FRONT of the entrance to the old warehouse that contained the Haunted Alien Catacombs attraction. A few were crying. Some looked confused. Several worried adults, including Devin's grandmother, Myrna Reed, and Charlotte and Rachel had formed a protective circle around the children and were talking quietly to them.

The dust bunnies were doing their part to calm the kids. They hopped from fairy to doctor to superhero, making soothing sounds.

Devin Reed spotted Cyrus and Sedona first.

"The chief said for you to go in as soon as you got here, Mr. Jones," he announced in official tones.

Cyrus nodded. "All right." He looked at Myrna. "What have we got?"

"Dead body," she said quietly. "Not a local. Must be

one of the tourists. Some of the kids found him when they entered the last exhibit inside."

"Actually the dust bunnies found the body," Devin said.

Cyrus nodded and turned back to Myrna. "Cause of death?"

"Mag-rez. Slade says it's a double-tap."

"Pro."

Myrna wrinkled her nose. "On Rainshadow. Who knew we'd become a tourist destination for that crowd?"

Lyle chortled a greeting to Sedona and waved the small gleaming object that he held in one paw. At first she thought it was a Halloween cookie wrapped in shiny foil. When she collected him from Annie, he offered her the gift.

She glanced at it and shivered. Without a word she handed Lyle's gift to Cyrus.

"It's an amber compass," Cyrus said. "Standard Guild issue."

"Look at the back," Sedona said.

He turned it over in his hand and examined the name and serial number that had been stamped on the flat metal surface. "This is interesting."

"Whose compass is it?" Rachel asked.

"It belongs to Kirk Morgan, the head of the Gold Creek Guild," Sedona said. "The jerk boss who set me up to be kidnapped."

Chapter 30

THE OVERHEAD LIGHTS WERE ON INSIDE THE OLD WARE-house, casting a bright glare on the tableaus. Sedona and Cyrus went through the heavily draped space, past Alien witches stirring their cauldrons and Alien vampires rising up from their coffins.

The small group of grim-faced people at the back of the warehouse was gathered around the scene of an Alien mad scientist working in his lab. Kirk Morgan's body, clad in Guild khaki and leather, was stretched out on the lab table as though about to be autopsied.

The lab apparatus arrayed around the exhibit was hokey and theatrical, replete with mysteriously bubbling beakers and an old-fashioned amber-generator that spit out harmless sparks. Just a melodramatic scene from an old horror movie, Sedona thought. Nevertheless it brought back fragments of her nightmares. She swallowed hard.

"Okay, this can't be a coincidence," she said.

"No," Cyrus agreed.

"I'd say the killer has a really warped sense of humor," Slade said. "Which, when you get right down to it, is not typical of the average professional hit man."

"It's not a joke," Sedona whispered. "It's a warning. Someone was sending a message to me."

Cyrus shook his head. "Why put you on guard like that? Sending a warning doesn't sound like the work of a pro, either. They do a job and get out."

"He's got a point," Harry said. "Wouldn't a pro have taken more pains to conceal the body?"

"That's easier said than done in a small town," Slade said. "Still, at the very least, you'd think a pro would have dumped the body into the bay to wash off some of the evidence."

Sedona glanced at him. "Did you find some? Evidence, I mean?"

Slade held up a small white card. "Nothing as helpful as a cell phone with Morgan's list of contacts but this was in his wallet."

Cyrus glanced at the card. "It's Morgan's. Just says he's the CEO of the Gold Creek Guild. What's useful about it?"

"There's a phone number on the back," Slade said. "I'll give it a call and see who answers."

Sedona was standing close enough to see the number written on the card. She stared at it in shock.

"Don't bother," she said. "It's Brock's private phone number. Only those closest to him have it." She folded her arms around herself. “But this doesn’t make any sense. Whatever else he is, Brock is not a professional assassin.”

Slade looked at the body. “Don’t bank on that. Pros are very, very good at wearing masks.”

Chapter 31

CYRUS'S PHONE RANG LESS THAN TWENTY MINUTES later, just as he and Sedona walked back through the door of her cottage.

"I found Prescott," Slade said. "He was at the marina, trying to find a private charter to take him to Thursday Harbor. He's confused and disoriented. I think he's on drugs. That would explain the over-the-top display of Morgan's body. I'll know more when he comes down off the high."

"*If* he comes down," Cyrus said. "Listen, if he's on the drug I'm thinking of, he'll either go crazy or else he'll be dead by morning. We need information from him. I've got a dose of the antidote. Can I see him long enough to give it to him?"

Slade thought about that. "This is about finding that drug dealer who kidnapped Sedona?"

"Yes."

"Come on down to the police station. I'll meet you there."

Cyrus ended the connection and looked at Sedona. "They picked up Brock. Slade says he's acting irrationally, as if he's on a drug high."

Sedona frowned. "Brock never did drugs while I was with him."

She set Lyle down on the floor and gave him the sack of candy that the kids had sent home with him in payment for his contribution to the evening. The sack was bigger than he was. It bulged with goodies.

Lyle chortled, thrilled with his haul, and dragged the sack off to a corner behind the reading chair.

Sedona straightened and looked at Cyrus.

"Do you really think Brock is on the formula?" she asked.

"It's a strong possibility." Cyrus went to the lockbox, opened it, and took out the case with the syringe. "His involvement in this thing would explain a lot, including why he never expected to see you again. I'm going to give him the antidote. It will put him to sleep for a few hours but he should wake up in the morning. I want answers from him."

"I'm coming with you," Sedona said.

"Of course you are. I'm sure as hell not leaving you here all by yourself."

BROCK WAS MORE THAN CONFUSED AND DISORIENTED. HE was hallucinating wildly by the time Cyrus and Sedona arrived. He raged back and forth in the small jail cell, alternately clutching at his hair and then the cell bars. When he saw Sedona he stared at her as if he could not believe his eyes.

"Dead," he said. "You're dead."

She moved toward the bars. "Brock, can you understand me?"

"Get away from me." He shuddered and lurched backward, eyes widening in panic. "You're a ghost. Don't touch me."

Sedona looked at Cyrus. "I've never seen him in this condition. You're right, he's definitely on something."

"The question is, what's he been using?" Harry asked.

Rachel spoke up. "Slade asked me to view Prescott's aura. There's a lot of violence and chaos in the pattern but that's typical of the effects of any strong mind-altering drug or steroids, for that matter."

"It's typical of that damned formula, too," Cyrus said.

"No telling exactly what he's on without a tox screen, and we don't have time for that," Slade said. "Not like we've got a handy-dandy forensics lab here on Rainshadow."

Cyrus held up the syringe. "If he's on the drug I think he's using, this should bring him down. If he's on some other drug this antidote won't do any harm, it will just put him to sleep for a while."

Brock started to scream. He stared at the floor of his cell as if it were the entrance to hell. "They're coming for me. You've got to stop them. Save me."

Slade made an executive decision. "Give him the antidote. Harry and I will restrain him."

Five minutes later Brock was unconscious on the cot.

"Now what?" Harry asked.

"Now we wait until he wakes up to get some answers," Cyrus said.

Chapter 32

"I CAN'T BELIEVE IT." SEDONA PACED PAST THE FIREPLACE, came face-to-face with a wall, turned on her heel and started back in the other direction. "Brock was in on this from the start? How in the world would he have gotten involved with Blankenship?"

Cyrus looked up from his computer screen. "There are a lot of questions here. We'll know more in the morning."

They were back in her cottage. He had poured some whiskey for both of them. Now he was sitting on the couch, running searches to see if the news of Morgan's death had reached Gold Creek Guild headquarters. On the other end, in Frequency City, Marlowe was searching for possible connections between Morgan and Brock Prescott. Blankenship was still missing.

Lyle was in the corner, gloating over his stash of

Halloween candy. Evidently unable to make a decision about which piece to eat first, he kept arranging and rearranging his mound of brightly wrapped goodies. He treated each treat as if it were a piece of precious amber.

Sedona paused at the far end of the room and swallowed some of the whiskey. "It certainly took a lot of nerve to kill Kirk Morgan. I mean, he's a Guild boss, for crying out loud. Brock had to know that would cause a stir. Good grief. The Chamber would have pulled out all the stops to find him. Why would he take such a risk?"

"Because he's on the drug and he's deteriorating," Cyrus said patiently. "At least he was before I gave him the antidote. The first thing to go is impulse control. According to the old files, users tend to take risks, believing that they are supermen who can get away with actions that would give any normal person second thoughts."

"Okay, if you say so. Sure doesn't sound like Brock, though." Sedona started back across the carpet. "I wonder why Kirk Morgan agreed to meet Brock on Rainshadow?"

"Brock probably promised to deliver you to him."

"But he didn't even try to grab me. He tried to talk me into leaving with him, but he didn't make any overt physical moves."

"Unless he is the one who set that psi-trap, after all," Cyrus said, thinking about it. "Maybe he developed a new talent for working Alien psi."

She winced. "Like me, do you mean?" She shivered. "And then he started to deteriorate."

"Not like you." Cyrus got to his feet and went to stand

in front of her. He gripped her shoulders and waited until she met his eyes. "You are stable. You're immune to the side effects of the drug, remember? That's why Blankenship wanted to get hold of you in the first place."

"But what if the side effects have simply been delayed in my case?"

"Trust me, you would be showing signs of instability by now. But if the worst happens, I'll give you the antidote. Marlowe tells me the second batch will be ready soon."

"We don't even know if the antidote would work on me, my para-psych profile being so abnormal."

"Stop it." He moved his hands upward to capture her face. "You're okay, Sedona. And you're going to remain okay. Rachel read your aura, remember?"

Sedona closed her eyes. When she opened them, she looked more composed.

"I know," she said. "Sorry. I guess this business of discovering that Brock was involved in the kidnapping has really rattled me. It's worse than finding out that Blankenship and Morgan set me up. I mean, one of them is a mad scientist and the other is an old-school Guild boss." She paused. "Sorry. No offense intended."

He pulled her into his arms. "None taken. The old-school bosses did not exactly cover themselves in glory."

"I think what's really bothering me, is the fact that my own judgment was so faulty when it came to Brock. I knew the relationship was never going to be long-term but I thought he at least liked me. To find out that he was just manipulating me all along is . . . unnerving. I feel like an idiot for not seeing the truth early on in our relationship."

"You said yourself you were pretty sure he had some talent for charisma."

"Yes, but he seemed like a nice guy—not perfect—but okay," Sedona said. "Now, if you're right, he's a full-blown psychopath."

"Because of the formula. Look, forget Brock Prescott, okay? I'm the one who's here tonight."

She managed a misty smile.

"Do you trust me?" Cyrus asked

"Yes," she said. "I trust you."

"And you will note that there is no weird blue psi in the atmosphere, right?"

"Right."

"And neither of us is in the grip of a post-burn buzz, correct?"

"Correct." Her brows snapped together in confusion. "Where are you going with this?"

"To bed with you, I hope."

He kissed her before she could say anything else. She seemed somewhat startled at first but as soon as he deepened the kiss she responded. She sank into him with a soft sigh. Her arms went around his neck. Her mouth softened; her lips parted.

The rush that he got whenever he touched her hit him. Anticipation rolled through him in waves. He was as hard as he had ever been in his life.

After a moment he picked her up and carried her into the bedroom. He did not turn on the lights. Instead, he undressed her in the shadows and got her into bed. He was peeling off his trousers when she suddenly looked down the hall toward the fire-lit living room.

"Lyle," she said. "He's out there with all that candy."

"Something tells me we don't want to try to take it away from him."

There were two small clinks when he set the mag-rez and the flamer on the bedside table. Moonlight glinted on the weapons.

Sedona glanced at them. "You're still worried?"

"Blankenship is out there, somewhere. So are his two assistants. I believe I mentioned that there's a streak of paranoia in the Jones family."

"Those of us who have been kidnapped by drug-dealing mad scientists totally understand the tendency."

He climbed under the covers, savoring the intimacy of the moment. The sexual energy in the atmosphere resonated with his senses, both normal and paranormal. When he touched her warm body and inhaled her intoxicating scent, he knew that she was also aroused.

He pushed back the covers and levered himself up on one elbow so that he could admire her in the moonlight. The silvery glow transformed her into a creature of magic; irresistible, enchanting, captivating.

He put his hand on her breast. "You are amazing."

She smiled and reached up to pull him down to her. "So are you, Cyrus Jones."

He smoothed his hand down to the curve of her waist and the graceful swell of her hip. He drank from her lips while he teased the hidden places of her body.

She explored him slowly. By the time she took his rigid erection into her hand he was sweating and close to the edge of his control. He could hear her quick little breaths. When he eased two fingers into her she clenched tightly.

"Oh, yes," she whispered.

Energy crackled in the atmosphere, challenging him.

He took a breath and slowly heightened his talent. The energy levels soared around them.

He drove slowly, deeply into her tight body in one long, relentless stroke. At the same time he released the last restraints on his talent. The dark, heavy waves of his aura clashed with the heat of her own energy field.

Fire and ice danced in the night. Heat blazed in the room. He could have sworn he saw flames. He was certain he felt them licking at his aura.

He looked around. Sure enough small sparks of paranormal fire were flashing in the bedroom.

"How are you doing that?" he asked, amazed. "You're not using your flicker."

"The fireplace," she gasped. "It's putting out a lot of energy. It's close enough to supply the currents I need." She giggled. "I didn't know I could ignite a fire from this distance, either."

He laughed. "You are one dangerous woman."

The amusement evaporated from her eyes. "But you're not afraid of me, are you?"

"How could I be afraid of you? Honey, you were made for me."

He kissed her again and began to move slowly,

deliberately, in and out of her clenched body. The energy in the atmosphere got hotter.

But in the next moment, their auras were resonating in the same stunning harmony that had occurred in the cave.

"Told you so," he said against Sedona's mouth. "No blue energy involved."

She opened her mouth—perhaps to laugh—but in that instant her release swept through her. Her thighs tightened around his waist. Her nails sank into his shoulders. Her head tipped back. Her eyes squeezed shut. And the only sound she made was a breathless cry.

Her climax pulled him into the vortex. For a timeless moment he was locked in the shatteringly intimate embrace. The past and the future no longer mattered. He was with Sedona. That was all that was important for now.

Chapter 33

HE CAME AWAKE SOME TIME LATER, DISORIENTED BY THE sudden rush of adrenaline that had kicked him out of a dream that had him chasing through dense fog, trying to find Sedona. It was a lot like getting lost in the tunnels without amber, he thought. Everywhere he turned in the dreamscape he was met with more fog. He knew she was there, somewhere, but he had no way to locate her.

He rezzed a little energy, pushing back the last fragments of the dreamscape, and lay still, listening with all of his senses. The first thing he saw were four eyes—two blue, two amber. Lyle was on the bed next to him, hunkered down on the pillow.

Sedona barely stirred but there was enough moonlight to see that her eyes were open, too. She looked at him across the short distance that separated them, silently asking him the question that he was asking himself. What had awakened them?

He heard it then, the faintest whisper of sound from the back porch. A moment later, a tiny draft of night air stirred the atmosphere. Someone had picked the lock on the kitchen door.

Lyle's growl was so low it was doubtful that anyone who was not right next to him would have heard it. But Cyrus touched Sedona's shoulder and shook his head. She must have gotten the message because she touched Lyle who immediately went silent.

Cyrus put his mouth on Sedona's ear.

"Over the side," he whispered. "On the floor."

She did not argue. He should have known she wouldn't, not in a situation like this.

She eased herself out from under the covers and over the edge of the bed. She lay prone on the floor.

He didn't have much time, Cyrus thought. The cottage was small. The intruder would be jacked to the max and he had probably already figured out the layout. He would be coming down the hall any second and he would be armed.

Cyrus slipped off the edge of the bed and crouched on the floor. He reached back and whipped the covers up and over the pillows, creating small bulges that, for a few vital seconds, would give the illusion of two people sleeping.

Lyle got with the program. He scampered silently off the pillow and down to the floor on Cyrus's side.

The figure of a man appeared at the end of the short

hall, silhouetted against the moonlit living room. He moved forward swiftly, the barrel of the mag-rez glinting in the shadows.

Cyrus raised his talent, slamming a dead zone over the intruder's aura just as he fired two shots into the bedding.

The intruder jerked and shuddered. He got off one more wild shot before the gun clattered on the floor. Then he seemed to fold in on himself. He fell beside the gun.

Cyrus waited a moment longer to make sure the intruder hadn't brought someone else along for backup. Then he got to his feet and rezzed the light.

Sedona rose and reached for her robe. She came to stand next to the unconscious man.

"Well, this certainly explains a few things," she said.

"HIS NAME IS PETE GRIFFIN," SEDONA SAID. "EVERYONE called him Griff. He was Kirk Morgan's chief lieutenant, an old pal from their days in the tunnels. Folks said that Griff was the only man Kirk really trusted."

"Obviously that proved to be a mistake," Slade said.

Sedona shivered. "Yes."

She looked at the two small darts that Cyrus had recovered from the pillows. Both contained little capsules containing an unknown drug. Griff had come to kidnap her, not kill her.

It was nearly four o'clock in the morning. Earlier Cyrus had helped Slade secure the unconscious Griff in Shadow Bay's only remaining cell. Then the two men had returned to the cottage. A couple of phone calls had brought Harry and Rachel and Charlotte. Now they were all gathered in the living room of the cottage, drinking the coffee that Sedona had made.

Lyle had lost interest in the proceedings now that the action was over. He was fully fluffed once again and back in his corner, reorganizing his stash of Halloween candy.

"Rachel says Griffin is definitely on some heavy-duty drug," Harry said.

"Something is disturbing the paranormal currents in his aura," Rachel said. "It may be a chemically induced disturbance, but the damage I saw is quite different from the damage I viewed in Brock Prescott's aura."

"No two auras are identical," Sedona said. "Maybe the drug affects different people in different ways."

"I'm sure that's true," Rachel agreed. "Still, if I had to take a wild guess I'd say that Griffin and Brock were using two entirely different drugs. The one Griff is on is doing considerable damage. But I think Brock Prescott will survive." She looked at Cyrus. "And not because you gave him the antidote. Whatever he was using isn't nearly as toxic as whatever Griffin was taking."

Slade looked thoughtful. "Maybe Blankenship has created more than one version of the formula."

"Either way, we've got a problem," Cyrus said.

They all looked at him.

"I only had one dose of the antidote," he said. "I gave it to Prescott. If Griffin is also on the drug, we'll probably lose him within twenty-four hours unless we let him have another injection."

"We can get him to the mainland in the morning," Slade said. "Your people can give him the antidote then."

Cyrus shook his head. "That won't do any good. Marlowe told me that it will be another forty-eight hours before the lab will have the next batch of the antidote ready."

Harry gave him a knowing look. "It's Griffin who could tell you what you want to know?"

"I think so, yes," Cyrus said. "He would have been the one closest to Kirk Morgan, who must have been running the operation. They may have used Prescott for cash and connections but they wouldn't have trusted him with all their secrets. I screwed up. I used the antidote on the wrong guy."

"You had no way of knowing there would be another hopped-up killer on the island," Sedona said.

Cyrus looked at her. "We need to keep Griffin alive at least long enough to wring some information out of him."

"He was carrying two filled syringes in an inside pocket of his jacket," Slade said. "I'll give one back to him when he wakes up and make it clear that if he doesn't talk, he won't get another one."

AN HOUR LATER THE PHONE RANG JUST AS SEDONA PUT two slices of bread into the toaster. Cyrus pounced on the device.

"Attridge," Cyrus said. "Griffin's awake?"

"He awoke a few minutes ago," Slade said, his tone grim. "I gave him one of the syringes. He seemed extremely relieved to get it. Gave himself an injection right away."

"This isn't going to end well, is it?"

"Griffin was dead within two minutes of the injection."

"These guys on the drug, they're not the suicidal type—not unless they are deprived of the formula," Cyrus said. "Someone murdered Griffin. Must have filled his last two syringes with a lethal compound."

"That's how it looks to me," Slade said.

"What about Brock Prescott?" Cyrus asked.

"He's awake, stable, and mad as hell. He's yelling for coffee and his lawyer. Says he doesn't remember a thing about what happened last night. Harry and I are convinced he's telling the truth."

"There's someone else involved in this thing and he's snipping off loose ends," Cyrus said. "He set up Prescott to take the fall for Kirk Morgan's murder. Then he sent Griffin after Sedona. But he gave Griffin a bad dose of the drug just in case the second kidnap attempt failed."

"No one left to tell us what's going on," Cyrus said. "Except the person who is now in charge."

"I'm guessing that individual took off in a private boat last night when the plan failed," Slade said.

Cyrus thought about that. "Maybe."

He ended the connection and gave Sedona a quick rundown of events.

She looked oddly satisfied.

"In other words, Brock really did come here to try to convince me to marry him just so he could get his hands on my money," she said.

"That's Slade's take on it."

"For some reason, that makes me feel a little better. I didn't want Brock to turn out to be pure evil. I mean, sure the guy was after my money, but somehow that's not nearly as awful as plotting to kidnap me so that I could be forced to undergo some horrible experiments."

Cyrus gave her a considering look. "You've got a real nuanced view of human nature, don't you?"

"I can forgive Brock for coming after me when he discovered that I might have access to the Snow fortune. He did that for his family, after all."

"That excuses him?"

"Well, you know how it is. When the chips are down you can't turn your back on family."

Cyrus hesitated. "Okay, I'll give you that point. But there are ways—"

"What I can't forgive," Sedona concluded, "is the fact that he didn't bother to look for me after I went missing."

Chapter 34

"YOU'RE REALLY NERVOUS ABOUT THIS RECEPTION, aren't you?" Cyrus said.

She met his eyes in the hotel room mirror. Her senses stirred at the sight of him. He looked shatteringly formidable in a black-and-white tux. The severe, clean lines of the jacket subtly underlined the power of the man, she thought—both the physical and the paranormal variety. When he walked into the reception tonight he would look as if he owned the room.

"Shows how much you know," she said, slipping on a pair of amber earrings. "I'm not nervous. I'm flat-out panicked."

He smiled. "Can't be any worse than a really hot gate or a Wonderland full of dinosaurs."

"See, there's where you're wrong. Tonight is going to be a lot scarier."

She studied her image in the hotel room mirror. She had gone with simple and elegant—a sleek, black silk boat-necked dress with long sleeves and knee-length hem. Black heels, discreetly trimmed with amber, the amber earrings, and an amber-studded bracelet finished the outfit. There was more amber set into the catch of the little black clutch bag she planned to carry. And all of it was tuned. *You'd think I'm preparing for a job in the Underworld.* In addition to all of the amber, she had tucked the flicker into the clutch. Really, you couldn't be too careful in the big city.

"You're still not convinced that your grandfather is sincere about drawing you back into the family?" Cyrus asked.

She wrinkled her nose. "Call me skeptical."

Cyrus watched her in the mirror, heat darkening his eyes. "You look spectacular, if that helps."

She flushed. "Thank you. Yes, that helps. A lot."

Lyle chortled approvingly.

She smiled. "Thanks, Lyle."

Her suitcase was open on the bed. Lyle was sitting inside, guarding his stash of Halloween candy. It had been clear that morning when she had started to pack that Lyle would not leave the sack behind. She had been forced to find room for it.

The bag of candy was still full. As far as she could tell Lyle had not made any inroads into his precious hoard. Instead, he continued to arrange and rearrange the treats. She wondered why he was saving his treasure.

"You're going to have to stay here by yourself tonight,"

she warned him. "Don't bite the maid when she comes to turn down the bed, okay? And don't run off and get lost."

Lyle bounced a little.

"He's not going anywhere without his haul," Cyrus said. "Which reminds me, I have something for you—both of you."

He took a small box out of his pocket and walked across the room to where Sedona stood. She glanced at the box and saw the logo of Charlotte's shop. A thrill of delight tingled through her from head to toe.

"A gift?" she said. "For me?"

"For you."

Cyrus handed her the box. She thought she caught a trace of veiled hope in his eyes. Did he really think she might not like whatever it was that he had given her?

She undid the ribbon. Her fingers trembled a little when she took off the lid. She caught her breath at the sight of the blue amber stone suspended from the gold pendant. Next to the pendant was another piece of blue amber. It was set in a shorter necklace that looked too large to be a bracelet.

"Oh, Cyrus," she whispered. "They're beautiful."

She felt tears gather in her eyes. She blinked hard. She must not cry, she told herself. If she did, she would have to redo her makeup. Besides, everyone knew that Guild bosses were notorious for giving pricey presents to their women.

Still, this wasn't just any piece of jewelry. It was blue amber from the cave in Wonderland. It had meaning. She looked up and saw Cyrus watching her.

"There's something I want you to know," he said.

She realized she was holding her breath. "What's that?"

"If you ever disappeared I would look for you and I would not stop until I found you."

She knew from the heat in his eyes that he meant every word. Cyrus was the kind of man who kept his promises, she thought.

"Thank you," she whispered, still fighting the tears.

He looked relieved; genuinely pleased.

"The regular-length necklace is for you," he said. "The smaller one is for Lyle."

Sedona smiled. "He will be so excited."

She turned back to the bed and dangled the shorter necklace in front of Lyle. "Here, this is for you."

Lyle hopped out of the suitcase, chortling madly. She draped the little necklace around his neck and then held him in front of the mirror so that he could admire himself. The chain and the amber all but disappeared in his fluffy gray fur but he didn't seem to mind. He was ecstatic.

She kissed him somewhere in the vicinity of the top of his head and set him down on the bed.

"Don't get into trouble while we're gone," she ordered.

Lyle chortled and resumed the task of organizing his treasures.

"Any idea what he's going to do with all that candy once he's satisfied with the filing system?" Cyrus asked.

"Not a clue," Sedona said.

Cyrus opened the door for her. "It's going to be okay, Sedona. You can do this. What's more, you're going to look fantastic doing it."

She touched the blue amber pendant and suddenly felt a lot better. She would not be facing a ballroom full of hostile relatives alone tonight.

They took the elevator down to the hotel lobby. The same sleek black limo that had picked them up at the airport was waiting for them. In addition to the driver, there was another man in the front seat. Sedona knew that both were probably armed. The Guilds were changing but the old ways died hard.

"How classy," she said. "The Guild-mobile matches our outfits."

Chapter 35

THE POWERFUL LIMO GLIDED TO A SMOOTH STOP IN front of the doors of the Snow mansion. Another flash of panic struck Sedona when she saw the crowd of tabloid reporters and Guild paparazzi waiting on the other side of the velvet ropes.

"Oh, crap," she said. "I forgot about the press."

"Ignore the media," Cyrus advised. "They love it when you do that."

The two Guild escorts got out of the front of the vehicle. One of them opened the door and assisted Sedona out of the backseat. She confronted a dazzling wall of lights and cameras. For a few seconds she was literally blinded.

Just one more Underworld gate, she thought. *I can do this.*

Cyrus took her arm. Together they went toward the front door of the mansion.

Hands holding microphones and cameras reached across the velvet ropes.

"Rumor has it that you and Mr. Jones, the boss of a new Guild territory, are romantically involved, Miss Snow. Care to comment?"

"How do the Snows feel about you dating a Guild boss?"

"Our viewers would love to know if there's a Marriage of Convenience in the offing, Miss Snow. Or maybe a Covenant Marriage?"

"The Snows disowned you years ago, Miss Snow. Can you tell us why you've been invited to rejoin the family now?"

"Does your family know you're dating a Guild boss?"

One of the Guild escorts moved forward and pushed the microphones out of the way. Sedona and Cyrus kept walking.

And then, mercifully, they were across the threshold. A very dignified butler closed the door and turned to greet them.

"Welcome, Miss Snow, Mr. Jones," he said. He took their coats and gave them to someone else, who disappeared into a coatroom. Then he turned back to Sedona and Cyrus. If you will follow me, please?"

They were shown into a chandelier-lit ballroom. A sudden, awkward hush gripped the crowd of elegantly dressed guests. All heads turned toward the new arrivals.

A moment later, everyone became very busy chatting and laughing.

"First time in my life I've ever made an entrance," she whispered to Cyrus.

A distinguished-looking man with a head of silver hair and amber-colored eyes came forward. Lean, with a stern, implacable profile, he wore his formal black-and-white evening attire with ease and authority, a master of his empire. This was what her father would have looked like if he had lived, Sedona thought.

"I'm so glad you are here, Sedona," Robert Snow said. "You have given me a great gift tonight. Thank you. Now, if you will come with me, there is someone I want you to meet."

He looked at a girl of about thirteen who was hovering just behind him. Her dark hair fell in waves down her back. Her amber eyes were bright with excitement. There was a whisper of energy in the atmosphere around her. Sedona knew the paranormal side of her nature would only grow stronger as the girl got older and came more fully into her talent.

"This is your niece, Gwen," Robert said. "She's been looking forward to meeting you."

"Oh, wow," Gwen breathed, fascinated. "You're the crazy aunt that everyone talks about, the one who's dating a Guild boss. This is so high-rez."

Chapter 36

ROBERT SNOW ROSE FROM HIS DESK AND WENT TO STAND at the floor-to-ceiling windows of his study. He looked out at the spectacular view of the glowing ruins.

The invitation to accompany her grandfather to his study had come just as the dancing had started. Sedona was not at all certain she wanted to have the conversation but she had to admit that her curiosity now outweighed every other factor. She had come this far. It was time to learn the real reason why she was here.

"Thank you, again, for attending my birthday party tonight," Robert said. "I know it wasn't easy for you. I am very much aware that you have inherited the Snow family pride. It is something of a curse, I'm afraid."

"I admit I'm bewildered," she said. "Why was it so important to you that I show up tonight?"

Robert turned away from the view to look at her. She

suppressed the old, wistful sense of loss, taking comfort, instead, in the knowledge that Cyrus was waiting for her downstairs. She touched the pendant at her throat again and straightened her already rigid shoulders.

"I am hoping that we can put the past behind us, Sedona," Robert said.

"What part of the past are you referring to?" she asked. She was proud of her ability to keep her tone cool and polite. "Would that be the part where you informed my father that if he did not give up his relationship with my mother you would disown him? Or would it be the part where you instructed your lawyer to tell me that I was being sent away to boarding school because the law required my parents' families to support me until I came of age? Or maybe you're talking about the part where my high-school graduation gift was a letter from that same lawyer letting me know that I was on my own and that I should not expect anything more from this family?"

Robert's jaw hardened. "I'm aware that, as the offspring of an illegitimate union, you were not to blame for the actions of your parents."

"Gosh, thanks."

Robert took a breath. "I understand that your mother's family treated you just as harshly."

"Yep. Fulfilled the letter of the law and then dumped me."

Robert's eyes sharpened briefly with anger and something else, a glint of uncertainty, perhaps. Evidently the interview was not going the way he had intended. Maybe he was also becoming aware that the one hold he had hoped to exert over her—acceptance as a full member of the family—was not working.

"You have every right to feel that you were not treated fairly," he said. "It's the truth. But I would hope that you are old enough and mature enough now to understand that you were not the only one who was hurt by your father's actions."

"Is this where I get the lecture on how my father embarrassed and humiliated the family? Forget it. I've had that from my mom's side."

Pain flashed in Robert's eyes. "My son did embarrass and humiliate this family when he walked away from his responsibilities. But as far as I am concerned, those were the least of his crimes."

"Is that so?"

"He broke his mother's heart," Robert said in a very tight voice. "She never recovered from the wounds that he inflicted."

Sedona froze. It took a moment for her to find her breath. "I see," she said when she could speak. "All these years you blamed my father for the death of his mother—your wife?"

Grandfather had himself back under control. "Martha fell into a deep depression after Gordon . . . left. He was always her favorite. She called him the child of her heart. After he went to live with your mother she was so certain that eventually he would come to his senses and return to us. But when you were born she realized that would probably never happen. Anger sustained her for a time; anger and false hope."

"She had two other sons, Vincent and Alton. They both gave her grandchildren and they gave you the heirs you needed to take over your empire."

"Vincent and Alton could never replace Gordon as far as Martha was concerned. When we learned that Gordon and your mother had been killed, Martha lost her will to live. To be honest, I don't know if she intended to kill herself when she took those pills or if it was an accidental overdose. But in the end it made no difference."

Understanding whispered through Sedona. "You don't blame my father for what happened to your wife, Martha. You blame yourself."

Robert looked at her for a long time. Then he turned back to the window. "That is . . . very insightful of you. You're right, of course. For years I told myself that Gordon was the one who had killed his mother. But I'm the one who drove him away from the family. I used lawyers to deal with you at every turn over the years because I knew that if I came face-to-face with you, I would have to confront my own guilt."

"Why the change of heart now?"

"There are two reasons why I hope you will accept your birthright. The first is Vincent's daughter, Gwen. The girl you met when you arrived."

"She's coming into some talent and you're afraid that you've got another female in the family with a para-psych profile like mine."

"The talent that Gwen is exhibiting runs in the female line and, yes, there is no denying that she will be powerful. We are fortunate to live in a time and place where psychic abilities are accepted, but you know as well as I do that those with a great deal of talent face certain social as well as psychological challenges."

"It can be rocky growing up with a lot of talent."

"Gwen needs guidance from someone who understands what she's going through," Robert said. "I'm hoping you will take on the responsibility."

"You're afraid you'll screw up with her the way you did with my father and in the end you'll lose Gwen, as well. I get that. You said there were two reasons why you wanted to bring me back into the family. What's the second reason?"

Robert continued to gaze out the window. "I won't say that age brings wisdom but sometimes life forces a man to look into the mirror and see the truth. A few months ago I had a health scare. In the end, it turned out that I was not going to die, after all. But in the process of working up the diagnosis some genetic tests were performed."

Sedona was having trouble breathing again. "Is this where you tell me that I'm not related to you, after all?"

"No." Her grandfather turned around. "This is where I tell you that I have recently discovered that my wife, Martha, had an affair with my business partner while I was busy building my empire. One of my two surviving sons is not my biological son."

"Are you certain?"

"I had the tests repeated three times."

Sedona hesitated. "I'm assuming Vincent is the one who is related to you by blood because Gwen is his daughter and she's showing the family talent."

Robert said nothing.

"Does Alton know that you're not his biological father?"

"No. Not yet. I've spent the last three months trying to decide how to handle the situation. One day I tell myself that there is no need to hurt him and the family with the truth. And in the next breath I tell myself that he has a right to know his genetics."

A rush of anger threatened to overwhelm her. She fought it with the same will she used to control her talent.

"Is this the reason you came looking for me?" she asked. "You've lost another son and suddenly the granddaughter who is proven to be a member of the bloodline is more valuable than you had realized?"

"No, damn it." Robert closed his eyes and made a visible effort to regain his composure. "I came looking for you because the shock of the initial diagnosis combined with finding out the truth about the past forced me to confront some hard facts. What happened all those years ago was my fault. I'm the one who ignored my wife and drove her into the arms of another man. I'm the one who was responsible for her death. I can't go back and put things right, but I can at least tell you that I am sorry for what I did to you. I don't have the right to ask for your forgiveness but I'm going to do it anyway, even though it is unlikely you will ever be able to grant me that kindness."

Sedona walked slowly across the elegantly appointed room and stopped at the windows a few feet away from him. Tears blurred the view of the radiant green ruins.

"What about Alton?" she asked after a while. "And Alton's children?"

"As far as I am concerned, Alton is my son in all the ways that matter," Robert said. "He lived in your father's shadow for years but he was there when the family needed him—when I needed him. He stood with me when Martha was buried. He would have preferred a career in academia but when called upon, he accepted the responsibility of running the company, instead. He's doing a damn good job of it, I might add."

"Yes, he is," Sedona said. "I keep up with the business news."

"His children are my grandchildren. I will not repeat the sins of the past by doing to them what I did to you and your parents. I will not cast them aside. If that is the price you ask in return for forgiveness, I cannot pay it."

She blinked away the tears and managed a shaky smile. "Right answer. I forgive you, Grandfather."

He turned toward her. She saw that he, too, was crying.

"Thank you," he said.

He opened his arms. She went to him and put her arms around him. He hugged her close.

"Welcome home, my dear," Robert said.

"I'm glad you're going to be okay."

"Thank you, so am I. But I regret that you are coming back to a family with so many secrets."

The past could not be forgotten, Sedona thought. Some doors could never be closed. But you didn't always get opportunities to take a new path into the future.

"Every family has secrets," she said.

Chapter 37

CYRUS WAS WAITING FOR HER IN THE HALLWAY OUTSIDE the study when she emerged from the meeting with Robert. At the sight of him she heard the chimes clash, clear and resonant. A bone-deep sense of certainty swept through her. She touched the blue amber pendant. It was the wrong time, the wrong place, and quite possibly the wrong man, but in that moment she knew what it was to love with all of her heart.

The shock of the realization filled her with an unfamiliar lightness. It was as if she had just been given a perfect gift. Like an armful of flowers or a summer dawn, it might not last but in that moment she experienced a quiet joy. She would never forget this sensation, she thought. The future would take care of itself. For now she had Cyrus.

He straightened when he saw her and came forward to take her arm in a protective manner.

"Are we staying or leaving?" he asked. But his eyes were on Robert who loomed in the doorway of the study.

"We're staying," she said. She smiled through the last of her tears. "For a while, at least."

"All right," he said.

"But I can't go back downstairs just yet." Sedona pulled free, grabbed a tissue from her little evening purse, and dabbed at her eyes. "I'm a mess. I need to repair my makeup. You'll have to excuse me. I'm going to find a powder room."

Robert angled his chin toward a shadowed hallway. "You'll find one there," he said.

Sedona nodded. She looked at Cyrus. "I'll meet you downstairs."

"Take your time." Cyrus switched his attention back to Robert.

She managed another watery smile and rushed off down the hall. Behind her, Robert spoke to Cyrus.

"I think you and I should have a talk, Jones," Robert said.

It was, Sedona reflected, more of a command than a suggestion.

"Yes, sir." Cyrus sounded amused but sincere.

Alarmed, Sedona paused and glanced over her shoulder in time to see Cyrus follow her grandfather into the study. The door closed firmly behind them.

"Damn," she said under her breath.

There was nothing she could do, she decided. She had the uneasy feeling that Robert had decided to go all patriarchal and conduct the "what are your intentions toward my granddaughter" chat. But Cyrus could take care of himself.

She hurried along the hallway and found an elegant guest suite. One glance in the mirror was enough to make her groan aloud. Dark circles of smudged makeup ringed her eyes.

The door opened just as she was using a tissue to wipe away some of the damage. Gwen peeked around the edge of the door. Her amber eyes were alight with curiosity.

"How did it go?" Gwen asked.

"The chat with your grandfather?" Sedona smiled at Gwen in the mirror. "I survived. So did he."

"So does that mean you're back in the family?"

"Sort of."

"Cool. You'll be able to teach me stuff about my talent."

"I'll do my best. But keep in mind that no two talents are identical."

"I know but still, you can show me things, can't you?"

Sedona gave her a misty smile. "Watch and learn, Gwen. Watch and learn."

"Can I come and stay with you on Rainshadow while I'm doing all the watching and learning?"

"That will be up to your parents, but you're welcome to visit me as far as I'm concerned."

Gwen giggled.

Sedona raised her brows. "What?"

"Did you see the look on Aunt Ellen's face when you walked in with Mr. Jones tonight? I thought she might explode."

"Well, she didn't."

"She's the one who calls you the crazy aunt, you know. Everyone else just tried to pretend you didn't exist. But Granddad says you can't ignore family. Are you going back downstairs now?"

"In a minute."

"I'll wait and go with you."

"Okay."

It actually took several minutes to clean up her tear-streaked makeup. Gwen used the time to ask an endless string of questions about the gatekeeper's art.

When they emerged from the powder room the door of the study was still closed. Sedona hesitated but feminine intuition warned her not to interfere. Men had their own ways of handling certain issues.

She and Gwen went downstairs together, Gwen still chatting animatedly.

Aunt Ellen was waiting in the first-floor corridor. She was alone. Tension tightened the lines of her face.

"I must speak with you, Sedona," Ellen said. "Run along, Gwen. This is a matter for adults."

Gwen did the kind of eye-roll that only a teenager could pull off successfully.

"Yes, Aunt Ellen," she said.

Reluctantly she went down the hallway toward the ballroom.

Ellen's expression sharpened. She turned and started walking briskly in the opposite direction.

"Please come with me, Sedona."

Sedona did not move. "What is it you want to say to me?"

Ellen stopped and looked at her. "What I have to say should be said in private."

Sedona reminded herself that she had known it was going to be a night for family drama. She stifled a sigh, mentally girded herself for another emotional conversation, and followed Ellen through a doorway into what proved to be an elegantly appointed library. Volumes bound in hand-tooled leather lined the walls.

Sedona inhaled the scent of old books and history. It mingled with the delicate fragrance of the exotic flowers arranged on an end table next to a chair. "This is Grandfather's library, isn't it? My father told me that he collected First and Second Generation manuscripts and books."

"Yes." Ellen moved to a small table where a teapot and two cups sat. "It has taken him decades to acquire this collection. I understand that he intends to leave it to the university library."

"I'm glad," Sedona said, meaning it. "That way the materials will be available for scholars and historians in the future."

"I did not ask you to come in here to discuss your grandfather's collection. I want to talk to you about the past. You have a right to the truth and there is so much that you don't know. Please sit down. Do you take milk or sugar in your tea?"

"I don't care for any tea, thank you." Sedona glanced at the door and then, reluctantly, sat down in one of the curved-back chairs. The scent of the flowers from the nearby vase was oddly soothing. "I don't wish to be rude but could you please say whatever it is you feel you must? Mr. Jones will be waiting for me."

"Mr. Jones." Ellen's jaw tightened. "Yes. Don't you find it somewhat odd that he has taken such an interest in you of late?"

"A lot of people have taken an interest in me lately."

Ellen carried her cup and saucer to the desk and sat down. She sipped at the tea. When she lowered the cup it rattled a little in the saucer.

"I'm sure you're aware that Cyrus Jones is no ordinary Guild boss," she said.

"A lot of people have mentioned that fact but as far as I can tell, he seems determined to do his job on Rainshadow."

Anger shadowed Ellen's eyes. "You have no idea who you are dealing with. I realize you must be thrilled that such a wealthy, powerful man has taken an interest in you. But believe me, he has his reasons and rest assured none of them are of a romantic nature."

"You're sure of that?"

"Of course. The Jones family has always been very secretive. It is said that there were strong paranormal traits in the bloodline long before the family boarded the colonial ships to settle on Harmony. Rumor has it that there is a great deal of psychic instability in that clan. The last thing a woman with your genetic heritage should consider is marriage into that family tree."

"I would prefer not to discuss Cyrus's family."

"Forgive me, my dear. You no doubt feel that it is none of my business." Ellen fortified herself with another long swallow of the tea. "But you are not accustomed to moving in the circles in which the Joneses and, for that matter, the Snow family moves. You have not had the advantage of learning the ropes, as it were. In our world, everyone has an agenda and in the end, that agenda must always be in service to the family."

"Gee. Who knew?"

Ellen stiffened. "I am very sorry to see that you are not going to take this seriously. I am trying to explain—"

"The facts of life in your world, yes, I get that." Sedona glanced at her watch. "But you can save your breath. Trust me, I am very well aware that everyone, including you, has an agenda. I'm sure that you asked me to come in here so that you could tell me yours. Why don't we get to that?"

"Very well." Ellen drained her cup and put it down with great care. "The Jones family is not the only clan that arrived on Harmony with a history of psychic talent in the blood."

"No offense, but that doesn't exactly come as a shock. My parents informed me that the Snows had a few talents on the family tree back on Earth."

"Yes. And more are developing in the bloodline here on Harmony. The problem is that some of those Snow talents were quite unstable."

Sedona gripped the arms of the chair very tightly. "This is about my connection to a woman named Arizona Snow, isn't it?"

Ellen rose to her feet and moved across the room to stand in front of one of the bookcases. She pulled one of the volumes off the shelf.

"This is a First Generation journal kept by one of your ancestors, the wife of Jared Justin Snow. Her name was Elizabeth. As you know, after the Curtain closed, cutting Harmony off from the home world, the computers began to fail. Elizabeth, along with many other colonists, considered it vitally important to transcribe as many family records as possible so that future generations—assuming the colonists survived—would have some sense of their own history."

"I told you, I am aware of my link to Arizona Snow," Sedona said. "I am also aware that any eccentricities she exhibited can most likely be explained by the simple fact that science at the time refused to acknowledge the existence of the paranormal. People born with talent back in those days were considered to be suffering from delusions or some form of mental illness."

"True but that is not the whole story of Arizona Snow." Ellen closed the book. "Elizabeth Snow discovered that Arizona Snow worked for a secret government agency that recruited people of talent. You see, not everyone back in those days refused to accept the possibility of the paranormal."

Chimes clashed somewhere in the distance and not in a good way this time.

"I know the story, thank you," Sedona said.

"Evidently Arizona Snow was one of their best operatives," Ellen continued. "However, at some point she began to deteriorate mentally and psychically. She became quite dangerous."

"That's not the way it was, damn it."

"Orders were given to terminate her but the head of the agency elected to allow his lab people to try an experimental therapy on her instead," Ellen continued. "The treatment was successful in that it saved her life. However, she was never again fit for clandestine work. She retired and went to live in a small town. Unfortunately, there were some drawbacks to the drugs that were used on her in the course of the therapy."

"Crap. This is about that damned formula, isn't it? Good grief, Ellen, please don't tell me that you are involved with Blankenship's project."

Ellen stiffened. "Dr. Blankenship contacted me, yes. He explained that after you were badly psi-burned on your last contract job they thought you would die of your injuries. Blankenship convinced his superiors to allow him to try to save you."

"That's a lie." Sedona found herself on her feet. "There was no therapy. I was forced into those damn experiments."

"Dr. Blankenship explained that, due to your peculiar psychic genetics you were given a modern version of the drug that was used on Arizona Snow. Unfortunately, there was a bad outcome."

"You bet there was—I escaped. Couldn't get any worse for Blankenship."

"He explained that you have developed a full-blown para-psychosis, which has manifested itself in the form of delusions, hallucinations, and an unstable profile," Ellen said.

"No kidding."

Ellen's mouth tightened. "Dr. Blankenship says he

was able to save your life but that you are now extremely fragile and a danger to yourself and others. You need regular doses of the drug to survive."

"I've had enough," Sedona whispered.

The scent of the flowers had become overpowering. The chimes clashed wildly. She started toward the door. Halfway across the room, she stopped and looked back over her shoulder.

"One question, Aunt Ellen. Does the rest of the family know about this?"

"Not the entire story, no. I warned Robert that because of your para-psych profile and the trauma you suffered when you were psi-burned, you may be somewhat fragile, but I didn't tell him about Dr. Blankenship or the experimental therapy that was used on you. Dr. Blankenship did not think that would be wise. Your grandfather, after all, has been obsessed with bringing you back into the family. He would not want to hear the truth about your condition."

"You mean you knew he wouldn't believe a word of it. Blankenship lied to you, Ellen. He and his people drugged me and held me prisoner in a secret Underworld para-psych lab for damn near a month."

Ellen sighed. "Dr. Blankenship told me that you were now prone to paranoid conspiracy theories due to the fact that you have missed several doses of the drug."

"That is pure ghost shit and you know it. You never wanted to do me any favors in my life. I think you would have been absolutely delighted if I had not survived Dr. Blankenship's so-called therapy."

A cold light burned in Ellen's eyes. "Unfortunately, you did survive, and so you leave me no option."

"Go to hell, Aunt Ellen. Do me a favor, take Dr. Blankenship and his crew with you."

Sedona reached out for the doorknob. She could not wait to tell Cyrus that she had a new lead on Blankenship.

But the doorknob was suddenly miles away and rapidly disappearing into infinity. The scent of the flowers was as thick as honey in the atmosphere. The library began to whirl around her. She lost her balance and flailed wildly, trying to stay on her feet. She went down hard on her knees.

"The flowers," she whispered. "Ellen, you poisoned me."

"It's for your own good," Ellen said. For the first time there was a hint of anxiety in her voice. "And for the good of the family."

Sedona wanted to scream her rage. She wanted to call to Cyrus. But she discovered that she could no longer speak.

She was vaguely aware of a door opening on the library balcony. Two figures wearing the uniforms of the catering staff came swiftly down the spiral staircase and crossed the room. One of them, a man, knelt beside Sedona and hoisted her over his shoulder.

"Got her," he said.

His voice came from a long way off but Sedona recognized it. Buzzkill.

"Take her outside to the van," Hannah Holbrook ordered.

Well, that certainly explained a few things, Sedona thought.

Hulk started toward a side door.

Sedona heard Hannah pause to speak to Ellen.

"Thank you," Hannah said. "We'll take care of everything now."

"What will happen to her?" Ellen asked. She sounded even more uneasy.

"Don't worry," Hannah said. "We'll take good care of her. She will get the medical treatment she requires to stabilize her, but I'm afraid her condition has deteriorated to such an extent that she will never be normal again. She will spend the rest of her life in a para-psych ward."

"The family will pay for the best care," Ellen said quickly.

"That won't be necessary. She is the Guild's responsibility. Miss Snow's family will be free to visit her, of course, but please don't expect a full recovery. That is no longer possible, according to Dr. Blankenship."

"I understand," Ellen said. "Please go. I must consider what to say when Robert and that . . . that Guild boss boyfriend of Sedona's start asking questions."

"There will be no need for explanations," Hannah assured her. "I am going to give you an injection of a hypnotic drug, one that will induce amnesia. You will not be able to recall anything that happened in this room tonight. You won't remember me or my associate. You may remember your meeting with Dr. Blankenship yesterday but that won't be a problem."

"No," Ellen gasped. "Stop. You can't do this to me. I'm a Snow."

Sedona caught a murky, dreamlike glimpse of what proved to be a very brief struggle. Hannah clamped a hand over Ellen's mouth and used a syringe to inject some substance into the back of Ellen's shoulder near the neck.

Ellen fluttered and then went limp.

Buzzkill paused. "Everything under control?"

"Yes. Hang on, I want to check her for live amber."

Hannah yanked the earrings out of Sedona's ears, stripped off the amber-studded heels, and tossed them onto the floor alongside the clutch purse.

She reached for the pendant around Sedona's neck. "This doesn't look like regular amber but better to be safe than sorry."

Hannah ripped off the necklace and dropped it on the library floor.

The door of the library opened. Sedona tried to cry out again for help. Then she caught a glimpse of the new arrival.

"What's going on?" Gwen asked. "Where are you taking Aunt Sedona?"

"I'll handle this," Hannah said.

She grabbed Gwen and clamped a hand over her mouth.

"No," Sedona managed to croak. "Don't hurt her."

Hannah paid no attention.

"Go," she ordered. "I'll bring the girl. She may prove useful."

Buzzkill went up the spiral steps with Sedona.

She tried to hold off the darkness but it was no use. The old dreams closed in on her like sharks scenting blood in the water.

Chapter 38

"I AM AWARE THAT THE JONESES HAVE A LONG HISTORY when it comes to talent in the bloodline," Robert said. "A history that goes back to Earth."

"Yes, sir," Cyrus said. "I believe the Snows also have a tradition of talent in the family that goes back to the home world."

He tried not to look at his watch. It wasn't easy. His intuition was stirring. He had the feeling that he should not leave Sedona alone with her relatives for too long. Most of those he had met that evening seemed merely curious. Only a few appeared actively hostile. When he had been introduced to Sedona's aunt Ellen, however, the tension in the atmosphere had been electric. It was clear not all of the old guard in the family were in favor of welcoming Sedona back into the fold.

Robert went to the drinks cabinet in the corner and

splashed scotch into two glasses. He carried both glasses across the room and gave one to Cyrus.

"You will understand that I am naturally concerned about your interest in my granddaughter," Robert said.

"I could say it's about time you took an interest in her welfare."

Robert bristled. Then he downed some of the scotch and exhaled heavily.

"I had that coming," he said. "You're right, of course. But the fact that I am late in assuming my responsibilities toward her does not mean that I don't intend to take them seriously. I will be blunt, Jones. I want to know your intentions toward Sedona."

"I hope to marry her," Cyrus said. "If she'll have me."

Robert looked at him for a moment. Cyrus felt a little energy sizzle in the atmosphere.

"Does she know that?" Robert asked.

"She's leery of marriage. I don't want to get no for my answer so I'm going to wait until the time feels right."

Robert fixed him with a sharp look. "If you're talking about a cheap Marriage of Convenience—"

"In my family we take marriage seriously."

"I see. I suppose I had that coming as well. But I hope you understand my concerns. I only recently discovered that Sedona had disappeared into the tunnels for an extended period of time. Her own husband believed her to be dead for a few weeks."

"That would be her ex–MC husband," Cyrus said. "And aside from Brock Preston, no one from either side of her birth families even noticed that she was missing."

"She has never been close to her families," Robert said coldly.

"You mean she never felt welcome."

"Damn it, man, I am not going to continue apologizing for the past, not to you, at any rate. All you need to know is that I intend to do my best to protect my granddaughter. There is every reason to believe that she was badly burned down in the tunnels. She is probably still somewhat fragile."

"Ghost shit. I spent a lot of time with her in a newly discovered, uncharted sector of the Underworld. We were stranded together. In the course of that situation we survived a psi-hot cave, an attack by a pack of predators that came out of some damn Alien biolab, and—just to round things off—your fragile, delicate granddaughter opened a tunnel gate twice and then sealed it with a psi-lock. If you know anything about psi-locks you know that gatekeepers have to be psychically stable to work that kind of energy."

"I'm relieved to hear that, of course, nevertheless, Sedona may be delicate at the moment."

A sense of knowing whispered through Cyrus.

"Who told you that she was so damned delicate?" he asked deliberately.

Robert frowned. "Is that important?"

"You may have spent the past few years pretending that Sedona didn't exist but it turns out that a number of folks have developed a whole lot of interest in her lately. Someone recently tried to kidnap her."

"What are you talking about?"

"Her former employer, a Guild boss named Kirk Morgan, was recently murdered on Rainshadow. Trust me, he didn't travel to the island for a vacation. He came for Sedona but someone else got to him first. Sedona's ex–MC husband also showed up on Rainshadow. And now we have all this sudden concern for her welfare from the Snows. You can see why I'm a little suspicious of everyone who is showing deep interest in Sedona. So, yes, it's important that I know who told you that she was psychically fragile."

Robert stared at him. Energy shivered in the atmosphere. No doubt about it, Cyrus thought, Sedona wasn't the only talent in the Snow family.

"You're serious, aren't you?" Robert finally said.

"I'm a Jones. We take stuff like attempted kidnapping and murder very seriously." Cyrus got to his feet. "Just like we take family responsibility seriously."

Robert hesitated. "To think that I brought you in here to interrogate you on the subject of your intentions toward Sedona. Obviously you had your own plans for this conversation."

"Who told you that Sedona might be fragile?"

"My sister-in-law, Ellen Snow, got a call from a Dr. Blankenship who is affiliated with the Gold Creek Guild."

Alarm twisted through Cyrus.

"Blankenship called someone in your family?" he said. "When?"

"Quite recently." Robert frowned. "Ellen was somewhat concerned."

"Does Ellen have a history of being concerned with Sedona's well-being?"

Robert shook his head. "To be honest, no. Look, I'm not blind to my sister-in-law's faults. Ellen's chief concern is to make sure that her son and daughter inherit their fair share of the family business. She's not thrilled that I'm setting up a trust fund for Sedona."

"Because she thinks that will mean that her son and daughter get a smaller piece of the pie," Cyrus said.

"There is plenty to go around."

"Not everyone thinks that way when it comes to money. You know that as well as I do."

Robert exhaled slowly. "It's no secret in the family that Ellen and my brother have not enjoyed a happy marriage. I'm afraid Ellen is a bitter woman. Years ago my wife informed me that my sister-in-law had hoped to marry me rather than Paul. But I assure you I never had any feelings for Ellen. I don't see why any of this matters."

Robert's phone rang. He glanced at it with a troubled expression.

"My private line," he explained. "It's Gwen's mother, Beatrice. It must be important. Please excuse me."

He picked up the phone.

Cyrus got to his feet and headed toward the door. There was an oppressive sensation in the atmosphere. He would not be able to relax until he found Sedona.

"No," Robert said. "Gwen isn't here. Neither is Sedona. What do you mean, they're both gone?"

Cyrus froze, his hand on the doorknob, and looked back over his shoulder. "What?"

"Hold on." Robert took the phone away from his ear. "Beatrice says she just found out that Gwen left the ballroom to look for Sedona. Beatrice wanted to warn me that Gwen might interrupt my conversation with my granddaughter. But Gwen never got here."

"And Sedona never made it back to the ballroom?" Cyrus said.

"Evidently not. She and Sedona probably met somewhere along the way."

"Where is Ellen Snow?" Cyrus said.

"Ellen?" Robert scowled "What does she have to do with this?"

"Ask Gwen's mother if Ellen is down there," Cyrus said.

Robert spoke into the phone. "Is Ellen in the ballroom? No? Where? Ask someone, Beatrice. Yes, I'll wait."

Cyrus watched time stretch out to infinity.

Robert ended the call.

"Ellen is gone, too," he said quietly. "Beatrice said a member of the staff saw her heading down the hallway that leads to the library."

"All three of them are missing at the same time." Cyrus opened the door. "Talk about your amazing coincidences."

"Where are you going?" Robert called behind him. "I assure you, Sedona is in no danger in this house. I have state-of-the-art security."

"I think Sedona is in more danger here than she was on Rainshadow," Cyrus said.

Chapter 39

CYRUS WALKED OUT OF THE STUDY AND WENT SWIFTLY down the stairs. The need to find Sedona had become overwhelming in the short span of time that he had spent with Robert Snow.

Mentally he put the pieces together in his head. It was no secret on Rainshadow that Sedona had decided to attend the birthday reception. Blankenship and whoever was working for him had concluded that the easiest way to get to her was to find a way into the Snow clan. The one person on Rainshadow who might have had that kind of insider information was Brock Preston. Odds were that he had either wittingly or unwittingly provided Blankenship with the name of a weak spot in the Snow clan—Sedona's aunt Ellen Snow, the wife of Robert's younger brother.

When he reached the first-floor hall he started toward

the ballroom. His intuition was flaring, rezzing all of his senses—which was why he became aware of the presence in the corridor behind him.

He swung around, telling himself that whoever was there probably had every right to be in the corridor. But the psychic side of his nature overrode the logical, reassuring explanation. He had not survived in the Underworld by ignoring his intuition.

The seriously bulked-up man who emerged from a darkened doorway was dressed in the black uniform of the catering staff. He had short, razor-cut hair and an amber stud in one ear. He had an empty serving tray under one arm. He came quickly toward Cyrus.

"Can I help you, sir?" he asked.

Energy shifted in the hallway. Heat burned in the waiter's eyes. Psi-light sparked in the narrow space. A split second later a hot ghost flashed into existence behind Cyrus, blocking any retreat.

The waiter produced the mag-rez that had been concealed behind the serving tray.

"Looking for the Snow woman?" he asked. His voice was harsh with a dark excitement that bordered on lust. "Forget it. She's long gone."

The intense, violent energy flaring around the waiter was echoed in the green fire that burned at Cyrus's back.

"Where is she?" he asked quietly.

"By now she's down in the tunnels. Won't be long before she's back in Dr. Blankenship's lab where she can continue making her contribution to science, as

Blankenship likes to say. Me, I was never much for science classes in school but I've got to admit Blankenship's wonder drug has made a new man out of me."

"How long have you been on the formula?" Cyrus asked.

"Couple of months now." The waiter paused. Uncertainty flickered in his eyes. "You know about Blankenship's formula?"

"More than you will ever know about it," Cyrus said. "Out of curiosity, what are the side effects with this new version? The usual instability and addiction problems, I assume? You do know that if you don't get regular doses you'll go insane and die, don't you?"

Rage laced with panic flashed across the waiter's face. "How do you know about all that shit?"

"Long story," Cyrus said. "We don't have time for it now. You're probably due for another dose soon and I've got a feeling you're not going to get it. Unfortunately, I don't have any more of the antidote so I need answers from you before you start to go crazy."

"You're wrong, you son-of-a-bitch. I've got enough of the drug to last me for a month."

"You've probably got a supply of something," Cyrus said. "But I wouldn't count on it being Blankenship's formula. See, the thing is, whoever left you here to deal with me is just using you as a distraction to buy time for your associate to escape with Sedona."

"You're lying, you SOB."

"You can bet your Guild pension that your associate spiked your next dose of the formula with something lethal. Hell, she wouldn't have needed to use poison. A shot of tap water will be more than enough to make sure you don't survive."

"Shut your damned mouth. Never mind, I'll shut it for you. I hear they call you Dead Zone Jones. Well, now you're going to be dead for good."

The energy ghost started to close in on Cyrus.

Cyrus jacked up his talent, neutralizing most of the energy in thc corridor. The ghost winked out of existence. The shock of having his talent iced transformed the waiter's face into a mask of terror. He dropped the mag-rez. Clutching his chest, he sank to his knees and then sprawled, unconscious, on the floor.

Cyrus shut down the dead zone, collected the gun, and then crouched beside the waiter to do a quick search. He found a small plastic case containing a syringe filled with a clear liquid and a Guild ID in one of the man's pockets.

Cyrus went to the doorway where the waiter had been concealed and rezzed a light. A woman was sprawled unconscious on the floor. Bits of amber jewelry glittered on the floor.

Robert appeared in the doorway. He took in the scene in a glance.

"What's going on?" he demanded. "What happened to Ellen?"

"Somebody tied up some loose ends," Cyrus said.

Robert picked up Sedona's amber earrings and bracelet and the clutch bag.

"They stripped her of her amber," he said. He stared at Cyrus, stricken. "How will we ever find her?"

Cyrus reached down to collect the blue amber pendant.

"I'm going to need a fast car," he said.

"I've got one. Where are we going?"

"To find Sedona."

Chapter 40

THE VOICES DRIFTED OUT OF THE DARKNESS THAT ENVELoped her.

"Is she awake yet?" Dr. Blankenship asked. Anxiety and tension vibrated in his thin, reedy voice. "Jones will be searching for her by now."

"Take it easy," Hannah said. "Arcane has been looking for the lab for days and hasn't come anywhere close. It's not likely they'll suddenly find it in the next few hours. We've got time."

Sedona opened her eyes and found herself looking up at a quartz ceiling that glowed with acid-green light. That answered one question. She was back in the catacombs.

She took a deep breath and pushed herself to a sitting position on the cot. Hannah, Blankenship, and Hulk all watched her as if she were an unpredictable lab rat. She ignored them and turned her head, searching for Gwen. The girl was hunkered down in the corner as if trying to make herself so small that no one would notice her. She brightened a little when she realized that Sedona was awake.

Sedona smiled reassuringly. "Hey. You okay?"

Gwen nodded, mute.

Sedona turned back to the others. "What a bunch of dumbasses you guys are. You're starting to feel some of the side effects of the drug, aren't you?"

"The good news is that you're here to fix that little problem." Hannah walked toward her. "You're going to unlock that gate and let Dr. Blankenship get the extra vials of serum and the crystal."

"And if I don't feel like opening the gate?"

"Then we won't need you or the kid anymore, will we?" Hannah said. "We'll send little Gwen off into the tunnels in one direction and turn you loose somewhere else."

"You're going to cut us loose without amber, regardless, after I open that gate," Sedona said. "I'm not seeing a lot of incentive here. You know us gatekeepers, we're all about the contract terms."

"If you do as we say, there won't be any need to kill you," Hannah said. "Blankenship and I will disappear into the tunnels."

Hulk jerked in alarm. "And me. I'm coming with you. That was the deal."

"Yeah, sure, you're coming with us," Hannah said

smoothly. She did not take her eyes off Sedona. "Goes without saying."

Hulk did not look particularly reassured.

"You're right about one thing," Sedona said to Hannah. "Cyrus will come looking for me. And when he finds me, he'll go after you and Dr. Bozo, here. Don't worry, Hulk, I'm sure he'll find you, too. You do know there's a reason they call him Dead Zone Jones."

"No talent," Hulk said quickly. "That's why they call him that. He's a Guild boss with no talent."

Sedona smiled. And said nothing.

Blankenship's eyes burned with fury. "You have no idea who you are dealing with, Miss Snow."

"Actually, I do," Sedona said. "You're the latest in a long line of idiots who believed that they could perfect the old Sylvester Jones formula. But there are side effects with your version, as well. I hear that there are always side effects."

"I'm almost there," Blankenship said, his thin voice rising. "The key is the crystal. I'm certain that with the properly calculated doses, the para-radiation can be used to stabilize the serum so that the side effects of the formula can be tolerated."

"What a dork you are. I survived the formula because I've got some natural immunity, not because of the crystal."

"Yes, your unusual genetics were the reason that you were selected for the study," Blankenship assured her. "The goal was to identify the exact frequencies in your aura that allow you to survive the drug and then use the crystal radiation to stabilize the serum so that it does not affect those particular frequencies. It was necessary to give you several large doses of the drug over time in order to calibrate the crystal."

"You think you've found the secret to making the formula work without side effects but you're wrong," Sedona said.

Blankenship glared. "I'm on the right track. I just need a little more time."

"And the stone," Sedona said.

"Which you are going to get for us," Hannah said.

Sedona remembered what Cyrus had said when he gave her the necklace. *If you ever disappeared, I would look for you and I would not stop until I found you.*

Chapter 41

THE FIRE GATE SEETHED WITH HOT PSI. THE HEAVY STORM of energy roiled and flared like a miniature sun.

"Oh, wow," Gwen said, wide-eyed with wonder. "That is so high-rez."

"Thanks," Sedona said. "Am I good, or am I good?"

"You're good, Aunt Sedona."

Hannah shot a disgusted look at Sedona. "What you are is a real annoying bitch."

"You're the one who goes around killing folks for fun and profit." Sedona smiled. "And you definitely aren't the sharpest knife in the drawer. You actually believed that Dr. Frankenstein, here, could turn you into some kind of Super Assassin, didn't you?"

Hannah hauled back the flamer and lashed out in a short, vicious arc designed to catch Sedona on the side of her face.

"Shut up," Hannah shouted.

Gwen screamed.

Sedona managed to move in time to avoid the full impact of the blow but the weapon caught her along the jaw and cheek. She staggered to one side but she managed to hang on to Gwen's hand.

Blood dripped on the green quartz floor. Gwen stared at Sedona as if she had never seen blood before.

Sedona wiped some blood from her face and shook her head. "You're really losing it, aren't you, Hannah? I'm told that impulse control is one of the first things to go when you're on the drug."

Hannah took a deep breath and seemed to steady somewhat. But her eyes were still unnaturally hot. "Close your damn mouth or I'll use the flamer on your niece."

"Stop it, both of you," Blankenship pleaded. He was shaking. "We don't have time for this."

Hulk stirred anxiously. "The doc is right. Make her open the gate, Hannah."

Sedona looked at Hannah. "I'll need tuned amber."

Hatred flashed in Hannah's eyes but she reached into the pocket of her khaki shirt and took out a small chunk of amber. "Open the damn gate."

"Sure, no problem," Sedona said. She took the amber and drew a still-stunned Gwen forward until they stood in front of the gate. "You know, I usually charge a lot of money for this particular service. First lesson in the profession, Gwen. Nail down the terms of the contract before you sign on the dotted line."

"Open the damn gate," Hannah said. Her voice was fraying again.

Sedona considered her options. Unless Cyrus arrived in the next fifty or sixty seconds, she had no choice but to open the gate. Hannah, Hulk, and Blankenship were all exhibiting a lot of frantic desperation. With luck, once the chamber was open, they might temporarily forget about their hostages and rush inside to grab the extra vials of the formula and the stone. If that happened, there would be an opportunity to reseal the gate before they realized that she and Gwen were still outside in the corridor. True, without amber, they would be lost, but if they stayed put Cyrus and Lyle would eventually arrive.

Okay, she thought, it wasn't much of a plan but it was a plan, which was better than having no plan at all.

Gwen gave her a sidelong glance, silently asking if there was hope. Sedona squeezed her fingers a couple of times.

"It will be all right," Sedona said.

Gwen swallowed hard but she just nodded once, accepting the promise.

"Hurry, damn you," Hannah snarled.

Sedona rezzed her talent, focused through the amber and set about unlocking the gate. It took just as much energy to unseal the chamber as it had to seal it in the first place. But she was much stronger tonight because she was not coming out of a waking dreamstate.

Just keep going, she thought. *You and Gwen will either make it or you won't but you can't quit. Not an option.*

The hot currents of the gate slowly started to falter and fade, revealing the psi-lit green chamber on the other side. The gleaming lab apparatus came into view. The glass-and-steel strongbox containing the Alien jewel still glowed with an eerie inner radiance.

Everything in the room looked exactly as Sedona remembered. Another chill of nightmare-fueled dread iced her blood. She knew she had shivered because Gwen squeezed her hand very tightly.

"Looks like something out of an old horror flick," Gwen whispered.

"Good description," Sedona said.

"The stone," Dr. Blankenship whispered. "It's still here."

He rushed into the chamber, heading straight for the glass-and-steel box.

Sedona held her breath and waited, hoping against hope that Hannah and Hulk would follow Blankenship through the open gate. Instead, Hannah waved the flame gun impatiently, motioning Sedona and Gwen into the chamber.

"Give me the amber and go inside," Hannah said. "I'm not leaving you out here."

Evidently comprehending something had just gone wrong with Plan A, Gwen cast another quick, searching glance at Sedona.

That was the problem with a really good plan, Sedona thought. It never worked the way it was supposed to work.

She surrendered the amber and walked into the chamber with Gwen. They halted near a lab bench.

Blankenship ignored them. He stared at the glass-an steel strongbox. Anger and fear shivered through him.

"No," he said. "No, damn it."

"What's wrong?" Hannah demanded. "Open the box. Get the stone and the extra serum."

Everyone's attention was focused on the strongbox. But Sedona knew there was no way she and Gwen could make it to the doorway. Hulk was standing guard.

"I can't open the box." Blankenship stared at Sedona, fury heating his eyes. "You locked it."

"Yes, I did," Sedona said. "Try to open the box on your own and your senses will get zapped. You might survive but you'll spend the rest of your days in a nice, comfy para-psych ward. No telling what the explosion will do to the crystal."

Blankenship studied the glass-and-steel box with horrified fascination. "She's right. She set a psi-lock. Make her open it."

"De-rez the trap," Hannah ordered. Her voice was tight with fury. She tossed the chunk of amber back to Sedona. "Do it."

Sedona caught the amber. "Right. Stand back, everyone. I'll open that box for you."

Hannah, Blankenship, and Hulk gave her some space. Blankenship was all but wringing his hands now.

"Hurry," he said.

Sedona looked at Gwen. "These little psi-locks a tricky. Watch and learn."

"Okay," Gwen said.

Sedona smiled. "You're very cool under pressure. You're going to make an excellent gatekeeper."

Gwen managed a shaky grin. "Like you?"

"Why not? It's in the blood, thanks to Arizona Snow."

Sedona rezzed her talent.

Flames exploded in the atmosphere, forming a psi-hot firewall between Sedona and Gwen and the others.

Someone screamed on the other side of the flames. Hulk, maybe, Sedona decided. She thought she caught a glimpse of him running toward the door of the chamber.

Hannah and Blankenship retreated from the flames, shouting in panic and rage. But they could not bring themselves to leave their crystal and the stash of serum behind. They were still there a short time later when Cyrus came through the door with Lyle on his shoulder. Robert and half a dozen hunters followed him into the chamber. One of the Guild men had Hulk.

"Shit." Hannah raised the flamer, aiming it at Cyrus.

But it was too late. Cyrus had already rezzed his talent, enveloping Hannah and Blankenship in a dead zone. For a moment or two, Sedona could have sworn that even the ever-radiant energy of the quartz walls dimmed.

Blankenship gasped and collapsed, unconscious.

Hannah dropped the gun and lurched to one side, trying in vain to keep her balance. The heat went out of her eyes. She fell to her knees and stared at Sedona.

"Bitch," Hannah whispered.

She sprawled, unconscious on the floor of the chamber. One of the hunters moved forward to collect the flam-

Sedona shut down the firewall.

Robert started across the room, "Gwen. Sedona. Are you both all right?"

"Yes, I think so," Gwen said. She threw herself into Robert's arms.

Lyle chortled, fully fluffed once more. He bounded off Cyrus's shoulder and dashed across the chamber.

Sedona leaned down to scoop him up and tuck him into the crook of her arm. She watched Cyrus come toward her, aware of a sizzling sense of certainty. She smiled.

"I knew you'd come looking for us," she said.

Cyrus's eyes burned. "Yes. Always."

Chapter 42

"MARLOWE SAYS THEY WERE ABLE TO GET TO BLANKENship, Hannah Holbrook, and the assistants you called Hulk and Buzzkill in time to give all of them the antidote," Cyrus said. "They're in jail, sleeping off the effects of what the authorities assume was just one more designer street drug gone bad. But some serious damage was done to their para-senses. The Arcane experts don't expect any of them to make a full recovery, but they will be able to stand trial for a whole lot of charges, including kidnapping and drug dealing."

"Well, that's something, I suppose," Sedona said.

It was the following afternoon. She and Cyrus were [illegible]her with Robert and Gwen in Robert's study. She [illegible] that with the exception of Gwen they all looked [illegible] the worse for wear.

[illegible]ecoming evident that in Gwen's mind the

entire affair was going down as a grand adventure. Sedona had a suspicion that her niece was already envisioning a career of daring exploits as a gatekeeper in the Underworld. Who knows? Sedona thought. Maybe that's exactly what awaited her. After all, she was a descendant of Arizona Snow.

Unfortunately, although the house was quiet once more, the gaggle of tabloid reporters and Guild paparazzi out in front had doubled in size. The morning papers had been filled with variations on the theme of how a visiting Guild boss had busted up a drug ring in the tunnels.

The photo on the front page of the paper on Robert's desk showed Cyrus looking quite dashing in his tux, his black tie undone around his neck, shirt collar open, jacket hooked over one shoulder.

The image showed her as well, but somehow she did not appear nearly as elegant and dangerous. Her hair was a mess. She was barefoot. The cut on her face had stopped bleeding but she looked like she'd been in a bar fight. She had Lyle tucked under one arm. He bore a striking resemblance to a rather tatty stuffed animal.

"What will happen to Aunt Ellen?" Gwen asked.

Robert glanced quickly at Sedona and then turned back to Gwen. "Your aunt seems to have suffered what the doctors sometimes call a nervous breakdown. Don't worry, she will be properly cared for. How are you doing today?"

"Great," Gwen said. "Aunt Sedona says I can visit her on Rainshadow if Mom and Dad agree."

"I'll talk to your parents," Robert promised. He turned to Sedona. "What are your plans, if I may ask?"

"Cyrus wants to introduce me to his family and then we are heading back to Rainshadow on the first available ferry," Sedona said.

"A little too much excitement here in the big city," Cyrus said. He smiled at Sedona. "We're used to the laid-back island lifestyle."

"Right," Sedona said. "On Rainshadow all we have to worry about is the odd prehistoric monster, weird Alien labs, and paranormal storms. Life is simple."

Robert looked at Cyrus. "You'll be staying on as the CEO of the Rainshadow Guild, then?"

"I think the job is going to be interesting," Cyrus said.

Gwen looked at Cyrus. "Last night, Aunt Sedona said you would find us down in the tunnels. How did you do that?"

"We followed Lyle," Cyrus said. "Caught up with him in the tunnels under the hotel. He was on his way to find Sedona but I convinced him we could make better time in your grandfather's car. So we drove to the ruin site and went down through that entrance."

"But how did you find Lyle in the catacombs?" Robert asked.

"The usual way. He was wearing amber. I plugged his code into a standard Guild locator."

Robert's silver brows rose. "You gave a dust bunny tuned amber?"

Sedona smiled. "Shows how much you don't know about Guild men, Granddad. When it comes to amber, if it's tunable, they make sure it's tuned."

Chapter 43

"WHAT HAPPENED TO LYLE'S CANDY STASH?" CYRUS asked. He closed his computer down and relaxed back into the sofa cushions. "I just noticed it's gone."

Sedona picked up the two glasses of brandy that she had poured and carried them out of the kitchen. The quartz pendant was back around her neck.

"Annie, Lyle's partner-in-crime on Halloween night, came by this afternoon. She said the kids were going to hold a big candy exchange in the old warehouse where the Haunted Alien Catacombs was set up. The dust bunnies were invited. Lyle took off with Annie, who was carrying the sack. That's the last I saw of either of them."

Cyrus glanced at his watch. "It's getting late. The candy-exchange event must have finished hours ago."

"Well, whatever Lyle and the others are doing, I

expect they're having an excellent time doing it. *Life is good* is probably a dust bunny motto."

Cyrus swallowed some brandy and watched the fire blaze on the hearth. "Life has been good for me lately, too."

She propped her arm on the back of the sofa and smiled. "You were telling Robert Snow the truth when you said you were going to remain on Rainshadow and run the local Guild, weren't you?"

"I've been one of the weird Joneses all my life. But somehow weird feels downright normal here."

"Even though you're dating a woman who was injected with a dangerous formula that has given her a talent for setting fires?"

"Like I said, life feels normal here." He looked at her, his eyes heating in the firelight. "It feels good. But here's the thing, I'd feel that way anywhere as long as you were with me."

She stilled. "Cyrus?"

"I was going to wait awhile to tell you that I love you."

"Cyrus."

"That would have been the best strategy. I realize that after all you've been through, you probably need time to discover exactly what you feel for me, time to trust me completely. Time for me to woo you. Usually I'm good when it comes to strategy. But I can't wait any longer to tell you. I just wanted you to know."

Joy threatened to overwhelm her. In another minute she would be crying, she thought. She managed a shaky smile.

"I'm so glad you didn't wait," she said. "Because I

love you with all my heart, Cyrus Jones," she said. Just saying the words out loud sent her senses soaring.

"You're sure of that?" he asked.

"Positive."

"In that case, will you please marry me? I'm talking about the real thing. In my family, we frown on Marriages of Convenience."

She looked at him through the tears that sparkled in her eyes. "Oddly enough, my family—both sides—frowns on MCs, too."

He pulled her into his arms. She touched the side of his face with her fingertips.

"What on earth would you have done if it had turned out I really was a dangerous, formula-enhanced multi-talent?" she asked.

Cyrus said nothing. He just smiled.

She winced. "Oh, yeah, right. I *am* a dangerous, formula-enhanced, multi-talent."

Cyrus laughed, joy and love heating his eyes. "Not a problem for this particular Guild boss."

He pulled her into his arms and kissed her until the fire burned low and then he carried her into the bedroom.

THE HAUNTED ALIEN CATACOMBS HAD BEEN CLOSED down at the end of Halloween Week but the tableaus were still in place. There was a move afoot by the town council to make it a year-round attraction. Meanwhile, the Alien ghosts and vampires and witches loomed silently in the shadows.

At the conclusion of the big candy-exchange event, the kids had left the contents of three bulging bags of carefully selected candy in the Alien Mad Scientist Exhibit. The pile of goodies sat in a glorious heap on the floor. Lyle, Darwina, and Rex, attired in their costumes, were ready to greet the guests.

The other dust bunnies arrived at midnight. They emerged from the catacombs and the Preserve.

The mountain of candy rapidly became a small hill and eventually disappeared altogether. Fueled by a sugar high, the guests played hide-and-seek amid the scary tableaus.

As usual, a good time was had by all.

Leave it to the humans to find a way to turn their nightmares and fears into an excuse to throw a party. Really, Halloween was the perfect holiday for Rainshadow.

piatkus